Contents

w/o

SPY MASTER

SILENT ENEMY

THE WALK OF DEATH

JAN BURCHETT & SARA VOGLER

Orion
Children's Books

Orion Children's Books
First published in Great Britain in 2018
by Hodder and Stoughton

1 3 5 7 9 10 8 6 4 2

Text © Jan Burchett and Sara Vogler 2018

The moral rights of the authors have been asserted.

*All characters and events in this publication, other than those clearly
in the public domain, are fictitious and any resemblance to
real persons, living or dead, is purely coincidental.*

A CIP catalogue record for this book
is available from the British Library.

ISBN 978 1 4440 1077 0

Typeset by Input Data Services Ltd, Somerset

Printed and bound in Great Britain by Clays Ltd, St Ives plc

The paper and board used in this book are from well-managed forests
and other responsible sources.

MIX
Paper from
responsible sources
FSC® C104740

Orion Children's Books
An imprint of
Hachette Children's Group
Part of Hodder & Stoughton
Carmelite House
50 Victoria Embankment
London EC4Y 0DZ

An Hachette UK Company
www.hachette.co.uk
www.hachettechildrens.co.uk

SILENT ENEMY

Ye can not see the wood for trees.
(John Heywood, 1546)

For Hannah Featherstone, who can!
With grateful thanks for her help and guidance.
And for Eileen and John May,
with many thanks to John for all the
useful information he gave us,
Jan and Sara

1

I was in trouble. I'd been summoned to the tiltyard by His Majesty, King Henry, and I had no idea why.

I charged through the Greenwich Palace gardens, scattering courtiers as I went, and skidded to a halt at the tiltyard gates.

'Move aside, you clay-brain!' someone shouted at me. 'This pageant has to be ready for St George's Day, not Christmas!'

A band of sweating men came staggering along under a huge model castle. I flattened myself against the gate as they passed.

I wondered what I'd done to anger the King. It wasn't difficult to upset our monarch. His Majesty's temper could erupt at the slightest of things. The page who'd brought the message had seemed terrified. Oswyn Drage had given me a very smug look across our scribes' table when the summons had come. He was

1

always hoping that I'd lose my position at Court. Had he been up to some nasty trick to ensure just that? It wouldn't be the first time. Or was it to do with my other job, the one that few people knew about, my job as a spy for the King's most important minister, Thomas Cromwell?

The jousting yard was heaving. Workmen, horses, guards and grooms were getting in each other's way and musicians in the corner were blasting out a deafening tune. But where was King Henry? He was so tall and so broad he was hard to miss yet I couldn't see him anywhere. The messenger had told me he was here, rehearsing for his part as St George, the heroic dragon slayer. That probably meant interfering and changing everything and storming about in a bad temper – which didn't bode well for me!

There was a roar from behind a couple of wooden trees and I heard a deep voice booming across the tiltyard.

'I ordered a forest. You will see to it before sundown!'

Frightened workmen scarpered out from behind the two trees and made for the gate. I wanted to scarper off with them. But it was too late. King Henry himself came striding into view, his eyes flashing with anger. Then they lighted upon me.

'Jack Briars!' he yelled over the sounds of shouting and hammering. 'About time. Come here immediately.'

My stomach churned as I dodged carpenters, painters and armourers to kneel at King Henry's feet. I kept my head bowed low, staring at the royal buckles.

'Where is Robert Aycliffe?' I heard him demand.

'Here, my Liege.' Two booted feet had joined His Majesty's.

Robert Aycliffe! If I'd been worried before, I was terrified now. I knew very little about Cromwell's other spies – it was safer for all that way – but I knew Aycliffe was a fellow agent. The summons had to be about my secret job. But what had I done wrong?

'Take a good look at this boy, Robert,' said the King. 'He's about the right height, don't you agree?'

'He is indeed, Sire,' replied Aycliffe.

I dreaded to think what I was the right height for!

'Stand up, lad,' King Henry commanded.

I obeyed, trying not to tremble too much. Then I saw that His Majesty was smiling! But so would a wolf sizing up a tasty lamb.

He clapped a gloved hand on my shoulder which nearly sent me sprawling. 'You'll be perfect as the young St George.'

I gawped at him, bewildered.

Aycliffe came to my rescue. 'His Majesty wants you to take part in the pageant,' he explained.

The King nodded enthusiastically. 'The pageant will start with a rousing joust. Then we will tell the story of the life of our patron saint and how he slew the mighty dragon and rescued the fair maid. You'll be wearing my boyhood armour and portraying St George as a boy.'

I must have looked like the village idiot as I stood there trying to take in King Henry's words. I wasn't in trouble. Instead I was being given a great honour!

'Thank you, my Liege,' I managed to croak at last.

'No, you fools!' the King suddenly bellowed over my head. 'I said the castle had to be on the other side. How did I come to have such dolts for workmen?' He grasped me by the shoulders and looked squarely into my face. 'I know you of all people won't let me down, Jack.'

'No, Sire,' I gulped. 'I am ever your faithful servant.'

'Be sure that you are,' he said. He beamed at me. 'Now stay, lad. I am about to call forth the beast that I shall fight.' He gave a command. 'Michael Dressler. Bring out the dragon!'

I'd nearly seen a dragon when I was little. Brother Matthew, my godfather, had planned to take me to a mystery play in Acton Village in which a fearsome monster was promised. I remembered how my excitement had grown and how disappointed I'd been when Abbot Busbrig had said we couldn't go. He said that orphan foundlings like me couldn't expect to enjoy themselves and that I was lucky to have a roof over my head at the abbey. I hadn't felt lucky. Apart from the kindness of my wise godfather, my chief memory of my twelve years at St Godric's was of the abbot's cruelty.

Still reeling from the news of my good luck, I looked towards the gates at the far end of the tiltyard.

They were slowly opening. I expected a magnificent, scaly, fire-breathing beast to emerge. Instead, a metal frame on wheels came wobbling towards us. I hoped His Majesty would think that my smile was pure admiration and not because I was trying to stop myself laughing.

A tall, muscular man was pushing the dragon from inside. He brought it to a halt in front of the King.

King Henry strode round the structure, inspecting all its joints. 'My armoury is doing a fine job in creating the monster. You can just imagine how it will be, Jack, when the trumpets sound and the dragon, covered in shining scales, appears from a swirling cloud of smoke!'

'Indeed, Sire,' I murmured. 'Truly terrifying.'

'Demonstrate the fire,' King Henry called to Michael Dressler. The man turned a large handle. The metal jaws of the dragon frame slowly opened. He thrust out a long piece of wood, flapped it about and pulled it back in again.

'When the mouth is arrayed with vicious teeth and the wood covered in bright flames it will strike fear into the sternest heart. What do you think, Jack?' The King looked like a young boy eager for praise.

'All those watching will tremble when they see their monarch fighting such a beast,' I said dutifully.

The man operating the dragon stepped out from the frame and knelt in front of His Majesty.

'Good work, Michael,' said the King.

'I am at your service, Your Majesty,' said the man. He spoke English but with a German accent.

I didn't know him but I guessed from his size and nationality that he was an armourer. The King only employed Germans in his beloved Royal Armoury. He maintained that they were the most skilled in Europe.

'The dragon is being built to my design,' King Henry explained to me. 'Tell the lad about it, Michael.'

Michael Dressler rose to his feet. He seemed very eager to list the merits of the dragon. 'As you can see, it is as high as two men and very wide so we made the frame from steel. Therefore it is strong but light enough for one man to push. We will add green cloth covered in gleaming metal scales and the dragon will be complete.'

'Excellent,' said King Henry. 'And it will of course be ready in time. Two days should be plenty.'

Michael bowed and began to push the dragon away.

I hadn't imagined the flicker of worry in the man's eyes although he'd managed to hide it from the King. I wondered what was going on. The beast looked nowhere near ready. Was there a problem in His Majesty's armoury?

2

'Well what are you standing around for, Jack?' demanded the King, a smile playing on his lips. 'Take yourself with haste to the armoury and try the suit on!'

I obeyed! But first I made a quick dash up the gatehouse stairs to the office. Mister Scrope would be wanting to know why I was away so long. Our Chief Scribe was ever quick to complain. Besides, I had to prove to Mark Helston that I wasn't in trouble. Mark was a good loyal friend who'd looked horror-stricken when I'd been summoned to the King. I knew he'd have been fretting over his copying all this time. And I admit it – I wanted to turn Oswyn's weaselly face green with envy.

Mark was delighted and terrified when he heard my news.

'Make sure you learn your part thoroughly,' he

warned. 'It would be awful if you got it wrong.'

I assured him that I'd try to avoid tripping up the King or being swallowed by the dragon. Unfortunately that just gave Mark more to worry about. He obviously hadn't thought of those particular catastrophes.

Oswyn kept his head down over his copying. I could see his ears were burning. He was so jealous he was ready to burst. It must have riled him that this lowly abbey foundling had been chosen for such an important role.

Mister Scrope wasn't impressed either. 'Just hurry back when you've had your fitting,' he grunted. 'There's plenty to be done here.' Perhaps he feared he might have to do some work himself for once, instead of dozing by the fire.

I bounded down the stairs, taking them three at a time, all the while imagining myself in gleaming armour, wielding my sword and bowing to the delighted cheers of the crowd. As I passed Master Cromwell's office on the floor below, the door silently opened.

'A word please, Jack.'

I followed my master into his room, eager to share my good news. As always his office was gloomy, despite the bright April sunshine outside. Just one candle was lit. It stood on his table and its glow gave the chamber an even more mysterious air. My master sat down in his carved wooden chair.

'I have heard you are to play the part of young St George, Jack,' he said. 'This is most fortunate.'

I should have guessed that he'd already know! There was little that escaped His Majesty's spymaster.

'Indeed, sir,' I replied eagerly. 'I feel very fortunate. I am on my way to try on the armour now. I pray I am worthy of the great honour the King has bestowed . . .'

'Spare me the flowery language.' Cromwell interrupted my dramatic speech. 'You clearly have little idea of the gravity of your situation.'

'Sir?' I gasped, wondering whether I was going to be fed to the dragon.

'This pageant has tested the King's patience to its limit,' said my master. 'It is his creation and he means to impress the whole of Europe with the spectacle of our patron saint. You must play your part impeccably. You will not let His Majesty down.'

'I'd never do that,' I declared.

'And now to business,' Cromwell went on. 'I also have an important job for you.'

My heart leapt at his words. I knew he didn't mean scribing.

'I am at your service, sir,' I said.

'We believe His Majesty may be in danger,' he told me. 'Several things have happened that could be thought accidents – a saddle girth cut almost through when the King was to ride to Eltham Palace, a loose slate slipping from a roof, even a plate of poisoned figs. His food taster was very ill as a result.'

'His Majesty has had some lucky escapes!' I

exclaimed. *Luckier than his food taster*, I thought to myself.

'Indeed,' said Cromwell. 'Naturally I have had agents investigate since the incidents and although they have prevented any harm coming to His Majesty, they could not discover the perpetrator.'

I wondered for one brief moment whether Cromwell was going to ask me to take over where his other agents had failed!

'Strangely, since the pageant was announced, the attempts have stopped. What do you make of that, Jack?' My master was challenging me to think – not so easy when my head was full of the excitement of my role as St George.

I tried to banish the images of my triumphant entrance in shining armour. 'Well, sir,' I gabbled, 'several possibilities come to mind. It could be coincidence, or the perpetrator could be ill, or dead, or has simply changed his mind.' I must have sounded flippant for my master raised an eyebrow. I reined myself in. 'Or, if he is determined to harm His Majesty, the announcement of the pageant could have made him decide to bide his time. He may have something very public and spectacular planned for that day.'

My master nodded. 'We must assume the worst. Therefore I have doubled the surveillance throughout the palace. I have everywhere covered.'

I didn't doubt this. Cromwell's army of agents was vast and invisible.

'But it has proved difficult to keep a close eye on the armoury,' he went on. 'I don't have any German armourer agents. This is where you can be useful, Jack. As the young St George, favoured by the King, you can move in and out of those workshops freely on matters relating to your armour. Your presence there will not be questioned.'

The memory of Michael's worried expression flashed into my brain.

'It may be nothing, sir,' I said. 'But I had the impression that the armoury is struggling with its work for the pageant. The dragon is still just a bare frame.'

'That is interesting.' Cromwell leaned back and pressed his fingers together. 'It should have been finished by now. Of course it hasn't helped that the King has changed his mind many times about the form it should take. However, that is His Majesty's prerogative and he is never wrong. We always work round his wishes.' He spoke calmly enough, but I imagined that the King's whims must be taxing his patience more than usual.

'Do you have any idea who could be behind the accidents?' I asked.

'The King always has enemies,' said Cromwell. He gave a heavy sigh. 'I am painfully aware that we do not have any information about the origin of this possible threat, nor any hint of a motive. It could come from a foreign power or from some madman working alone.

We simply do not know. Find out what you can. It goes without saying that you will report anything you discover straight away. King Henry's safety must not be at risk.'

'I will play the young scribe eager to try on his armour and explore the armoury,' I said.

'I have the feeling that won't take much acting,' said Cromwell wryly.

3

When I stepped into the huge armoury workshop the heat hit me like a solid wall and the noise of hammer on metal battered my ears. Half-finished helmets, gauntlets and breastplates covered the workbenches. I almost forgot that I was under orders from Cromwell in the anticipation of seeing my armour.

A team of dark-haired men in leather aprons were striding back and forth round a central fire, heating, beating and shaping pieces of steel, and shouting to one another in German, sweat pouring from under their caps. I didn't know whether they always wore such grim expressions but most looked ready to snap. I gave an anxious glance about for the Master Armourer. I'd seen David Hartmann around the palace. He was a lion of a man with fierce eyebrows and an even fiercer beard, who often seemed in a temper. Old Brother

Jerome back at the abbey had a saying for most things. He would have said that Hartmann was as fiery as his furnace! To my relief, the Master Armourer wasn't there.

I spotted Michael Dressler. He was standing at a workbench with two other men, shorter than him but looking just as strong. They were wielding shears and cutting sheets of thin metal into large leaf-like shapes. I guessed these would be dragon scales. I went over and tapped Michael on the arm.

He looked at me blankly for a moment. Then my face seemed to fit.

'You are to be young St George,' he shouted over the tumult.

'That's right,' I exclaimed, playing the eager young scribe. 'I've come to try on the armour. I can't wait to see it.'

His companions glanced my way. I wondered if they were expertly sizing me up, just like the King had. The younger man winked at me. His friendly blue eyes twinkled as if he was remembering what it was like to be a boy.

Michael gave a weary laugh. 'You'll have to find the armour yourself,' he said. 'We're too busy to look. There is so much to be done what with the dragon and so many in the pageant needing armour – and this morning we're a man down.'

'It's probably in one of the storerooms,' said the younger man helpfully.

'It's unfortunate that you're a man down,' I said, hoping no one would question why I hadn't gone straight off in search of my armour. A missing worker could explain why there was such tension at the armoury. I couldn't ignore this opportunity to glean information. 'Is he ill?'

'I wish we knew,' said Michael. He cut forcefully into his metal sheet, then swore as his blades went too far. He threw the sheet to the floor, kicked it into a pile of scraps and took another.

A worker with a lined face looked up from riveting an elbow joint. 'Samuel Bohn has gone missing, lad,' he told me, his accent heavier than the others. 'I am worried for him. Not one of us has seen him since we settled down to sleep here last night.' He turned to his companion who was holding the joint in place for him. 'Did he get up after that, Vincent?'

'I don't think he came to bed,' said Vincent, the man who'd winked when I arrived. 'I'm nearest the door. I'd have woken if he'd stepped over me.'

Michael slapped down a finished dragon scale. 'You're making too much of it, Albert. Samuel's just shirking when we've so much to do. That's typical of him!'

'You would see his bad side,' said Albert. He frowned and his lines grew deeper. 'And all because he bested you in that fight last month.' He tutted. 'The two biggest men in the armoury at each other's throats.'

'*You'd* see his bad side if he'd taken payment for a

15

'helmet you'd repaired!' retorted Michael.

'Quiet,' hissed Vincent. His eyes flashed a warning. 'There's enough trouble here without adding to it.'

'Anyway,' Albert muttered grumpily, 'I think it is not in Samuel's character to shirk.'

'Master Hartmann was angry with him yesterday,' said Michael. 'Samuel was shaking in his boots. Perhaps he ran away.'

'Nicht Samuel,' protested Albert. 'He is no coward. Our master can be fearsome when roused.'

'I agree,' said Vincent. A look of horror came over his face. 'You don't think the ghost had something to do with him disappearing?'

His two companions flashed worried glances at him.

'What ghost?' I asked. I knew the palace was meant to be stuffed with phantoms – the most famous being Duke Humphrey. The gruesome details of his death depended on who was telling the tale – he'd been seen everywhere from the privies to the Presence Chamber.

'Don't speak of it,' whispered Michael.

'The lad will be in and out of the armoury,' protested Vincent. 'We have to warn him. And we'd be ready for the pageant by now if we weren't too scared to work at night.'

A missing man and a spectre that seemed to be spreading fear among the workers. I couldn't see how this might endanger the King but I made a mental note. My work for Cromwell had taught me not to ignore anything.

'Do tell me more,' I urged them. 'But only so I can take care to avoid it.' I wasn't sure how I would do that, as ghosts are apt to pop up unexpectedly, but luckily Albert took this as permission to go on.

'We did not know that these workshops were haunted until recently,' said Albert in an awed voice. 'Then we started to see strange lights and to hear things – after dark fell.'

'Turns out the workshops were built on the site of an ancient armoury,' said Michael. 'An armoury that was here long before the palace.'

'They say it was haunted by the ghost of a murderous armourer,' added Vincent. 'Something has stirred it and it walks again. To see it means certain death.'

'I heard that in the old King's day, a fire on this very spot took two lives,' said Michael. 'It must have appeared to them.'

'And in one week alone a worker drowned in the Thames and another fell to his death off the roof when he was fixing loose bricks in the chimney,' added another armourer, who'd brought Albert a fresh basket of rivets. The man rubbed his red cheeks. His hands were scarred. I noticed that all the armourers bore burn marks from their trade. 'It can only have been the ghost that caused that.'

'I remember hearing the story too, Wilhelm,' said Vincent. 'It would have been a terrible time, losing workers to a vengeful spirit.'

'I pray God we none of us set eyes on it,' muttered Wilhelm, crossing himself.

'And don't forget the tale of the thief,' said Michael. 'The story goes that a worker at the armoury was found to be stealing and was sentenced to have his hand cut off. He died of his punishment. There's only one explanation for that, if you ask me. The ghost must have been seen by him too.'

I thought it was most probable that a man could die from losing a hand without the help of a phantom, but I kept my mouth shut.

'The Master Armourer was the only one of us here then,' said Albert. 'We should ask him what happened.'

'That's not a good idea,' warned Vincent. 'He gets angry at the slightest mention of ghosts.'

'I wonder what's woken it,' I said. 'It's an intriguing mystery. Perhaps the older servants remember it.'

'Don't speak of it outside of the armoury,' said Vincent. A worried look flashed across his face. 'Master Hartmann does not wish the tale to go beyond these walls.'

'Why?' I asked.

'If the King gets to hear that we are disrupted by this terrible story, he'll think his pageant is in jeopardy.'

He turned away. The other armourers bent their heads over their work. This ghost was certainly disturbing the preparations for the pageant. It might have nothing to do with my mission, but it would help everyone if it could be laid to rest.

'I mustn't forget my orders from the King!' I said brightly. 'Does anyone know where his boyhood armour is kept?'

'It was in here only yesterday,' said Albert, hammering another rivet. 'Samuel was polishing it.' He looked me up and down. 'It will be a good fit, I think.'

Vincent gestured towards a passageway leading from the workshop. 'Try one of the storerooms,' he suggested, putting a candle into my hand and giving me an encouraging pat on the back. 'But don't go to the far end.'

'Why not?' I asked.

'That's where the ghost walks,' Michael whispered.

'And it is where the lights come from,' added Albert. 'And the sounds also.'

Vincent nodded. 'Unearthly sounds.'

In spite of my eagerness to see my armour, their fear made me shiver. I set off, glad of the candle's light in the long, gloomy passageway. The other end was in deep shadow.

The first room held sheets of unworked metal. It felt very cold after the heat of the workshop. For a second I wondered if the ghost was making its awful presence felt. Then I noted that there was no fire here, and that a breeze was blowing through a cracked window. I hunted in vain for my armour. I remembered to cast an eye over the room for anything that might arouse my suspicions. Brother Matthew had channelled my natural nosiness into a keen sense of observation, and I examined every nook and cranny. I found nothing. I broke off from my examination of the second storeroom to gaze at the swords and shields and magnificent suits of men's armour that stood like soldiers on their stands. But as none of them was small enough to be the one I was searching for I left – reluctantly.

The next door was firmly padlocked. I peered along the passage. The end was in darkness. I felt a shiver. There was the room where the ghost was said to walk. I hoped my search wouldn't take me that far.

I opened the fourth door to find a flight of steps leading to a sort of cellar.

I stopped halfway down. Pale wax legs stood in eerie rows on a workbench along the edge of the room. Mark had told me that some courtiers would send exact models of their legs to the armoury to save themselves the trouble of coming to be fitted.

I turned to leave and my candlelight caught a leg that had fallen to the ground. I decided to be helpful and return it to its place on the bench.

The next instant I was reeling back in horror. The leg was not a model. It belonged to a man – a man wearing a shirt and breeches and lying motionless on his front, head to one side. I put my candle on the floor and felt for a pulse of blood. But there was no beat in the stone cold flesh.

4

I scrambled up the stairs, yelling for someone to come. Footsteps thundered towards me. Albert and Vincent appeared, looking frightened.

'Did you see the ghost?' quavered Albert, casting his eyes around as if he might glimpse it at any moment.

I shook my head. 'I've found a body.'

Vincent went slowly down the steps. 'Samuel!' he said, hoarse with shock. 'Dead.'

Albert shouted to the workshop for help.

There were more footsteps as the other armourers came running. They took in the scene below and hurried to join us but Michael hung back, his huge frame filling the doorway.

Albert rounded on him. 'The poor soul has been lying here all the time while you were speaking ill of him.'

'Ruhig sein, Albert!' muttered Michael.

'Do not tell me to be quiet,' snapped Albert. 'You cannot pretend that you are sorry.'

Michael gulped and wiped a hand over his forehead.

'Poor Samuel,' said Vincent. 'I wonder how it happened.'

'Perhaps he was visiting the jakes before going to his bed—' said Albert.

'And he saw the ghost,' put in Wilhelm. 'And when he tried to flee, he fell and broke his neck.'

Wilhelm bent to close Samuel's eyelids, but the body was stiff with rigor mortis. I noted this. Samuel must have died hours ago.

'Do not talk of phantoms,' declared Albert hurriedly. 'Samuel simply missed his step.'

'It's possible.' Vincent didn't sound as if he believed this theory. 'But what reason would he have to be here late at night? It's nowhere near the jakes. No, I agree with Wilhelm. This is the work of the ghost.'

I stared down at the body while they argued about the armourer's last moments. Something jarred in my head, like the lid of a chest that won't shut properly. I had a sudden image of the old bell ringer back in Acton Village when I was a small boy. He'd taken too much ale, gone to ring the bell for evensong and tumbled down the church belfry to his death. Brother Matthew had been called from the abbey to help lay out the body and I'd gone with him. The poor bell ringer was covered in cuts and bruises. Samuel had none, although the stairs in the storeroom were every bit as hard as the ones in the belfry.

A bellow from the top of the stairs made us jump. The Master Armourer came storming down.

He looked from one worker to the next, his eyes blazing under his fearsome eyebrows.

'Mein Gott!' he shouted, his face purple with fury. 'What are you all doing standing around there? You're supposed to be working, or have you forgotten we've got a pageant to prepare for and my neck will be on the block if we're not ready?' He pushed through the huddle of workers. 'Now Samuel's run off and that fool of an artist is sure to demand some more ridiculous new engravings for the King's armour and . . .'

The men turned, heads bowed, and parted silently. Master Hartmann's eyes widened with horror as he saw the body. The next minute he was on his knees in front of it.

'Samuel!' he cried. 'How could this have happened?'

'He must have fallen,' said Michael. Fear flickered in his eyes. 'Fleeing from the ghost,' he muttered under his breath.

The Master Armourer put his head in his hands. 'A fine worker. I cannot believe it.'

He looked up, tears in his eyes, and seemed to see me for the first time. Again his mood changed abruptly. 'Who are you?' he demanded, with a piercing gaze. 'And what are you doing here?'

I explained my orders from the King.

'Very well,' growled Hartmann. 'You'd better go to the workshop and wait until we can deal with your request. Who knows when it will be,' he added. 'We have enough to do without that.' Suddenly he leapt to his feet. 'And as for the rest of you – on with your tasks. I'll get someone to see to Samuel.'

I made sure I was last to leave. I let my livery cap fall to the ground next to the body and caught up with the armourers. As we got to the workshop I gave a loud curse. Vincent and Wilhelm turned to me.

I clapped the top of my head. 'I've lost my cap. It must be in the storeroom. I know I had it before.' Candle sputtering, I turned to retrace my steps. 'I have to find it,' I called over my shoulder. 'I'll be beaten if I lose it again!'

Alone in the storeroom, I was suddenly aware of the regimented rows of wax legs around me. Motionless, of course. But they made me uneasy. I shook myself, stuck my cap on my head and looked hard at the dead man. I didn't have long. Any moment now, the Master Armourer was going to send someone to deal with Samuel's body. I got on with my examination, checking the arms, face and legs. There didn't seem to be a wound of any kind. However I couldn't throw off the niggling feeling that something was wrong.

Carefully I lifted up Samuel's shirt. I didn't need to bring the candle closer to see the huge bluey-purple bruise that spread right across his back. I'd been wrong.

Here was an injury that might have been caused by a fall.

I had another sudden memory of the bell ringer. I'd been helping Brother Matthew prepare the body for burial. There'd been a bruise like this on his back too. I remember being shocked, it was so large and dark. My godfather told me that it was a normal occurrence on a corpse. The bell ringer had not been found for many hours. If a body was left lying in one position for a while, then the blood would sink to the lowest point, he said. It would make a large, even bruise like the one I was looking at, but always after death.

That was all well and good but for one thing.

Samuel was lying on his front.

It wasn't a fall that had killed him. He'd died some other way and been left on his back – long enough for the blood to pool. Then he'd been placed in this position to make it appear that he'd fallen down the steps.

I hoped the men in the armoury were too busy to have noticed my long absence. I had to stay and discover more while I had the chance. I checked for any other indication of how Samuel had met his end. Keeping a keen ear open for approaching footsteps, I put the candle down and heaved him over. It wasn't easy. The armourer had been a tall, muscular man and now I was getting the full meaning of a dead weight. The rigidity of his body made moving him even harder.

His eyes stared as if in shock. I tried not to look at

them, concentrating on his neck instead. There was no sign of a rope burn. He hadn't been strangled.

I pulled up his shirt. There was a small mark in the centre of his belly. At first I thought it was an old scar and went to pull the shirt down again. But something made me look closer. I held the candle near. The mark was open and seemed deep. If this was how Samuel had died, then the wound had been made by a thin blade of some sort – a blade no wider than my little finger. And yet to have killed him, it must have been long enough to plunge deep into his body.

But the scene still wasn't right. There was no blood – not on his skin nor on his shirt. And not a drop on the floor. And a dead man doesn't move his own body and rearrange it in another room.

Someone had stabbed Samuel and cleaned every speck of blood away while he lay on his back. The killer had changed his victim's shirt which no doubt had been bloodstained and perhaps even torn from the knife. Then, after some time, he'd moved him and placed him here to make it look like an accident. I checked the man's hands and arms. They were unharmed so there hadn't been a fight. In fact there was no sign that he'd defended himself at all. Had he been killed in his sleep perhaps? But Vincent had said that Samuel had not come to his bed last night.

One thing I was certain of – Samuel Bohn had not died from fright running from a ghost.

I heaved the body over to lie as I'd discovered it. I

had no idea if this murder was related to the accidents close to the King but I had to report it to my master immediately.

A blast of trumpets reached my ears. I'd have recognised King Henry's harbingers anywhere. His Majesty was on his way!

I could not be found lurking round a dead body.

5

I hurried back to the workshop and joined the armourers. We all fell to our knees as His Majesty swept in, flanked by his yeomen guard. Behind him came Robert Aycliffe and Thomas Cromwell. As usual when we met in public, my master gave no sign that I was anything more than a lowly scribe. I was desperate to report what I'd found but this was not the time.

The last to enter was a thin, arrogant man who curled his lip as his eyes fell on Hartmann. I noted that the Master Armourer had tried to tame his wild hair before the King's arrival. He still looked fierce.

I knew well enough who the thin man was. King Henry had commissioned an artist to make a visual record of the pageant. Ever since Giles Thorpe had arrived at Greenwich Palace to paint the St George portrait, he'd been wafting about the place as if he owned it. Mark had noted his rich clothes and lengths of gold chains and worried that he would spoil them by getting paint on them. I tried to allay Mark's fears by saying that although the man was a strutting peacock in public, he would surely change before he worked on the portrait. There certainly wasn't a speck on the fine white cuffs and velvet doublet.

Thorpe immediately stepped up to the King, gave him an elaborate bow and began to talk about breastplate engravings.

'We always shudder when that Mister Thorpe comes here,' Vincent whispered to me. 'He puts our master into an even worse temper. As well as doing the portrait, the King asked him to draw up designs for Master Hartmann to engrave on the new royal armour. The trouble is, Thorpe keeps proposing more patterns every day, or so it seems. He's run our poor master ragged with his unreasonable demands. To tell you the truth, it makes his blood boil and he's not been slow in telling Thorpe what he thinks.'

Now I understood the sneering glance the artist had given Hartmann. And I imagined the armourers had borne the brunt of Hartmann's temper. It wasn't as if he could take it out on the artist, a man chosen by King Henry himself.

'By the stars, it's Jack Briars!' The King had spotted me. 'This is most fortunate. Come here, lad. How did you like your costume for the pageant? I trust it was a good fit.'

With a sudden jolt I remembered why I'd come to the

armoury in the first place! King Henry was beaming, fully expecting me to say that of course the suit fitted me perfectly, and to add fulsome praise about the wonders of its construction and how impressive it would be in the pageant.

Around me, every armourer held their breath. They must have been hoping I wouldn't mention the dead body.

'Forgive me, Sire,' I said. 'I was so lost in amazement at Your Majesty's Royal Armoury that I have not yet tried the suit.'

Cromwell's piercing eyes were on me. He often seemed to be able to read my thoughts and I wondered if he knew that I was hiding something.

There was relief on the faces of the workers as I made my excuse. Vincent squeezed my arm in thanks.

The King guffawed at my words. 'I understand, Jack. You will not find such another marvel in the world!' He waved his gloved hand at Master Hartmann. 'Let me see my new armour,' he commanded. 'Where is it?'

'As ever, it is safely under lock and key in my workshop, Sire,' replied Master Hartmann.

We bowed as he led the party away down the passage, towards the room where Samuel lay. He stopped at the locked door before it.

Hartmann opened the padlock and stood back for the King to enter.

Cromwell, Mountford and Aycliffe followed His

Majesty. Thorpe made sure he wasn't left behind. Hartmann went after them.

'Where is Jack Briars?' we heard King Henry call. 'Come, boy. I warrant the young St George is keen to see my suit.'

Keeping my eyes averted from the fearful room at the end, I shot along the passage and was through the door before His Majesty could change his mind. The chamber was small, and even hotter than the main workshop, thanks to the fire crackling away in the corner.

Something tall and bulky stood in the centre, covered in a silk cloth. Hartmann pulled the cloth away.

I couldn't help gasping at the sight before us. The armour was magnificent. Each section of the suit was edged with bands of black and gold, and the steel shone in the light of the forge flames. Three lions, identical to those on the King's coat of arms, flashed their claws on the helmet. A pattern of falcons entwined with lilies covered the elbows and arms. The falcon was the Boleyn Family symbol, added no doubt in honour of the King's beloved – Lady Anne Boleyn.

I had never seen anything like the breastplate. Instead of being rounded, it came to a point just below the middle, sticking out as if it was a big fat belly! A Tudor rose emblem adorned the raised centre. The King ran his hand admiringly over it.

'I am most content with the new shape you have devised for this breastplate, Master Armourer,' he said.

'Thank you, my Liege,' said the Master Armourer proudly.

I stole a glance at the artist. If he'd been a dog, his hackles would have risen.

'Look Thomas,' declared the King, turning to Cromwell. 'See the double layer of steel that I told you about. It gives extra protection. There is not another such in the whole of Europe. Let me try it on.'

'Of course, my Liege,' said Hartmann, bowing deeply.

The King took up a stance in the middle of the workshop, his arms wide, while Aycliffe and Mountford helped him take off his coat and doublet. Before the Master Armourer could move, Giles Thorpe had snatched up the padded lining that lay ready, and was simpering round the King as he helped him to put it on.

I saw an angry vein throbbing in Hartmann's temple.

Soon the King was encased in the breastplate.

'You have done a fine job, Master Hartmann,' said Cromwell, as the Master Armourer made the final adjustments to the buckles on the shoulders and sides.

'Aye, it fits to perfection,' beamed the King. 'But we must give it a test.' He turned to Aycliffe. 'What better than the moment in the pageant when the dragon strikes me with its fire?'

'An excellent idea, Your Majesty,' said Robert Aycliffe.

'Fetch a sword,' instructed the King. 'That will serve as well as the wooden flames. For I doubt you have a fierce dragon to hand, Master Hartmann.'

He chuckled at his own joke and we all joined in dutifully.

'Jack Briars will be the one to wield the sword. On the Tudor rose, boy. That's where the dragon's fire will strike.'

'Yes, Sire,' I gulped, feeling equal parts of pride and terror at being chosen.

Hartmann brought out a sword from a chest and wrapped the blade in a thick cloth.

'To keep the breastplate unmarked for the pageant,' Aycliffe told me.

I took the sword and faced the King.

'Have at me!' he ordered.

I gently waved the sword at him. There was a muffled thud as I tapped the rose.

'Have at me, I said!' boomed His Majesty. 'The armour needs a good test. Imagine you are a deadly dragon, Jack, not a feeble measle.'

I swung the sword and slammed it onto the central emblem. I was not prepared for what happened next. To my horror, the King staggered back. Arms flailing, he swung round to clutch at a workbench but missed and collapsed to the floor.

I felt as if the ground had opened up beneath me. What had I done to the King of England?

'Your Majesty,' I gasped, rushing forward to help him. 'I am deeply sorry. I didn't mean to hit you so hard.'

I was astonished to see King Henry leap to his feet!

'You did nothing wrong, young scribe.' His eyes were dancing with merriment. 'I was playacting.'

I heaved a sigh of relief. Yeoman Mountford gave me a reassuring wink.

'I was rehearsing the dramatic moment when the dragon seems to have the better of St George,' the King went on. 'It worked well, don't you think so, Thomas?'

'Very impressive, Sire,' said Cromwell. Even my master was almost smiling.

'It was a superb piece of acting, my Liege,' said Robert Aycliffe. 'The ladies will swoon to see you fall.'

'And nobody is to whisper a word of what they have seen,' said King Henry. 'Those watching the spectacle will believe St George is doomed to a fiery death. I shall be lying, a broken man, with the dragon looming over me. All will look lost. Then at the last I shall rally and kill the beast.'

Everyone clapped. And of course no one pointed out that he would be changing the legend if the dragon won!

'The breastplate is strong as well as unique in design, my Master Armourer,' the King went on. 'I scarcely felt the boy's blow though it was a fine one.'

Giles Thorpe stood sulkily in the corner. He reminded me of a child who wanted all the attention.

However, as soon as the King was back in his finery, he waved the artist over. 'Mister Thorpe, I thank you for your wonderful engraving designs.'

'I am honoured, Sire.' The man lowered himself into

a toadying bow. 'Might I be so bold as to show Your Majesty more of them? Images that will add to the glory of your magnificent breastplate. Master Hartmann has done a good job with my ideas, I suppose, but I have a suggestion that will make it great. I'm sure that the Master Armourer will be happy to carry out any further engraving that may be required . . .'

David Hartmann started at this and I saw his look of horror at the thought of the extra work.

Cromwell caught his expression and began to speak. 'My Liege, the armoury has so much to do that . . .'

'Nonsense, Thomas!' chortled the King, waving away his objections. 'My armourers have never let me down yet. Pray show us your ideas, Mister Thorpe.'

Giles Thorpe produced a large roll of parchment from his bag. He opened it with a flourish and laid it out on the nearest workbench. 'Sire, other parts of this suit may have been embellished, but surely the front should be the most majestic. My idea is to add a bold engraving to the centre of the breastplate. Here, around the Tudor rose. I could never hope to reflect the true magnificence of my King, for that is something beyond any man's ability. . .' His Majesty nodded in delight at the flattery. '. . . yet I wish to try, in my humble way, to exemplify the splendour of our esteemed monarch.'

I'd seen some grovelling at Court but Thorpe outgrovelled the lot!

The Master Armourer was frowning at the drawing. 'Your Majesty, I am certain you do not need such fancy embellishment,' he dared to say. 'The armour speaks for itself, surely.'

But the King was lost in admiration of Thorpe's design. 'This is wonderful!' he exclaimed. 'Look Thomas. Not one, but two mighty dragons, both pierced by lances bearing the banner of St George!'

Hartmann sagged as if he was carrying a burden that threatened to crush him.

'And once the extra engraving has been done,' Thorpe went on, 'I will also add it to my painting. But as for the engraving – in no way would I wish to inconvenience Your Majesty's Royal Armoury.' He stared unblinking at Master Hartmann. 'If it cannot manage the new commission, I could do it this minute. I am equally as skilled an engraver as I am an artist.'

The Master Armourer reddened under his bristling beard. I'd warrant it was only the presence of King Henry that kept him from leaping on the artist.

'As I command it, then Master Hartmann will do it,' said the King, his tone suddenly cold.

'It will be done immediately, Your Majesty,' replied Hartmann in a strangled voice.

The King strode to the door. 'This glorious armoury was built to my design, you know, Jack. I have many suits here – and each is a creation of unique artistry. Would you like to see the whole place?'

I was speechless. I could hardly say no – and yet it felt as if the dead body was calling out, begging to be discovered. David Hartmann couldn't stop the panic that flashed across his face.

Cromwell was watching us intently. He turned to the King. 'An excellent idea, Your Majesty,' he said smoothly. 'Although I would beg to remind you that you were eager to start rehearsals this morning after all the delays.'

'You are right, good Thomas,' said the King. 'It will have to wait, Jack. Be sure to be ready when you're summoned to the rehearsal.' He swept out through the main armoury, closely followed by Cromwell, Aycliffe and the yeomen guard.

I watched them as they passed. I found myself wishing that I had no urgent obligation to tell Master Cromwell what I'd found. I simply wanted to trail along behind the King until he called me to rehearse my part as the young St George. At once I felt guilty at the thought. The grim discovery in the armoury was far more important. All the same, I hoped I'd be able to make my report as brief as possible so that I would be ready for the royal summons to the tiltyard.

Giles Thorpe was the last to leave. He wore a triumphant, gloating look. As he passed close to David Hartmann, he stopped and hissed something under his breath. I did not hear it all but I would swear to these words: 'You will soon discover what I am capable of. Don't stand in my way.'

6

I hurried after the royal procession. They were already out of the armoury and disappearing through the gatehouse into the Inner Court beyond. Cromwell was deep in conversation with the King so I followed at a distance, waiting for a chance to see my master alone and report Samuel's death to him.

Nicholas Mountford turned to me and smiled.

'You are lucky indeed to be in the pageant, Jack,' he said, peering down from his great height.

'I can hardly believe it,' I told him, keeping one eye on Cromwell.

'My father was a yeoman guard and he would often tell me how he'd seen King Henry, a prince then, of course, fighting in that very armour.'

I had a brief image of myself as the young sword-wielding St George standing bravely in the centre of the pageant, repelling all the enemy.

'His Majesty was an excellent swordsman even at such a tender age,' Mountford went on. 'It's a great honour for a young scribe like you to be wearing the King's boyhood armour. Especially one who was nearly thrown in the Thames when he came to Court!'

Yeoman Mountford would never let me forget the day I'd first tried to enter the King's service.

By the time he'd finished laughing about how he'd chased me all over Whitehall Palace thinking I was a vagabond, Cromwell had left the King's side and was nowhere to be seen. I took my leave of the yeoman and dashed into the Inner Court just in time to see the tail of my master's cloak disappear through the doorway on the other side. I sped after him, sensing he would be waiting for me.

I was right.

He said nothing but led me up the wide staircase to the chapel near the Royal Apartments. He pushed open the heavy carved door and went inside. I followed and we made a quick search. When he was satisfied that no one lurked behind the pillars or in the pulpit, he gave me a nod. He knelt before the altar, his head bowed as if in prayer. I took a seat in a front pew. If anyone should come in, I could not be seen praying side by side with His Majesty's most important minister.

'Why was the idea of the King's inspection so unwelcome?' he asked without turning.

'Because he would have come across the dead body of one of the armourers,' I told him.

My master made no movement of surprise at this news but listened as I described how I'd found Samuel Bohn.

'The killer made it look like an accident,' I finished, 'so I believe I am the only one who knows that it was not.'

'Do you have any theories about who the murderer could be?'

'I've given it some thought, sir,' I admitted. 'David Hartmann has a fearful temper. With the pressures of the pageant, it is possible that he cracked under the strain and acted in a rage.'

'I think that would be unlikely, Jack,' said Cromwell. 'The Master Armourer is renowned for losing his temper. It has never yet led to violence. However, you are right to consider the possibility.'

'I have another theory,' I went on. 'There was bad blood between Samuel and a fellow worker, Michael Dressler. They'd had a fight over a payment that Samuel took when Michael said it should have been his.'

I had a sudden memory of Michael's behaviour as we'd stood over the corpse.

'Dressler looked very nervous when the body was found,' I said. 'And he was quick to blame the appearance of a ghost for the death.'

Cromwell turned, his hooded eyes gazing at me questioningly. I explained about the reappearance of the ghostly armourer.

'I think we can rule out a ghost as a suspect! However,

keep a close eye on Dressler. Have you anything else to report?'

'I'm sure you already knew that there is ill feeling between Hartmann and Thorpe,' I said.

'Indeed. It is lucky for them that the King is so consumed by his pageant that he has not noticed. Is there something further I should know?'

I repeated the threat the artist had made to the Master Armourer. 'I feel it could be more than coincidence that Thorpe was using those words when a murder had just been done.'

'Gather your evidence, Jack. I pray to God that neither Giles Thorpe nor David Hartmann is involved in anything sinister. The King would not take kindly to accusations about either of those trusted men. We must hope this death was the result of a simple argument between armourers that went too far. However, everything you find must be treated as if it could be linked to the threats to the King.' My master's shoulders sagged and he looked tired all of a sudden. 'If we are right to suspect that an attempt will be made on His Majesty's life at the pageant we are running out of time. Keep up your "boyish nosiness" in the armoury.'

'I will, sir. I still have to try on my armour.'

'It will be interesting to hear how many "fittings" you can manage,' he muttered. 'I'm sure you will be most inventive with your reasons.'

'The suit must be comfortable,' I replied solemnly.

'The heroic young St George could not think of limping out before the audience.'

'Limping?' questioned Cromwell equally solemnly. He turned to look at me. 'There will be no call for that. You will be on horseback!'

I tried not to show my shock. When I'd arrived at Whitehall Palace and persuaded him to give me a job, I'd claimed I could ride. I'd always suspected that he knew I couldn't!

'Surely it will be no problem for an accomplished rider like you, Jack,' said my master. I could tell he was enjoying this.

'No indeed, sir,' I answered. I left quickly before I gave myself away.

I needed a riding lesson before the big day. When I had time I would seek out my friend Cat Thimblebee in the sewing room. She'd been trying to teach me to ride ever since I'd made my foolish boast to Cromwell. No one else knew that she was an expert horsewoman who even borrowed one of the King's own horses to charge about on.

I headed off, intending to go straight back to the armoury and start my mission. Then I remembered that I was expected at the pageant rehearsal this morning. If I was going to be called, they'd come to look for me at the office. And besides, I would be needed there to do some scribing! I was constantly having to balance my office duties with my other, secret job, and if I was gone for too long I feared that Oswyn would find a way to have me dismissed. He was always watching for any opportunity to have me kicked out. He had a younger brother salivating for my position. And if I lost my position in the office, then I would have no reason to stay at Court. And Cromwell would not use me as a spy any longer.

I began to retrace my steps towards the gatehouse, passing the stairway that led down to the kitchens. Tantalising aromas were wafting up and my belly flipped with hunger but I couldn't spare time searching for a snack.

'I've told you, Oswyn Drage,' came a cross voice. 'There isn't a pie for you.'

An old woman in a snowy white apron was bustling up the steps, carrying a covered platter, and followed closely by Weasel-face. She stopped when she saw me and her eyes lit up.

'Jackanapes!'

'Hello, Mrs Pennycod,' I said, grinning.

The pastry cook turned to Oswyn. 'There you go. You said you wanted to find Jack and here he is.'

'I've been searching everywhere, Briars,' snapped Oswyn. 'As senior scribe, I shouldn't be taken from my work to run around with messages for you.'

'Who made you senior scribe?' demanded Mrs Pennycod before I could answer. 'I'll warrant that's in your head.'

Mrs Pennycod's good opinion was hard won. I'd been very lucky she liked me and had taken me under her wing. But she loathed Weasel-face and had even been known to chase him away with her ladle!

Oswyn eyed the pastry cook warily – probably to make sure she had no kitchen implements on her. 'You know little of Court matters, old biddy,' he sneered.

'I expect you're right,' answered Mrs Pennycod, her lips tight. 'To be honest, I'm so stupid I can't even count my pies properly. For now I find I *do* have one spare.' She delved under the plate cover, pulled out a thick-crusted pie and thrust it into my hands. 'Don't want you going hungry, Jack.'

'Thank you, Mrs Pennycod,' I said, taking a large bite. 'It tastes delicious.'

'The abbey foundling's getting better treatment than I am!' spluttered Oswyn.

'Shame on you,' said Mrs Pennycod fiercely. Oswyn backed away. 'Jack may not have any family but he has the manners of a gentleman – unlike some!'

'If you give me the message now, Oswyn, you can get back to work without more delay,' I suggested helpfully.

Oswyn opened his mouth – then shut it again. A cunning expression came over his weaselly face. 'I've forgotten it,' he said with a shrug. 'I've spent so long looking for you that it's gone right out of my mind. It can't have been important.'

He sauntered off whistling.

'He's a pain in the neck,' said Mrs Pennycod. 'If he causes you any more trouble just come to me.

44

Anyway, what have you been up to?'

I hesitated. However grateful I was to her for getting the better of Oswyn, I couldn't tell her I'd been finding dead bodies in the armoury.

'I'm going to be the young St George in the King's pageant,' I said.

'Well there's a fine thing and well deserved,' she chuckled.

I had a sudden thought that as she knew Greenwich Palace from basement to battlements – not that there were any battlements – she might know more about the haunting that was disturbing the pageant preparations.

'The workers were telling me about the deadly ghost that walks in the armoury.'

If I was expecting information, I was disappointed. A blank look came over the pastry cook's wrinkled face.

'I've never heard of it,' she said. 'And I've heard most of the tales. There's Duke Humphrey, of course. He appears on the top of his tower in the park and waves his severed head. Then there's the spectre of the spit boy who . . .'

She regaled me with grisly tales. Not one mentioned an armourer, ghostly or otherwise.

'I reckon they were pulling your leg, Jackanapes,' laughed Mrs Pennycod when she'd gone through her list. 'You wait till I see them. I'll give them what for – teasing my favourite scribe!'

'Please don't,' I begged her, pretending to be embarrassed. 'I'd never live it down.'

'I understand,' whispered the old cook conspiratorially. 'Your secret's safe with me.' She suddenly remembered the platter in her hands. 'I'm just taking a pie to Master Cromwell. He often misses his meals because he's working so hard and I can't have that. I've been chatting away while the poor man is starving to death!'

'He was in the chapel just now,' I said.

'Then that's where I'm going.' With a cheerful goodbye, she scuttled off.

I finished the rest of my pie and hurried back towards the office. I couldn't help the rising feeling of excitement that I'd soon be at my rehearsal, finding out exactly what heroic deeds would be required of the young St George.

I found myself caught up in crowds of courtiers as they headed for their lunch. To avoid them, I pelted down the stairs to the ground floor and dashed along the dark, deserted passageway that would lead me to the gatehouse.

I heard a faint sound behind me and turned. A shaft of sunlight picked out the small, eerie figure of a woman in an old-fashioned gown with long flowing sleeves and a pointed hat with a veil. She was floating towards me. All the stories of palace ghosts flooded back into my head. Her voice echoed along the passage.

'Jack!'

It was all I could do not to run in terror.

7

'Jack, you clodpole! It's me!'

I knew that voice. The apparition gave me a cheerful wave, tripped on its gown and let out a very unspectral curse. It was Cat Thimblebee.

'Your face!' she spluttered, pulling up her veil as she reached me. She was grinning in a very annoying manner. 'Anyone would think you'd seen a—'

'I was just surprised to see you,' I cut in. 'Why are you dressed in' – I waved a hand at her outfit – 'all that?'

Cat looked round furtively. 'I'm not supposed to be wearing it here,' she admitted. 'I've got my own clothes on underneath – just in case. It's Lady Anne Boleyn's costume that she'll have on at the pageant – you know, when she sits in her tower and the King rescues her. It'll be so romantic. He'll be declaring his love for her in the story and in real life.'

47

'Talking of the pageant,' I began. 'I've got to get back to work. The King has asked me to . . .'

But Cat wasn't listening. 'Anyway, you're holding me up. I have to take this dress to that dreadful artist Thorpe. He wants to look at the shade of blue in the light before he finishes the dress in his painting.' She raised her eyes to the ceiling as she spoke. 'Trouble is, he's always "finishing" his stupid painting. "A great artist's work is never done!" he says if I dare make a fuss. Pompous windbag! He thinks I have nothing better to do than jump to his every whim. I have to keep coming to his studio and modelling the dress for him – being the only girl in the sewing room – and I've nearly worn the flagstones out with running to and fro these last few days.'

I was about to try again to give her my news and get away when we heard footsteps along the passage. Cat hastily pulled down her veil to cover her face. She was about to leap for the shadows when a page came into view. As he passed us he stopped short in front of Cat and bowed respectfully.

The moment he'd gone Cat began to preen herself. 'Seems I'm a grand lady now,' she said imperiously, 'so you'd better start being more . . .'

She was interrupted by an almighty bellow from down the passage. Without a word I hurried towards the angry sound. Cat was close on my heels, bunching the trailing dress in one fist to keep from tripping.

'It came from the artist's chamber,' she hissed. 'But

48

it wasn't him. Whoever it is should beware of shouting at that man. Mister Thorpe was chosen by the King himself. He's protected.'

We reached the open door of the studio and peeped in. Two terrified assistants were crouching behind a table of pots and brushes. A log boy was frozen by the fire, wood in hand.

In the middle of the room David Hartmann and Giles Thorpe stood facing each other defiantly. The whole scene could have been straight out of one of the artist's paintings!

'I will not deface my breastplate with these scribbles,' spat Hartmann. He thrust a piece of paper at the artist's face. 'I don't interfere with your daubing so keep your nose out of armoury business. The design of the breastplate is perfect and I've already done enough extra engraving thanks to your whims. It does not need this stupid embellishment.'

Giles Thorpe slowly smiled. It wasn't a pleasant sight. 'I wonder what His Majesty will have to say,' he said, a smug tone to his voice. 'I imagine he won't be very happy to hear you are disobeying his direct instructions. I would like to be there when you tell him.'

The Master Armourer opened his mouth but he could find no answer. Boiling with anger, he scrunched the drawings in his fist.

The artist strutted over to a huge canvas on an easel. It showed a magnificent King Henry in the very armour I'd seen earlier. He was delivering the fatal blow to the mighty dragon while an unfinished Lady Anne leaned adoringly from her tower. 'My "Victory of St George" is just the first of hundreds of commissions from His Majesty,' he said gloatingly. 'I have worked for many noble families all over Europe, and now that I have the favour of the King of England everyone of importance here will be begging me to paint them. As for my engraving designs, there won't be a suit of armour in the kingdom without a Thorpe embellishment.'

Lips pressed tightly together, David Hartmann made as if to go. He looked beaten.

'One more thing,' said Thorpe. 'I want something else added to the engraving.'

'I will do the dragons and no more!'

'But this is the most vital part of the whole design,' said Thorpe smoothly. He snatched the drawing from the Master Armourer's hand, smoothed it out and drew something with a piece of charcoal. 'My initials. A true artist always signs his work.' He thrust the paper back at Hartmann.

Master Hartmann roared like an angry bear and threw himself at Giles Thorpe. Thorpe stumbled backwards, knocking the table flying. But Hartmann was on him. They crashed about the place, punching and kicking like urchins in a street fight. The poor log boy was nearly knocked into the fire.

Cat gave a gasp of horror as a large pair of scissors appeared in the artist's grasp. He waved the point in Hartmann's face.

'Think you can beat me, do you?' he taunted.

Hartmann snatched up a poker, spilled in the fight. His features were distorted with anger.

I didn't think about my next move or I'd never have done it. I threw myself between them.

'Remember your duty, gentlemen,' I said, hoping they didn't hear the wobble in my voice. 'This will not get the armour or the painting finished for the King.'

A moment passed. It felt like an hour. Then Hartmann, his face still a mask of fury, lowered the poker and let it fall with a clang. He snatched up the crumpled designs and stormed towards the door. 'I will do the dragons and no more!'

'Heed my warning,' Giles Thorpe snarled at his back. 'Don't cross me!'

The Master Armourer flinched at the words but quickened his step and was soon gone from our sight. Thorpe tossed down the scissors and went over to his painting.

'Leave the dress here, girl,' he snapped at Cat. She hurriedly pulled off her costume and laid it on a chair. 'Now go and give me some peace. All of you!'

The log boy beat everyone to the door, running as if the devil himself was after him. I'm sure I didn't imagine the whiff of singed clothing as he passed.

Cat caught up with me in the passage, pulling her seamstress cap on over her wild red hair.

'That was exciting!' she said. 'I knew there was no love lost between the two of them, but I never expected to see such an explosion. You're lucky you're still alive! They had murder in their eyes!' She elbowed me in the ribs. 'Are you listening, Jack?'

Her words were hanging in the air. *Murder in their eyes!*

8

Cat pinched my arm. 'Jack! Do I get an answer?'

'Sorry,' I muttered. 'I've got something on my mind.'

'I know that look, Jack Briars! You're on a mission – without me.' She sounded offended. She considered herself as much one of Cromwell's agents as I was although he'd never recruited her. Nor had I, come to that.

'I'll tell you how it started,' I said, resigned to sharing my investigation with her. 'This morning the King asked me to play the part of young St George in the pageant.'

I half expected Cat to scoff that this was old news – like Cromwell she usually had her ear to the ground. So it gave me a moment of smug pleasure to see her mouth drop open in surprise.

'What's that got to do with your mission?' she

demanded, obviously annoyed that this bit of palace gossip hadn't reached her already.

I quickly explained about the attempts on the King's life and how I was to be Cromwell's eyes in the armoury. When I told her that I'd found Samuel Bohn's body with the stab wound, she cut in.

'Poor Samuel!' she gasped in shock. 'He was a nice man. Who do you think killed him?'

'Michael looked very guilty when the body was found,' I said. 'And he was no friend of Samuel's, by all accounts.'

'You're not going to bring up that silly fight they had, are you?' she declared. 'I can't imagine him or any of the armourers doing a murder.'

I should have guessed that Cat would be acquainted with the armourers. She seemed to know every worker in the palace.

'What do the other men think?' she asked.

'They think it was an accident,' I told her, 'and Cromwell has ordered me not to tell anyone any different. They believe he fell down the stairs fleeing from the armoury ghost.'

'What armoury ghost?' she demanded. 'They haven't got a ghost there, have they?'

As I told her the story, I made a mental note that neither Mrs Pennycod nor Cat – both reliable sources of spectral stories – knew of the ghost.

'Master Hartmann doesn't want it spoken about,' I said quickly. 'He doesn't want the King to know that the armoury has any problems.'

'I won't tell a soul,' said Cat. 'What did the men say about it?'

'They said it's only just started walking again.' I explained about the strange noises and the fear that one sight of the phantom was fatal.

'Then surely it was the ghost who killed poor Samuel,' said Cat.

Cat was always ready to blame the supernatural for any disaster.

'Samuel was stabbed,' I reminded her patiently. 'Ghosts don't generally wield knives.'

'That's true,' Cat had to admit. 'Do you have any other suspects?'

'There's Master Hartmann,' I said. 'He gave a show of sadness when Samuel's body was found but his temper changes by the second. And now we've witnessed that he can be violent.'

'I've always thought the Master Armourer was a shouter, not a thumper,' she said. 'Until just now. But in his defence, Thorpe would drive St Edgar the Peaceful to violence! In my opinion Thorpe's the murderer. I'd believe anything of that man.'

I was beginning to dislike the artist as much as Cat did, although I couldn't allow the feeling to rule my head. 'We have no proof. But whoever did it, Cromwell said we must treat the killing as if it's linked to the attempts on the King's life.'

'Let me stop you there,' said Cat. 'You say David Hartmann is one of your suspects. What possible reason would he have to kill the King? And even if he did, he's had years to do it.'

'That's true,' I admitted. 'But we can't rule him out.'

'Thorpe's your man,' said Cat decisively. 'I know I'm right . . . Wait a minute. He only turned up at Court when the pageant was announced. Cromwell told you that the so-called accidents happened before that.'

I thought about this. 'Thorpe might have got an accomplice to act for him,' I said. 'And then the pageant came as a lucky way for him to ooze into his trusted position at Court and get to the King in person.'

'Like the nasty little snake he is,' declared Cat. 'But why would he kill Samuel?'

'Maybe Samuel was Thorpe's accomplice,' I said. 'When Thorpe came to Court he didn't need him any longer so he decided to silence him before he could give away secrets.'

'As much as I hate to say it,' said Cat, 'that doesn't work either. Thorpe's been here for weeks doing his painting. If I was him I'd have killed Samuel the moment I arrived.'

'Then perhaps the murderer's motive is simpler. Samuel discovered something he shouldn't.' I sighed heavily. 'Giles Thorpe, David Hartmann and Michael Dressler. All suspects but I have no evidence that links any of them to Samuel's death, or to the attempts on the King.'

'It's lucky you've involved me,' said Cat, 'because it sounds rather complicated!'

As usual, Cat had appointed herself my spying partner. I didn't fight it. I'd learnt it was impossible to stop her.

'I'll concentrate on Thorpe,' she went on. 'As I've said, I'm always in and out of that studio. I shall report to you straight away if I discover anything that proves his guilt. You can keep sniffing round the armoury. Now – I must get on.'

She made to scamper off.

'Wait!' I called after her. 'You don't know what you're looking for yet.'

'Yes I do,' retorted Cat. 'I'm looking for a knife with blood on it.'

'It's probably not even a proper knife,' I said. 'More likely a very thin, narrow blade of some sort.' I held up my little finger. 'No wider than this. And don't make it obvious you're snooping. We can't have Thorpe suspecting you.'

'I'm not daft, Jack,' said Cat scathingly. 'I shall pretend I've lost a needle or something. That'll give me a good excuse to nose around. And I'll get his apprentices to search too. That way they won't notice if I poke about in odd places. And the artist usually has his big swollen head in the clouds when he's working so he won't think anything's going on. Don't you worry – I've got it all figured out.'

'But what if his apprentices are in on the murder too?' I asked.

'They won't be,' said Cat. 'They didn't come with him – it seems he left his men in Foreignland when he came back from doing his fancy paintings abroad. The King got them for him and is paying their wages. I've been in that place so often I've got to know them both.'

'Then keep chatting to them,' I said. 'They might have seen something odd.'

'If they know anything, I'll soon have it out of them,' she said.

I didn't doubt it!

'There is one more thing,' I said, suddenly remembering the pageant. 'As the young St George I shall be in full armour and riding a fine steed.'

I waited for her to exclaim in admiration at the importance of my role.

Instead she snorted with laughter. 'You have enough trouble sitting properly on a horse when you're in your breeches. You'll never manage it in armour. It's much harder.'

'How do you know,' I retorted. 'When have you ever tried it?'

'I haven't, of course, but it stands to reason.' She suddenly looked very pleased with herself. 'I've got an idea. I'll do it for you. No one will know it's me inside the helmet and at least *I* won't make a fool of myself!'

'It was the King's command that I wear the armour

and we're not going to disobey him.' I felt annoyed at myself for being such a poor horseman, and at Cat for goading me about it. 'And you can help by giving me a lesson.'

'I'm not sure one lesson will be enough!' said Cat. 'But it's better than nothing. Meet me by the stables tomorrow morning at sunrise. Now I must get on. Some of us have work to do!'

9

As I hurried to the scribes' room, I tried to focus on what had happened this morning. An armourer had been murdered and it had been made to look like a tragic accident. The Master Armourer and the artist favoured by the King were at each other's throats.

Something scratched inside my head. The ghost. Cat knew Greenwich Palace almost as well as Mrs Pennycod but neither of them seemed to have been aware of the old tales of the phantom armourer. This begged the question, did it really exist? A seed of an idea came into bloom. Had someone invented the story? I needed to check with one more reliable source – my timid friend Mark. He had a mental list of every ghost past and present so that he could plan safe routes round the palace.

I had very little to go on, but if some terrible thing

was going to happen to His Majesty at the celebrations, I had only two days to find out what it was.

I pushed open the door to the scribes' room. I was ready to counter any complaints from Mister Scrope at my long absence – after all, I'd been busy on the King's business. And I was determined to ignore the snide remarks that Oswyn would surely make about pies. To my surprise Oswyn wasn't there.

Mister Scrope was guzzling a dish of eels by the fire. 'You're back quickly, Jack,' he said, without a hint of sarcasm.

'Yes, sir,' I replied, wondering if he'd been asleep and lost all sense of time.

I took my place, trimmed a quill and began to copy an order of new platters for the kitchen into the accounts book.

'Where's Weasel-face?' I whispered across the table to Mark.

After an anxious look at the Chief Scribe sucking fish bones, Mark whispered back, 'We haven't seen him since the messenger came for you for your rehearsal. Oswyn wasn't very pleased when Mister Scrope told him to go and find you. But he should have been back by now. How was the rehearsal?'

I stared blankly at him. 'He didn't give me any message,' I said. Alarm bells began to ring in my head. Oswyn was up to something.

The door opened and Oswyn himself breezed in. He

looked like a cat that had got the cream – or rather, a weasel that had got the biggest mouse.

'Ah there you are, Briars,' he drawled. He turned to Mister Scrope. 'I did as you said, sir. I looked everywhere for him. But in vain. I heard later that he'd been begging for food in the kitchen.'

'Disgraceful!' said Mister Scrope, wiping fish oil from round his mouth.

'It's not true!' I insisted.

Oswyn gave a sorrowful shake of his head. 'Don't make it worse for yourself, Jack,' he said in a horribly false kindly tone. 'Anyway, in the end I did the only thing I could. I went to the tiltyard and explained to His Majesty that I couldn't find you. I won't repeat his angry oaths.'

My heart sank. The King could not abide being kept waiting. 'Oswyn did find me!' I protested to Mister Scrope. 'But he gave me no message.'

'Don't be silly, Jack,' Scrope said wearily. 'Why on earth would Oswyn say he didn't find you if he did? You're always running about the palace on some pretext or other when you should be working. It's little wonder he couldn't track you down.'

I realised that it was useless to appeal to him. Our lazy Chief Scribe was never one to bother himself with our disputes. It was clear now why he'd thought I'd returned early. He must have believed I'd been at my rehearsal and so hadn't expected me back so soon. And all the while Weasel-face had been taking revenge for the pie incident.

I glared at him. 'You're a liar,' I said quietly.

'I think you must be feverish, Jack,' said Oswyn. 'You're talking nonsense.'

Mark was fidgeting in his chair. 'There's nothing wrong with Jack!' he burst out. His hand flew to his mouth. He looked shocked at his own boldness.

'Naturally I pleaded your cause,' said Oswyn, ignoring this interruption. 'But His Majesty would have none of it. In fact, I'm sorry to be the bearer of bad news. You are no longer in the pageant.'

I could feel myself growing red with fury. I knew what was coming next.

'I am taking your place.'

10

I stared at Oswyn's smug expression.

'But the King himself gave me the part!' I gasped.

Oswyn shrugged. 'And now it is mine. His Majesty has chosen wisely. He knows he can depend on his senior scribe.'

A knot of anger and fear twisted my insides. Anger at losing something I badly wanted. Anger at being bested by Oswyn. And fear at what the King thought of me and what punishment he might decree.

The door was flung open. Mister Scrope hid his eels and jumped to his feet as Thomas Cromwell stormed in.

'Jack Briars,' he said coldly.

I leapt to my feet, ready to go with him and put forward my side of the story. I didn't get the chance.

'You have seriously displeased His Majesty,' he said. His words cut me like a sword. 'He bestowed a great honour on you and you have thrown it aside as if it were nothing.'

'But sir . . .'

'Silence!' he thundered. I had never before witnessed my master's rage. 'I told you exactly how important this position was and you have failed me.'

Out of the corner of my eye, I saw Oswyn squirming with pleasure.

'I beg permission to go to the King and explain,' I bleated.

'Impossible,' Cromwell snapped. 'The King has decreed that you stay far away from the pageant. You can count yourself lucky that His Gracious Majesty has not had you thrown out of the palace all together.'

'But sir, I . . .' I tailed off. I could hardly argue against a royal decree.

'Stick to your scribing, Jack Briars.' His words were slow and clear. 'Do you understand me?'

He fixed me with a fierce glare. I understood only too well. My master believed I'd let him down. With only two days to go until the pageant he had lost his vital link to the armoury.

I could forget about investigating anything for him ever again.

He slammed the door behind him.

'What a shame,' gloated Weasel-face. 'If only you hadn't been running around the palace when you should have been at your rehearsal. You've been stripped of a great honour, Jack.'

Little did he know just how much I'd been stripped of!

'Well,' said Mister Scrope, 'you'll be here to do some work for a change, Jack. I would make you miss supper tonight to catch up but I don't need to. In two days you'll be doing all the work while we all go and watch the pageant.'

It was no good trying to plead my cause. Scrope's one care – apart from food – was that the scribing work got done without any bother to him.

I sat in misery, hardly able to put pen to paper. I could see Mark's sympathetic face across the table. I pretended to ignore Oswyn's expression of utter triumph.

Weasel-face had barely done a stroke of work when he threw back his chair with a grating sound.

'I'm off to my afternoon rehearsal, Mister Scrope,' he said, staring insolently at me. 'Just think, on St George's Day you'll be watching me performing my important role . . . well, apart from you, Jack.' He jogged our table as he passed. I sat on my hands so that I didn't leap up and throttle him.

I tried to go back to my copying. I was glad the work wasn't a Court letter that required my best secretary hand with all its loops and flourishes. I was making enough mistakes with a simple list. As I worked it slowly dawned on me that a disgraced spy couldn't stay at the palace. He would not be trusted. My days at Court were numbered. As soon as Cromwell had done with the pageant he would be done with me too. Returning to my childhood home at St Godric's Abbey was out of the question. Father Busbrig had made it very clear I wouldn't be welcome there again. Everything I had would be taken from me. I laid down my quill and put my head in my hands in despair. What was I going to do?

And then a white hot anger welled up inside me, turning my skin to fire. I raged against Oswyn but mostly I raged against myself.

I'd been wallowing in self pity while a man lay murdered and the King's safety could be in jeopardy.

Now I knew exactly what to do. I would carry on my investigation. I had nothing to lose. As old Brother Jerome back at the abbey would have said, my cup of poison was already overflowing. A few drops more wouldn't make any difference.

I might not be able to leave the office at this moment, but I could ask Mark about the ghost. I leaned across the table and spoke in a low voice. 'You know everything there is to know about Greenwich Palace, Mark. The armourers are all in terror of a deadly phantom. What have you heard about it?'

He dropped his quill in fright. 'I have never heard of it,' he quavered. 'Is it a new one?'

'No, an ancient one that was thought to be at peace, but now it walks again.'

'That's strange,' said Mark. 'There's Duke Humphrey who rides a ghostly steed around Greenwich Hill and the laundry maid who laments her lost love – that's why I never go near the laundry after dark – and there's . . .' He recited his long list of palace spectres.

Suddenly he broke off and grabbed my arm.

'I heard of a boy who hadn't heard of a ghost when everyone else had and the ghost was so angry it appeared and scared him to death just to teach him a lesson.' He looked around wildly. 'You don't think that will happen to me, do you?'

'Don't worry,' I told him. 'It hasn't been seen outside of the armoury so you'll be all right if you don't go there and don't tell anyone else about it.'

'I won't,' he gulped.

My mind was racing. None of my three ghost experts had heard of the armoury ghost. Was I right that someone had invented the story to cover up something far more sinister?

11

'It's six o'clock and time for supper.' Mister Scrope brought me out of my thoughts. 'You can run an errand on your way, Jack.' He flapped a piece of paper at me. 'This needs to be delivered to Doctor Cathcart.'

He'd only just finished his last eel but hurried off as if he was in danger of starving.

'I'm so sorry you're not in the pageant any more, Jack,' said Mark, following me to the door. 'You would have been much better than Oswyn. I'll come with you to deliver the message and then we can go to the Great Hall together.'

Good old Mark. I thanked him and we set off along the passageways to the doctor's chamber.

I knocked boldly on the door.

'Enter,' came a voice.

The doctor was sitting at a table eating his supper, surrounded by bottles with strange and unpleasant-looking things inside. He was reading as he chewed and absently brushing crumbs off his black robe. The open page showed a woodcut in full colour of a body being dissected. I saw Mark back away. I thought about the cut I'd seen on Samuel's body. How precise would a stab wound have to be to ensure the victim bled to death? Would the killer have to be an expert in the human body to be sure of success?

Here was the person to ask.

'Excuse me, sir,' I said politely as he glanced up. 'Mister Scrope asked me to deliver this message to you.'

The doctor scrutinised the parchment through his glasses. 'No reply,' he said. 'You may go.' He turned back to his book.

At this, Mark stepped smartly to the door. I hung on to his arm.

'My friend is anxious to leave, sir,' I laughed. 'And I know why. We have a wager and I'm hoping you can tell us who is the winner. He fears that it will be me.'

Mark looked bewildered. I prayed he wouldn't argue – he was used to going along with my strange ideas but I could see he wanted to get out as quickly as possible.

I rushed on. 'Mark here claims that a murderer's blade wound to the abdomen would kill more quickly than one to the foot. But I say it's the foot. It stands to reason. The blood would drain away much better – being at the bottom of your body.'

70

'Boys are so bloodthirsty!' exclaimed the doctor with a chuckle.

Mark looked anything but bloodthirsty. He was so pale I thought he was going to faint. I felt guilty that I was using him in this way. Luckily the doctor was too busy pointing at the picture in his book.

'Your friend is right,' he told me. 'There's a big artery in the abdomen, here.'

He ran his finger along a long red tube that ran right down the body, dividing below the waist.

'I have seen blood spurt out like a fountain from such a wound,' the doctor went on. 'Few men survive it. An injury to the foot is not so often fatal, unless the tar isn't applied quickly enough when the foot is cut off, of course.'

'But wouldn't the murderer need to know exactly where to strike to hit this artery?' I asked, as if I was hoping to wriggle out of losing the bet.

'Not with a good wide sword blade,' replied the doctor.

'Thank you, sir,' I said, remembering to look cross at having lost my wager. 'Well Mark, you win. It seems I must run to Limehouse with my jerkin on back to front.'

'Oh, good,' croaked Mark. He was trying his best to go along with my invention – and trying not to be sick at the same time.

I bowed to the doctor, hooked my arm through Mark's and marched him out before he collapsed.

'I won't ask why you wanted to know those horrible things,' said Mark, leaning against the passage wall, 'but I hope you found out what you wanted.'

'I did,' I assured him. 'And now to supper.'

'I'm not sure I have any appetite now,' groaned Mark.

'That's a shame,' I said. 'I was going to bet that you couldn't finish the food on your platter. If you do, I'll run to Limehouse with my jerkin on back to front for real!'

He managed a laugh and we headed to the Great Hall. Some people gave me strange looks along the way. It would be all round the palace now that I'd lost my part in the pageant and was in disgrace. Weasel-face had probably helped the story along.

As we turned a corner, I nearly cannoned into Weasel-face himself. He was walking very stiffly. I hadn't tried on the King's boyhood armour but both His Majesty and Albert had thought it would fit me. Oswyn was taller and wouldn't be finding it so comfortable! I had a moment of pure satisfaction at the thought.

This was quickly dispelled when I spotted the gloating look on his face.

'Ah, Briars,' he drawled. I noticed that as soon as he saw me he made great efforts to walk normally. He didn't succeed. Now he limped along as if he had brambles in his breeches. 'I've just been telling Mister Scrope that His Majesty needs me at the tiltyard all day tomorrow. As you know, the young St George has a major part in the pageant. *I* don't want to let our monarch down.'

'Of course,' I said smoothly while I seethed inside. 'But should you risk it?'

'What do you mean?' snapped Oswyn.

'You are walking strangely, if I may say so,' I told him. 'It looks as if you've injured yourself in a rather delicate place. As the young St George, I'm sure the King would allow you to see his physician. Though I hear that doctor's methods are rather painful.'

Weasel-face winced. 'There's nothing wrong with me,' he said haughtily. 'You will see that at the pageant. But wait.' He tapped his forehead as if he'd forgotten something. 'You won't be there!'

At that he swept – or hobbled – past me.

I came within a whisker of knocking him to the ground.

Mark had gone on ahead and was already at the supper table, deep in conversation with one of the pages. I sat down next to him. No one spoke to me. They kept their gaze averted. Mark saw what was happening.

'Are you all right, Jack?' he asked anxiously.

I was pleased he had the courage to talk to me when no one else would.

'I could strangle Oswyn,' I murmured. 'I might lose my job because of him.'

A shadow passed over Mark's face. 'If you strangle him you'll definitely lose your job,' he said. 'Try to ignore him. That's what I do when he's rude to me.'

'I am trying,' I growled. 'But I believe he'll never stop goading me about the pageant.'

To my surprise, Mark grinned. 'This will gladden your heart,' he said in a low voice. 'The news is all round the Court. James here has just told me. Oswyn is already having trouble with his role.'

'I could see he was having trouble with his bum,' I said.

'It's worse than that,' Mark answered with glee. 'Apparently he wobbles about like a sack of turnips on his horse. And because of the armour, he can't even mount on his own. A hoist had to be rigged up from the ceiling of the tiltyard storeroom. He gets pulled up and dropped into the saddle.'

'Thanks for cheering me up, Mark,' I laughed.

'So you don't feel like strangling him any more?' said Mark.

'There's no need. It would appear that Oswyn is getting his just desserts without any help from me.'

I let the chatter at the table go on around me. I wasn't included but for the moment I couldn't worry about the disapproval of the other servants. It gave me a chance to think about Samuel's wound. It could well have been in the right place to pierce that artery. Doctor Cathcart had said it would bleed copiously so somewhere there might be traces of blood – on the ground, or on a cloth perhaps. However, he had mentioned a good wide blade and Samuel's wound had been very narrow. It had proved fatal nevertheless.

Again I came back to the question I'd asked myself in the doctor's chamber – would the murderer have to be an expert in the human body to be sure of killing his victim? It seemed likely – unless he'd been lucky in his aim.

One thing I was sure of, the murder had happened at the armoury. The killer couldn't have carried a dead armourer around the palace without being spotted. My next move was to search the armoury for the weapon and the place of death. But I had no business that could take me there. It would have to be at night then, when all were asleep. The armourers were too scared to work through the night because of the ghost.

I fervently hoped I was right about the ghost not being real.

Mark suddenly stared over my shoulder in fright. I looked up and saw why. Cat had appeared at the door, and Mark was more frightened of her than of any spectre. She flapped her hand frantically to beckon me over. I hurriedly finished my pottage and went to meet her.

'What is it?' I asked. 'I was in the middle of my meal.'

'You'll forget all about your supper when you hear what I have to say,' said Cat mysteriously.

12

Cat led me to the stables. The sun was just setting and there was a chill to the air. It wasn't until we were squatting in the shadows outside and listening to the faint chomping and snorting of the horses that she spoke again.

'First of all,' she said sternly, 'what's this I hear about you not being in the pageant?'

'You've brought me here to talk about that?'

'No, you dalcop!' said Cat. 'But I want to hear it from you. There's hundreds of rumours flying around and some are very unkind.'

'It's thanks to Oswyn!' I said. It was hard to keep the bitterness from my voice as I told her what Weasel-face had done. 'And it's not only the pageant,' I finished. 'Cromwell has dispensed with my services as a spy as well. No more investigating for me.'

'That's terrible!' Cat burst out. 'I'm going to tell

76

your master that he's a dalcop as well.'

I wouldn't have put it past her! Her loyalty was heart-warming.

'Then we'll both be out of our jobs,' I laughed.

She fixed me with an earnest gaze. 'You're disobeying him, aren't you?'

I nodded. 'I have to investigate this murder.'

'Why are you doing it, Jack?' asked Cat. 'Is it to prove to Cromwell that he needs you?'

'Certainly not!' I said hotly. 'I have to discover what's going on. Our King could be in danger.'

Cat looked at me, her head on one side.

'Well, yes, there is a part of me that's determined to show Cromwell that he can't do without me,' I admitted. 'But the King's safety is the most important thing. Until I hear that someone has been arrested, I'm going to carry on.'

'Good,' said Cat. 'And now to my news. I've been in Thorpe's room.'

My spirits rose. 'Did you find anything useful?' I asked hopefully.

'I didn't find any knives – the sort that could have killed Samuel, anyway. But then he keeps his special engraving tools locked away somewhere. One of his assistants told me that, but he didn't know where. By the way, neither of those assistants have any time for the dreadful man, but they didn't seem to know anything suspicious about him – and don't worry, I was careful how I asked. Anyway, I decided to take a look at the cuffs of the old shirt Thorpe always wears when he works. It's a disgrace, quite honestly, but I thought he might have worn it if he sneaked off to the armoury to do the evil deed.'

I held in my irritation. Cat loved to draw out a dramatic story. And she'd make it even longer if she knew I was impatient for the end. But I did note what she'd said about Thorpe locking his tools away. Did engravers use long thin blades by any chance? In that case David Hartmann could easily have one too. And even Michael might have got hold of one at the armoury. It didn't narrow down my list of suspects!

'So I had to use a bit of cunning,' Cat went on. 'I told Thorpe that my granny's special ointment was marvellous for an artist's precious fingers and his looked like they could use some. Before he could do anything about it I'd whipped a bottle of pig lard from my apron – I'd brought it along specially – and grabbed his hands and smeared it all over them.'

'How lovely for him,' I muttered, wondering where this was leading.

'And do you know what I saw?'

'A very cross artist?' I ventured.

'Apart from that!' said Cat impatiently. 'I saw his cuffs. They had something on them. And do you know what that something was?'

'Pig lard,' I said promptly.

'Don't be silly,' said Cat. 'It was blood.' She wagged a finger. 'There. That's stopped you in your tracks!'

'Are you sure it was blood?' I dared to ask. 'He uses different coloured paints. Could it just have been from his palette?'

It seemed Cat hadn't thought of this. She shrugged. 'Could have been,' she said. 'But I bet he'd think that everyone would think it was paint so he wouldn't bother to wash it off. That wasn't the most exciting thing I saw while I was there though. A letter came for Mister Thorpe and he looked really shifty and I could tell he didn't want anyone else to have sight of it because he threw it on the fire. *And* he said he was going out straight away afterwards! When he'd got the pig lard off his hands anyway.'

'Then I must get after him!' I exclaimed, silently cursing Cat for taking so long with her tale. 'This could be important!'

'No hurry,' said Cat.

'Why not?'

'For one thing he'll be on foot because, despite his big talk of being so successful, he doesn't own a horse.'

'Surely he could have left by now though!' I insisted.

'I don't think so,' said Cat. 'I hid his cloak. He was still looking for it when I left.'

I had to admit this was a stroke of genius.

'We'll borrow the dung man's pony and cart,' Cat told me. 'That's why I brought you here. Thorpe's sure to use the garden gate into the park so he can slip away without a fuss. We'll wait along the road.'

'He'll hear us when we follow him,' I protested.

'Of course he will,' answered Cat. 'So we'll offer him a lift. Then with luck he'll tell us exactly where he's off to.'

'Giles Thorpe is an observant man, being an artist,' I said doubtfully. 'He'll spot my livery. And he's seen you often enough.'

'I'm one step ahead of you, as usual!' She led me into the stables and threw me an old hooded jacket hanging on a peg, followed by a battered old cap. 'Put these on instead of yours.' She took a smock and picked up a hat lying nearby and stuffed her mass of hair under it. The battered brim flopped over her face. 'Ready to go?'

I nodded dumbly. She seemed to have taken charge of the investigation. And she was doing a good job!

Soon we were sitting on the seat of a smelly, rickety cart and trotting towards the gate that led to the Dover Road. A lantern swung from the front, as far from our faces as possible. Few people were about, and none of them was the artist.

'I think we've beaten him to it,' said Cat. As we got to the gate, she urged the pony into a trot and nodded to the guard. He waved us through without checking who we were.

'He recognised Daisy and the cart,' explained Cat. 'The dung man's got a huge family. There's always someone different in and out with the horse dung.'

We went along to the road. East for Dover and west

for the City of London. Cat steered the cart under some trees and we stopped in sight of the gatehouse. Daisy seemed content to stand, chewing at her bit.

Cat rummaged in her apron pocket. 'I nearly forgot,' she said. 'The letter!' She produced it with a flourish. It was singed around the edges. She'd obviously rescued it from the fire.

'Why didn't you give this to me before?' I said.

'I knew you'd be in a hurry to set off after him,' said Cat.

This was too much – especially as she was right! I tried in vain to make out the writing by the light of the moon so I held up the lantern.

'Come on, Jack,' said Cat impatiently. 'You know I can't read. What does it say?'

'Son,' I read, 'that dreadful Gadbolt called again. How could you put your poor mother in such a position? I was frightened for my life. Remember what you're trying to achieve. It'll all come to nothing if you don't deal with this man at once. For the sake of your father's memory do as I say. He would turn in his grave if he found you being so lily-livered.'

I turned to stare at Cat. 'This Gadbolt's threatening Thorpe.'

'So he must know that Thorpe's up to something,' said Cat. 'Could he be blackmailing him?'

'Could be,' I said. 'Or Gadbolt might be forcing Thorpe to carry out his deeds . . .'

I broke off at the sound of a footfall. The guard was

speaking to someone. Cat picked up the reins and then dropped them again.

'It's only Jenny from the dairy,' she whispered. 'She'll be going home.'

Long moments passed. I began to worry that we were waiting in the wrong place. Then we heard a man's voice and the guard answering.

'I wish you a good night, sir.' His tone was polite and deferential.

He was answered with a growl.

'That could be Thorpe,' hissed Cat. 'He sounds rude enough and the guard knows he has to be polite to him or the King will hear of it.'

She was right. A moment later, Giles Thorpe strode past our hiding place. He carried a lantern and seemed in a hurry. He headed towards London. Cat waited a little and then gave an encouraging click to the pony. We set off after him at a fast plod. Cat pulled her hat further down over her face and I did the same with my cap.

As the pony came up behind him, I expected he would step aside but he whipped round and put up his hand.

'Take me to London Bridge,' he demanded.

'That'll be sixpence,' said Cat. She'd made her voice low and gruff.

Thorpe merely grunted.

I jumped into the back so that he could climb up beside Cat. He hunched down, holding his lantern, and stared at the road ahead without another word.

'You were lucky to see us, sir,' said Cat cheerfully. 'We'd normally be home by now but my brother made us late.'

Thorpe grunted again. Undeterred Cat went on.

'Are you seeing someone on the bridge?' she asked. 'A sweetheart perhaps?'

'It's none of your business,' he growled. 'I'm in a hurry. Can't you get this dilapidated cart to go any faster?'

Cat flicked the reins and Daisy put up her ears and began to trot. But almost at once, the poor nag caught a hoof in a pothole and stumbled. We were all jolted and I nearly fell off the back.

'Easy, Daisy,' called Cat.

The pony found her footing and continued on her way.

But Thorpe was staring hard at Cat. The jolt had made her huge hat slip and some of her curls had come tumbling out. He held up his lantern to examine her face. His expression was pure suspicion.

'Don't I know you?' he demanded. 'Do you work at the palace?'

'Lord love you, sir,' squawked Cat, turning away. 'That would be a fine thing.'

Giles Thorpe moved the lantern nearer.

13

'You dunderhead, Susan!' I yelled, giving Cat a push from behind and knocking her away from the light. 'You should keep looking at the road. We could have been killed.' I made my voice as rough as hers.

'Come up here and take over then, Will!' Cat yelled back.

'I've got better things to do than drive a cart and an old nag,' I retorted, shoving in between them.

'Hark at Mister Bighead!' Cat's bellow was so loud that Giles Thorpe clapped his hands over his ears.

'Enough of your bickering!' he cried, thumping his lantern onto the floor of the cart. 'Or you'll get no pay.'

We both fell silent immediately. I could guess what was going through Cat's mind. The thought was screaming in mine. We'd had a lucky escape.

By the time the lights of London Bridge came into

view, the moon was up, though clouds were billowing in front of it. Cat steered Daisy under the bridge's archway. I was glad it was too dark to see the severed heads always displayed above it. I shuddered as I wondered whether the traitors that I'd hunted in my secret work as a spy had ended up there. I couldn't help the terrible feeling that Thorpe could be joining them.

The narrow street between the tall, overhanging houses and shops was still busy. The taverns were full, and drinkers swayed and stumbled between them. Lanterns outside the shops made it almost as bright as day. If I hadn't known we were on a bridge with the river flowing beneath us, I'd have thought we were in any old London street.

'Where do you want us to stop?' I asked, hoping to hear a name.

'This'll do.' Before Cat had had a chance to bring the cart to a halt, Thorpe snatched up his lantern and jumped to the ground.

'Oi!' shouted Cat. 'What about our money?'

He gave a dismissive wave and headed off.

'Wait here,' I said.

I slipped down from the cart. Luckily Thorpe wasn't yet out of sight. I saw him stride along to one of the taverns, glance up and down the bridge, and go in.

I made for the tavern. By the time I'd managed to squeeze through the crowd of men in the doorway, the artist was already seated at a table in a gloomy corner, opposite a wizened little man with sharp eyes.

I edged towards them and slumped into a seat under a window, keeping my face turned away, and pretending I'd already drunk more than was good for me.

'You got my letter then, Mister Thorpe,' said the man. He gave a harsh laugh.

'I don't take kindly to it, Gadbolt!' The artist was at his haughtiest. 'My mother is a poor widow and should not be involved in this matter.'

'I will involve anyone I want to,' snarled his companion. 'You sit there in your fancy clothes and pretend to be my better. Who paid for it all? When will I see some results?'

Thorpe shifted uneasily in his seat.

'You needn't fear that you won't get your money back,' he muttered. 'Just be patient.' He straightened and the proud look was back on his face. 'Remember I am engaged in work for His Majesty and am to be paid handsomely. My name will soon be known throughout London. It will be good for credit anywhere in the city.'

'You said that when you borrowed the money,' growled Gadbolt, 'and I'm still waiting to be paid.'

I felt deflated. I'd been sure we would discover something of Thorpe's plans. But this Gadbolt was a mere moneylender.

'How dare you doubt my word!' growled Thorpe. There was a thud and a rattle of tankards. I guessed he'd thumped the table. 'I have plans – and no one is going to get in my way, do you understand? You would do well to remember it.'

There was silence for a moment. Then the moneylender spoke. 'And you'd do well to remember what happens to people who don't pay their debts. There's a baker in Clerkenwell who has a pile of ashes instead of a house. And all because he forgot to cough up on time.'

I risked a peek at Thorpe. His face looked pale in the flickering candlelight and he swallowed hard.

'You know I'll soon be good for the money,' he said, a slight tremble in his voice. 'Once everyone has seen my latest painting, I'll be turning away commissions, I'll have so many.'

'Very well,' said the man. 'I'll give you one week. I'll be wanting double interest of course.' He gave a dry chuckle. 'Seeing as you're going to be rich with your important connections.'

'I agree to your terms,' said Thorpe. 'Just don't bother my mother again with all this.'

'I won't,' said Gadbolt. 'But bear in mind that if I haven't been paid in seven days' time, then it'll be *you* causing her all the bother – trying to scrape the money together for your funeral!'

I digested this threat. Giles Thorpe wasn't the rich, successful artist he pretended to be. He'd had to find a way to pay for his fine clothes and jewels. He must have been desperately in need to risk borrowing from this dangerous man.

A woman pushed past, her hands full of empty tankards. She turned and stared down at me.

'What's your game?' she hissed, waving the tankards in my face. 'Lurking down there. We don't shelter vagrants.'

'I know him!' Thorpe's voice cut in. 'He gave me a lift on his cart. What's he heard? I can't have anyone spreading rumours.'

There was a horrible grating sound as a chair was thrust back.

I leapt to my feet to escape.

'Stop him!'

There seemed to be a wall of people between me and the door. The street was still very busy and the passers-by didn't take kindly to an urchin trying to cut a path through them.

'There he is.' That was Thorpe.

I had the fleeting thought that at least he hadn't recognised the palace scribe. But he was close. Too close.

I felt his hand grip my shoulder.

14

Brother Matthew had often worried that I was too thin. He hadn't realised how useful bony elbows could be. I thrust back, catching Thorpe in the belly, my elbow as good as any stick. He gave a groan and lost his grip.

I tore away through the crowds, desperately searching for Cat. The running footsteps behind spurred me on. Then I heard a piercing whistle. It came from the direction of the arch with the severed heads. A heavenly sight awaited me. Cat, Daisy and the cart were standing at the entrance to the bridge.

'Thorpe's after me,' I yelled as I clambered on board. 'Go! As fast as you can!'

Cat took me at my word. I doubt Daisy had ever had such excitement but she was a game little pony and we left the crowds and my pursuer behind.

I told Cat what had happened in the tavern.

'So everything he said about his work abroad – it's all lies!' she gasped. 'He's not rich and successful after all!'

'Looks like it,' I said. 'It turns out this commission for the King is vital to his career – and possibly to his life! He's relying on the fee for his work to pay his debts.'

'Then if he's that desperate,' said Cat, 'I bet he'd go as far as murder to warn off Mr Hartmann and protect his position as the King's favoured artist. I've always said it. He's the one who killed Samuel.' She stared into my face. 'You don't look very pleased that we've solved the murder.'

'Unless I've missed something this evening's work hasn't got us any further in finding out who is planning to harm His Majesty,' I said. 'If Thorpe is simply ambitious it can't be him. He'd be stupid to kill the goose that lays the golden egg!'

'At least we know now that he's a liar and a fraud,' said Cat.

'He's even more of an odious man than we thought,' I agreed. I stared into the darkness. 'But that alone doesn't make him the man who's intending to harm the King. Unless of course his ambition is just a device which he's using to get close to His Majesty. Not for the motive of fame and fortune but for a much darker one. But I still have no evidence! What am I missing?'

I felt as if I was swimming through murky water and trying in vain to reach the bank.

Cat suddenly swung round and glanced nervously behind. 'What's that?'

I could hear them too. Hoof beats and wheels clattering on the rough road. They were coming up behind us.

'It's Thorpe!' hissed Cat. 'He's got himself another free ride. He's after you.'

I dived into the back, choking on straw and the remains of the dung, hoping that Daisy had it in her to outrun the fast approaching horse.

But in an instant the cart had shot past. I felt a jolt and heard Daisy give a frightened whinny.

'He nearly had us in a ditch,' gasped Cat, pulling the pony to a halt.

'Perhaps he has something important to do back at the palace.' I scrambled up to join her. Thorpe was a speck in the distance now. 'He's forgotten about me, I hope.'

'Please God!' exclaimed Cat. 'So what's our next move?'

She flicked the reins and we set off again.

'The moment we get back, I'm going to search the armoury,' I told her.

'Have you gone mad?' Cat demanded. 'What about the ghost? One sight and *phit* you're dead!'

'I don't think there is a ghost,' I said. Cat looked doubtful. I explained my theory that the phantom was a smokescreen to keep people away. 'It's certainly stopping the armourers working at night. But I need to find out if it links to Samuel's murder and the attempts against the King.'

'So you think one of our suspects spread the story amongst the armourers?' said Cat.

I nodded. 'Fear of the phantom keeps them away from the room at the end of the passage,' I said. 'Albert insisted that Samuel was no coward. I wonder if Samuel went to investigate, saw something he shouldn't and was silenced. I want to see what's inside there.'

'Even if that ghost isn't real, you're still mad,' said Cat. 'You're going to the armoury where there could be a killer on the loose. Thorpe most likely. He'll probably be lurking in the dark, knife at the ready.'

Until this moment I hadn't given a thought to how dangerous my night-time mission might be. But I wasn't about to let on that I suddenly felt huge shivers up my spine.

'I'll be fine,' I insisted. 'Of course if I don't turn up for my lesson tomorrow, you must go straight to Master Cromwell and tell him what I was up to.'

'I'm coming with you,' said Cat gruffly. 'I won't take no for an answer.'

15

'Follow me,' whispered Cat. We'd sneaked into the palace by a small door near the stillroom. Cat had nipped inside the stillroom and swiped a candle stub and tinderbox. Now we were creeping down the steps to the basement. 'The guards will spot us if we try to cross the courtyard.'

She brought us out by the kitchen compost heap. We skirted round and headed for the armoury, keeping to the shadows. Torches burned here and there and we were able to see our way.

'If I get any warning of that ghost I'm going to shut my eyes,' Cat whispered as we drew closer to the armoury. 'I won't die if I don't see it. I advise you to do the same.'

'I've told you,' I muttered, trying to sound patient. 'I don't think there is a ghost. I reckon it's been made up to account for Samuel's death.'

'You can't be sure!' Cat was trembling and I didn't think it was from the cold.

'I've got something to tell you,' I said, hoping to distract her. 'Mark says Oswyn is making a mess of being the young St George. And the armour fits him so badly it's hard for him to sit down, let alone sit on a saddle.'

I could see that laughter was winning over her fear of the phantom. 'He's a sneaky little worm!' she exclaimed. 'If I was you, Jack, I'd go to the King and demand my part back. I'm sure His Majesty will forgive you. He doesn't want his pageant ruined by Oswyn Drage.'

'I can't risk it,' I said. 'He'll throw me in a dungeon as soon as he sets eyes on me.'

'Oswyn's the one who should be in a dungeon,' said Cat darkly.

We reached the armoury wall.

Cat hung back. 'Perhaps this wasn't a good idea,' she said. 'It's late. And you want me to give you that riding lesson before work tomorrow. I'll hardly have time to sleep! What will Mister Wiltshire say if I'm nodding over my hemming?'

I had the answer for that one. 'Not a problem,' I told her. 'Thanks to Weasel-face I don't need my lesson now so you can stay in bed a bit longer.'

'You always need a riding lesson,' Cat retorted. 'And it will be good for you. Take your mind off being thrown out of the pageant. You'll be too busy trying to control Diablo to think about anything else. Tomorrow morning at dawn.'

'You can have fun watching me fall from that devil stallion on one condition,' I said quickly.

'What's the condition?'

'That you don't run away now.' When it came to it, I found I wasn't relishing the thought of making my search alone.

'I never run away,' said Cat, haughtily striding off in front of me.

The walls of the armoury loomed up ahead and we fell silent. I beckoned Cat to a small, cracked window. I recalled seeing that window when I was looking for my armour. It had been in the first storeroom I'd searched. The armourers all slept in the main workshop. I hoped they wouldn't hear anything from there.

Gingerly I felt the glass. A triangle of it was loose. I eased it away from the frame and carefully pushed my hand through the gap. The catch inside gave suddenly, with a squeak that made Cat press herself into the shadows in fright.

No one stirred. Once the window was open I squeezed in, wondering if she'd dare follow.

There was a frantic scrabbling and she appeared on the ledge. 'You're not leaving me outside on my own!' she hissed.

She dropped down beside me and we crouched together, listening for noises.

'Quiet as the grave,' I whispered.

Cat gave me a nervous prod in the ribs. 'Don't remind me!' She pulled out the candle stub and tinderbox. 'So where do we start?' She looked as if she'd rather have stayed where she was.

'We'll go to where I found Samuel,' I told her as I tried to get the candle alight. 'I don't believe he was murdered in the cellar, but the murderer might have hidden his weapon somewhere in that room when he placed the body there.'

I held the lit candle up. A large shape loomed in the corner.

Cat gave a gasp and crossed herself.

'It's just an armour stand,' I said breezily. The wooden frame had given me a start too but I wasn't about to admit it to Cat.

We crept into the corridor. And froze. A man was standing there. The hooded figure had a candle and bag at his feet and was hunched over the lock of Master Hartmann's workshop. I licked my fingers and pinched out our light, hoping he wouldn't hear the hiss. Cat and I melted back into the darkness. She was trembling again. I think I was too.

Who was this, trying to get access to the Master Armourer's private room?

We heard the faintest click as the lock gave and the figure was in. He pulled the door to behind him. I crept along the passage. Cat was so close she seemed stuck to my back. We listened at the doorway. There was no sound inside, nothing that gave a clue as to what the man was up to. But the door was slightly open. I peered through the crack. The man was facing away from me.

'I have to get in there,' I whispered to Cat.

She nodded, her eyes full of fear.

I eased the door a little further open. Luckily the hinges made no sound as I slipped in. I took refuge under the nearest workbench, making sure I didn't disturb the discarded pieces of metal I could feel at my side. In the small pool of candlelight I saw the intruder approach the King's armour in its velvet cover. He ripped off the cover and flung it from him.

The man threw back the hood of his cloak and I could see enough to recognise him. Now I knew why he'd flown back from London Bridge.

It was Giles Thorpe.

The artist held his candle up to the breastplate. I could see that despite David's Hartmann's angry talk, he'd set to and done the new work the artist had demanded – or at least some of it. Two dragons impaled on lances were engraved on either side of the Tudor rose just as Thorpe had shown the King in his design.

The artist placed the candle close and pulled a tool from his bag. Now I could hear tiny scratching sounds. He was engraving something onto the breastplate. A quick look at the short blade told me that it wasn't one that could have made Samuel's deadly wound.

After many minutes Thorpe delved into his bag to find a different tool. I had to see what he was up to. Holding my breath, I slipped out from my hiding place and crept forward a little. The initials 'GT' had been beautifully carved in the curl of one of the dragon's tails. Thorpe must have known Hartmann wouldn't do it and was determined to have his way. This was simply part of their petty power struggle. We were no closer to proving that Giles Thorpe wished the King harm. I retreated as he began to engrave again, adding a final flourish with an equally small knife. At last he gave a satisfied grunt and put the tool back in his bag. This was my moment to escape. I had to leave the room before him or be locked inside.

But my foot caught on a loose piece of metal. The sound was so tiny that I hoped he hadn't heard it but he stiffened. I shrank back under the workbench as he whipped round. The candle held high in front of him, he crept towards my hiding place.

16

I quickly picked up a piece of metal and tossed it across the floor. It made a loud clank at the far end of the room. Thorpe turned towards the sound with a startled oath. I was out of the door in a flash. Cat and I scampered back to the storeroom. We heard the click of the padlock and hurried footsteps dashing away.

In a low voice, I told Cat what I'd seen.

'He knew the Master Armourer wouldn't add the initials so he did it himself,' she muttered.

'It seems very odd,' I went on. 'Is his pride so huge that he'd risk being caught just to put his mark on the armour?'

'It is strange,' agreed Cat. 'Although he is a right bighead.'

I lit my candle stub again and, shielding it with my hand, led the way to the room where I'd found Samuel's body. We crept down the stairs. Cat saw the wax legs and gave a shiver.

'It's scary in here.'

'We won't be long.' I put the candle down. 'We're just looking for a thin blade.'

I scoured the floor but all I found were dust motes that threatened to have me sneezing loudly. I joined Cat who was poking about among the rows of model legs.

'These wax things are bringing me out in a cold sweat,' said Cat. 'I keep expecting them to come alive and kick me! Have you seen everything you want to?'

She wasn't going to like what I had to say next.

'Now I'm going to the room at the end of the passage,' I said. 'But you don't have to come.'

I could see Cat's face in the candlelight. It was taut with fright. 'Count me out,' she quavered. 'I'll stay here.'

'Very well,' I said as if resigned to my lonely fate. 'I'll do it on my own. Remember, if the ghost appears, don't look at it. Although it might be too late, of course . . .'

'All right, all right!'

Feeling not one whit of guilt at my ruse, I led the way down the passage. There was a little light shining in at the windows from the torches outside. Cat jumped at every moving shadow. I was hard pressed not to do the same.

We came to the door.

'Looks as if it's dark in there,' I reassured her in a whisper. 'Silent too.'

Cat didn't answer but gripped my arm tightly. Trying not to let my hand tremble I felt for the latch and gradually eased the old door open. There were no windows here and as soon as I closed the door behind us the darkness hit me like a solid black wall.

We stood stock still, straining for any noise. I could hear my own ragged breathing and the blood thudding in my ears. Nothing stirred. I held up the candle. It might have been my imagination but it seemed to flicker – even though there was no movement in the air.

The flame lit up a small, square room. An old anvil stood in the centre and I made out a forge fireplace with a chimney above, built into the wall. There was nothing else that I could see, not even any armourer's tools, let alone the long, thin blade I was searching for. I inched my way around, Cat clinging to my side. No blood stained the bare earth floor. Samuel had not been killed here.

'Look,' Cat hissed suddenly in my ear. 'What's that?'

In the fireplace stood a solitary pot, half filled with a dark liquid.

'Is it blood?' She drew back as I put my finger into the pot.

'It doesn't feel like it,' I whispered, rubbing the liquid into my palm. 'And it doesn't have that sort of metallic smell.'

Cat picked up the pot and sniffed the contents. 'It's got a funny smell,' she murmured.

The grate was full of ashes. And something else. I brushed the ashes aside to reveal a piece of half burned paper. I pulled it out. I put my candle down and held the page up to the light. The lines of scribbled writing were hard to decipher but here and there a word became clear.

'What have you got there?' asked Cat.

'It's a sort of note that someone tried to burn,' I whispered.

'Thorpe trying to get rid of more secrets maybe?' said Cat grimly.

'Listen to this. *Eltham Palace.* I can't read the next bit. Then it's a list of plants, *foxglove, laburnum, hellebore . . .*'

I stopped. There was a deep sound, followed by another and another. The room echoed with soulless banging that reverberated like a funeral toll. I knew what it was – the thud of a hammer on an anvil. By her face, I could see that Cat recognised it too. As one, our eyes were drawn to the old anvil in the middle of the room. There was no one there. I put the paper back where I'd found it and covered it with ash again.

'Is the ghost invisible?' whispered Cat. 'Striking with his hammer and watching us all the while?'

The hammering stopped as suddenly as it had begun. The silence that followed was almost worse. It was broken by a slow, ominous creaking sound. I pinched out our candle flame and we were plunged into darkness.

Then I saw it. A vague shape in the dark of the far corner. Cat's gasp told me I wasn't imagining things. I reached for her hand and grabbed it. The shape was becoming clearer now and I wished it wasn't.

A figure stood in the furthest corner of the room. If it had been human once it was devilish now. The body seemed to be nothing but shadows, but the face filled me with terror. Its gaping mouth and staring eyes glowed with a hideous green light.

I felt my fear turn me to ice. Without a sound, the figure's awful gaze bored into our eyes. I couldn't move, transfixed by the terrible sight. As we watched, its mouth slowly opened and it let out a sound that surely came from Hell itself.

Hauling Cat after me, I turned and fled.

17

All night I saw that terrible image in my head. It had been very real and very gruesome and in the darkness I found I was struggling to hold on to my conviction that the ghost story had been made up by the murderer. My tired brain felt as if it was tethered to two donkeys who both wanted to go their own way. I forced myself to think logically. What had I discovered? Thorpe had been in the armoury last night and we hadn't seen him leave. So it could easily have been him playing the ghost.

I tried to turn my thoughts to the burnt note I'd found. Only five words, but there was something about them that I sensed was important. *Eltham Palace. Foxglove, laburnum, hellebore.* Where was the link? I recalled that Cromwell had mentioned the cut saddle girth when the King was to ride to Eltham Palace. And as for the list of plants – I'd helped in the Abbey physic room often enough to know that foxgloves, laburnum and hellebores were all poisonous. Surely this was how the culprit had poisoned the King's figs. Here at last was proof that attempts had been made on His Majesty's life – attempts that had been planned by someone who worked in the armoury or knew it well! Someone who had spread the false story of the ghost. Someone dangerous who had tried to kill the King and might well have already carried out one murder. But who was it? I had to remember that I had not found good reason to eliminate any of my three suspects – Michael Dressler, David Hartmann or Giles Thorpe. But the more I discovered, the more the artist seemed the most likely. I had to go to Master Cromwell with the few facts I had – and face any punishment for carrying on with my investigation when he'd expressly forbidden it.

I must have slept in the end because I was jerked awake at first light by Oswyn's snores. Although it wasn't until he farted loudly enough to chase away any lurking phantom that I felt able to move my blanket from over my head and slip off to meet Cat for my riding lesson.

Cat was waiting for me by the stables. She looked exhausted. Her eyes were sunken in her white face. I could tell from her expression that I didn't look much better.

'I'm surprised I'm here to meet you,' she whispered, gazing fearfully around. 'I've not slept a wink. We're under a death sentence, you and me. We've seen the ghost.'

'There is no ghost—' I started to say.

'If there's no ghost then what did we see?' she demanded. 'And why did you run as fast as me to get out of the armoury? You didn't stop until we were back in the palace.'

'I had to get *you* away,' I blustered. The scornful expression on her face showed me what she thought of my excuse. 'It was horrible,' I agreed reluctantly. 'But it's not real . . . it can't be!'

'Then it's Thorpe,' said Cat. 'It always comes back to that awful man. He was there just before, remember.' She clutched at my sleeve, her eyes wide. 'Did he see us in that room, do you think? Did he recognise us?'

'No,' I said firmly. 'It was too dark.'

Cat suddenly stared at my hand. 'That stain's still on your palm!' she gasped. 'It's dark brown like blood. I bet it *was* blood in the pot after all. It was wet so it must have been fresh. Perhaps it *was* a ghost we saw. And that stuff is fresh life's blood from its victims. It didn't smell like blood because it comes from beyond the grave. The touch of a ghost from hell. And now you bear the mark . . .' She stopped suddenly. 'Hold on a minute. I've remembered what the smell was now.'

'Not blood contaminated by a ghost from hell then?' I asked.

'Don't be silly,' scoffed Cat, as if it had been my idea. 'It was hair dye!'

'Hair dye?' I managed. 'Are you sure?'

'Of course I'm sure,' said Cat. 'Peg in the laundry uses it. I've seen her. She'd have a white streak like a badger if she didn't. So it's nothing to do with the ghost then.'

'It could be!' I exclaimed. 'At least – the man pretending to be the ghost. As you said, it was fresh – so as no one else dares go near that room it must have been him who put it there.' I thought hard. 'He needs a safe place to go and make his plans – whatever they are – without being disturbed, so he invents a ghost story. He cleverly spreads the tale of the ghost which haunts that very room to frighten all the others off.'

'So you think the hair dye is his?' said Cat doubtfully. 'But how does it help him pretend to be a ghost? All I know is Peg uses it to try and stay young looking.'

'I don't think he's using it when he plays the ghost,' I replied. 'Perhaps our murderer simply wants to hide his natural hair colour.'

'Well it can't be to disguise himself,' said Cat. 'I'd know Peg with or without her badger streak.'

'It's a puzzle,' I said. 'But at least we know more about the murderer. We're looking for someone with dark brown hair.'

'Thorpe's got brown hair,' Cat retorted.

'True,' I admitted. 'But so have Master Hartmann – and Michael for that matter. The burnt note I found might give us more of a clue. We now know that the murderer is also playing the ghost.'

107

'You could be right, Jack. The King was setting off for Eltham Palace when he had his so-called accident. But what about the list of flowers?'

'They're all poisonous,' I said. 'Remember the poisoned figs?'

'It all fits,' agreed Cat.

I nodded. 'So now I must tell Master Cromwell what I've found.'

'Good luck with that,' exclaimed Cat. 'He won't want to see you!'

She jumped out of her skin at the sound of approaching footsteps.

Yeoman Mountford came into view, a grim expression on his face. Two of his men were following. They were carrying a limp form between them.

'Looks like a dead body,' whispered Cat, recoiling from the sight.

She was right. The man's head lolled and although his eyes were open, they would never see anything again in this life.

'It's Michael Dressler,' I gasped. The shock made me forget for a moment that Michael had been one of my suspects.

David Hartmann came running from the armoury. I watched him closely. He looked as if he'd slept no better than Cat and I. His eyes were red-rimmed and his hair was wild. This was something to think about. The man playing the ghost would not have had a full night's rest. His horror at the sight of the body seemed genuine, yet I couldn't help remembering how, despite Cromwell saying Hartmann would not act on his temper, he'd been quick to throw himself into a fight with the artist. What else might he be capable of?

'Bring Michael in,' he said hoarsely. 'You can lay him in a storeroom for the moment.'

Cat and I slipped in behind the sorry procession.

'What's happened?' I asked Nicholas Mountford.

'The poor soul was found in the carp pond,' replied the giant yeoman. 'He must have slipped and drowned.'

A desolate silence filled the air in the workshop. Every man took off his cap in respect as Hartmann opened the door to the nearest storeroom and the yeomen took Michael's body inside. The Master Armourer remained with the body, closing the door behind him. Was he giving himself time to make sure there was no evidence of a killing?

I hoped no one would notice Cat and me standing in the corner. We had no business to be there. And even less reason to go into the storeroom. But I had to find a way to do just that. I wanted to inspect the body. I was willing to bet my year's wages that Michael had been murdered.

Albert, the older armourer, was wiping a tear away. 'This will surely be the work of the ghost,' he muttered darkly.

Cat gave an involuntary shiver beside me.

The men around him nodded and crossed themselves.

Encouraged, Albert went on. 'Michael tried to flee just like Samuel.'

'It didn't do him any good.' That came from Vincent. His face was solemn and his normally bright eyes dulled with grief.

'He would have been doomed from the moment he caught sight of the ghost,' sighed Albert. Cat was now shaking. 'It hounded him to the pond knowing that he could not swim.'

'The poor fellow would have been terrified,' murmured Vincent.

David Hartmann burst out of the storeroom and saw his workers in a huddle. 'Get on with your tasks!' he snapped. 'We're another man down. Vincent Lang, I want those dragon scales finished.' He pulled at his beard as he stormed round the workshop. 'What have we done to deserve this?'

Vincent took up his shears. The others pulled their caps back on and hurried off. The room was filled with a resounding clanging.

Hartmann suddenly spotted us. 'Jack Briars! What do you want? You've been thrown out of the pageant so you've no business messing around here. Get out! And you as well, Cat Thimblebee.'

'We've come to offer our help,' I said quickly. 'We have an hour or so before we must start our duties.'

I hoped he wouldn't wonder how we'd managed to pop up just when the armoury particularly needed some more hands.

'Help?' I thought the Master Armourer was going to explode. 'You think that a seamstress and a boy spurned by the King can be of use to me?'

'We can fetch and carry,' I said.

'They could be useful, Master Hartmann,' called Vincent. 'The fire needs stoking.'

David Hartmann threw his arms in the air. 'Very well. There's wood out in the store.' He pointed to the empty basket by the fire. 'Fill that first and be quick about it. And keep out of our way!'

'Thank you very much,' muttered Cat as we scuttled off to do his bidding. 'I hope you have good reason for keeping me in this dreadful place.'

I picked up an armful of logs. 'I want you to be lookout,' I told her, 'while I go into that storeroom to get a good look—'

'At the body,' Cat finished for me. 'I thought as much. You reckon poor Michael was murdered, don't you?'

We staggered back into the workshop and put the logs into a basket by the fire.

As we left to get another load I noticed Cat glancing anxiously at the long corridor that led to the haunted room.

'If you'd rather not help, I'd understand,' I said.

'I know there's no ghost,' she retorted. A tiny quaver in her voice made me think she was still trying to convince herself.

We filled the basket and headed back through the

111

workshop. Hardly anyone gave us a glance, but one or two looked at me as though I was vermin. All had heard of my disgrace. After feeding the fire and giving it a good poke, I led Cat to the storeroom. We slipped in and she stayed in position by the entrance, glancing nervously into every shadowy corner and occasionally remembering her job and peering out through the crack in the door.

Michael lay here, silent and lifeless.

I began to check his body. It did not have the bloated face of a drowned man. And when I lifted his shirt I had to stifle a gasp.

I felt as if I was living in a dream, or a nightmare. Michael had a wound in exactly the same place as Samuel's! The only difference was, this one was a little wider. The murderer hadn't even needed to clean the blood from the body. The water had done that. The sad irony was that by becoming a victim, Michael had been proved innocent of Samuel's death.

'His shirt looks wrong,' said Cat. 'A bit small.'

'I reckon his own must have been bloodstained,' I said.

'Blood stains cloth easily,' agreed Cat. 'All the pond water in the world wouldn't get out every mark.'

'And his own shirt would probably have had a hole where the blade tore it,' I added. 'So it had to be changed. It's got to be someone in the armoury like Master Hartmann or—'

'Or someone who was in there last night!' said Cat before I could finish. 'Giles Thorpe!'

'We always come back to Giles Thorpe!'

'I'm going to get my hands on those engraving tools of his and see if there's anything that could have done the job,' said Cat. Her eyes suddenly lit up. 'In fact, there's no time like the present! He's sure to want Lady Anne's dress again. I'll have a snoop round while I'm there.'

Before I could protest, my trusted sentry was gone. She'd found the perfect excuse to leave the armoury!

I checked for bruising on Michael's body though I knew there'd be none. One thing was clear. Neither he nor Samuel had put up a fight.

The door suddenly crashed open.

'Was machst du?' David Hartmann stood there looking daggers at me.

18

I jumped back from the body.

'What are you doing?' demanded the Master Armourer.

'I was just paying my respects.' My words came out in a rush. I could be standing between a victim and his murderer. I hoped the fear didn't show on my face.

'There's no time for that,' growled Hartmann. His fists were clenched as he ushered me back into the main workshop. 'How many more is this . . . thing going to claim?' he muttered.

The hammering had stopped. Now the workers were carrying pieces of armour to a cart outside. Their heads were bowed and their movements slow. It must have been very hard to carry out their tasks with another comrade dead and their fear that the ghost was responsible.

This new discovery made it vital that I speak to Master Cromwell – whatever the consequences.

'Where do you think you're off to?' The Master Armourer stopped me at the door. 'There is still a lot of work to be done. Find Albert and help him.' Hartmann stalked off to supervise the loading. I could hear him bellowing at someone for not taking enough care.

I had no choice but to do as he told me if I didn't want to risk his wrath – or worse! I found Albert in the second storeroom. It was crammed with armour and weapons ready for the final rehearsal. Vincent and Wilhelm, the red-cheeked armourer, were there too, packing swords into a box.

'What can I do?' I asked.

Albert gave me a frosty look. 'Why would you wish to?' he said, his voice surly. 'The boy who thinks the King's pageant is not important.'

I opened my mouth and closed it again. I wanted to shout to the rooftops that I'd been cheated out of my role as the young St George but that would mean that the King had been wrong to dismiss me – and the King was never wrong. 'Master Hartmann sent me,' was all I could say.

Albert sniffed in disapproval. 'You can take the cart up to the tiltyard when it is loaded,' he said.

'I'm sorry,' I said. 'But I can't do that. I'm not allowed near the pageant preparations.'

'Gott im Himmel!' Albert nearly dropped the armour in anger.

Vincent placed a lid on the box of swords. 'You're being very harsh with the lad, Albert.'

The older armourer flashed me a furious look and muttered something else under his breath.

'Remember how Jack kept Samuel's death from His Majesty?' Vincent went on. 'We were all glad of him then. And he's much more polite than that Oswyn Drage. You'd think Oswyn was the King himself the way he behaves when we go to help him into his suit.'

'He treats us like dogs not worthy to lick his shoes,' said Wilhelm.

Albert grunted. 'I am grateful for your help, boy,' he admitted grudgingly.

He gently lifted some armour off a stand. I noticed how much smaller it was than the others.

'Is this what the King wore as a boy?' I asked with a sinking feeling at the thought that I would never wear it.

Wilhelm shook his head. 'His own suit is far too precious to be used for a rehearsal.'

'Has this one been made specially then?' I was constantly amazed at how much work was going into the pageant.

'No, this was forged years ago at the same time as His Majesty's,' said Vincent. 'It was for his whipping boy.'

Mark had once told me that the job of a whipping boy was to be whipped in a prince's place, when the prince had done something wrong.

'Why did the King's whipping boy need armour?' I asked.

116

Albert rubbed a smudge on the breastplate with his sleeve. 'It was when King Henry was a prince. It ensured that he had someone his own size to fight with.' He handed me the gauntlets and helmet. 'You will hold those while I finish here.'

I wished I had a whipping boy. Oswyn would fit the role perfectly.

Wilhelm and Vincent began packing another case. We'd be loading the cart soon.

David Hartmann appeared at the door of the storeroom. He looked agitated. 'We'll need to work through the night,' he announced. 'Tell the others.'

Aghast, everyone stopped what they were doing.

'But the ghost . . .' Vincent began. He was silenced by a furious look from the Master Armourer.

'What choice do we have?' he snapped. He stared at the men's mutinous faces. 'And even then we need another pair of hands.' He turned to me. 'Jack Briars, put those things down. God help me, I have no wish to use a disgraced scribe but I need a new worker and I need him now.'

For a brief moment I wondered if he'd gone mad – his eyes were certainly wild enough. I thought he was going to throw me a pair of tongs and set me to work at the forge!

'You are to go to the armoury at Chelsfield,' he told me. 'Ask for a man called Peter Keller to come here. He is a friend of mine and a good armourer. He'll help us out – and he'll pay no heed to ghostly talk.'

'We'll be glad to have extra hands, sir,' said Wilhelm. 'Come, Vincent. We must take the rest of the dragon scales to the tiltyard. Excuse me, Jack.'

I moved out of their way, barely noticing them. I was furiously trying to think of an excuse not to go to Chelsfield. I needed to be here, at Court, to see my master.

'What are you dithering about for, boy?' snapped Hartmann. 'I will inform Mister Scrope that you are working for me today. Be off to the stables!'

'Stables, sir?' I blustered. The idea of a horse ride filled me with dread. I'd never had my lesson and there was no time to seek Cat's help. 'I thought I might walk it.'

'It's at least four hours on foot!' exclaimed David Hartmann. 'You will ride. Go!'

He gave me rapid directions. I left the armoury at a run, dodging round the crowds of servants that were now heading for the tiltyard. They looked as harassed as the armourers, trying to get everything ready for tomorrow. I was barely out of the place when I caught sight of Mrs Pennycod flopping down onto a stone wall. She let her basket drop to the floor. I couldn't go by without making sure she was all right.

'What's wrong, Mrs Pennycod?' I asked anxiously.

'I'm just tired, Jackanapes,' she said, managing a smile. 'Sweet of you to ask. I was up all night at a deathbed. You wouldn't have known old Ted. He was a servant here before your time. He had a peaceful passing just as St Alfrege's clock struck six. I've been sorting things out and now I'm off to my bed. They can do without pastries today.'

'I wish I could carry your basket for you,' I said. 'But I'm on an errand for Master Hartmann. It's really urgent.'

'How is David?' she asked.

I was surprised for a moment that she was asking and then cursed myself. She knew everyone, even irascible armourers.

'He looked tired too,' I began.

'That's not surprising seeing as he sat at the bedside with me for the whole night,' said Mrs Pennycod. 'Old Ted was a friend of his.'

It was as if Mrs Pennycod had dropped a hammer in a monastery. All my suspicions about the Master Armourer were shattered. While the ghost had been terrorising Cat and me, while Michael had been stabbed and taken to the pond, David Hartmann had been with Mrs Pennycod, one of the most reliable witnesses I knew.

I was left with just one suspect – Giles Thorpe.

I said my farewells to Mrs Pennycod and hurried to the stables. By the time I got there the blood was pounding in my veins – and not just from the run. The thought of being on horseback without Cat to help me, was beginning to loom large. I made my request to the stable lad on duty. I saw him try not to laugh as I swallowed my pride and asked for a quiet mount. He brought out a stocky round pony, assuring me that Dumpling would be a very calm ride.

Dumpling and I set off. The day was still and as I passed the tiltyard I could hear a rehearsal in full swing, with the King shouting orders above a tumult of snorting and horses' hooves. Unfortunately Dumpling seemed to think it was the call of the herd. Before I could stop him, he'd kicked up his hind legs, turned around and charged through the tiltyard gates.

I caught a brief glimpse of the faces of the astonished yeomen guards trotting around on their mounts as we flashed past. I clung to Dumpling's neck for grim death. Suddenly he saw the dragon. He gave a terrified neigh and skidded to a halt. I didn't stop. I felt myself somersaulting through the air.

I landed heavily on my bum – at the feet of the King.

19

There was silence. It was suddenly broken by Dumpling giving a frightened whinny. The stupid nag had set off again, crashing through the wooden forest and into the basket of metal scales. Vincent had one in his hand, ready to fix to the dragon. He only just jumped out of the way in time.

'Jack Briars!' The thunderous voice needed no identification. I scrambled off my bum and into the deepest bow I could make without actually digging a hole.

I peeked a look at the royal shoes. They appeared to bristle with rage like their owner.

'What is the meaning of this?' the King demanded. 'First you treat my pageant with disdain and now you try to ruin it!'

'I'm so sorry, my Liege. It was an accident. I never meant . . .' The words tumbled out. I was terrified. He was so angry he sounded ready to run me through with the sword of St George.

'Your Majesty, if I may.' Robert Aycliffe had come to stand beside the King. 'It did seem like a clumsy mishap to me.'

King Henry grunted. I couldn't tell what that meant.

'Perhaps I have been unfair on these stupid scribes, Sire,' Aycliffe went on. He was speaking, as Cromwell might have done, in an attempt to calm the situation, but it was obvious he had a very low opinion of me. 'Being able to write in a clear hand does not make you able to perform well in a pageant. They are such dullards. I should never have chosen either of them for such an important role.'

I knew he hadn't but was wisely taking the blame.

'They are the very plague!' answered the King. 'We're saddled with the other dolt now but this one can get out of my sight, like the worm he is.' His voice was deadly cold. It hurt me as much as a beating. 'Carry on with whatever paltry errand you were about, Jack Briars. And then you are to stay in your little office. I do not want to hear that you've left it – not even to use the jakes – until after my pageant is safely done. You will have no chance to sabotage my spectacle. I will deal with you once my celebrations are over.'

A guard caught Dumpling for me and helped me to mount. I never thought I'd be pleased to be on horseback. Oswyn was lurking by the gate as I passed, standing proud and sneering while Wilhelm buckled him into the whipping boy's armour. I kept my eyes firmly ahead as we passed.

The journey to Chelsfield seemed very long. I barely noticed the places I was passing. I just re-lived the dreadful scene of my disgrace. I tried instead to think about the mysterious deaths and how they linked to the equally mysterious accidents but Oswyn's gloating face kept popping up to taunt me.

I found the Chelsfield armoury just off the road in the centre of the little village. It was one small workshop, very different from the huge armoury at Greenwich Palace. As soon as I made my request, and explained the reason for it, the Master Armourer, Johann Engel, sent Peter off to fetch his tools ready for the journey. While I waited, I became the centre of attention with his fellow workers, all eager for details of the pageant. They fed me bread and cheese as they plied me with questions about the King's new armour. I played my part well, enthusing about the glories of the day to come without letting on how heartsick it made me.

It was early afternoon when we set off back to Greenwich. Heavy clouds blocked the sun making it feel like twilight. Peter lit the way with a small lantern. We rode side by side in the growing darkness.

'I will be pleased to see my old friend David,' he told me. Like all the other armourers I'd met, he spoke with a German accent. 'I've known him since we learned our craft together in Augsburg. We came to England from

Germany many years ago and it's a long time since we've seen each other. David is an excellent worker. He well deserves his position as the King's armourer.'

'Do you know a man called Giles Thorpe?' I asked.

Peter shook his head. 'Why do you ask?'

I told him about the quarrel between Hartmann and Thorpe.

Peter laughed. 'My friend always had a fiery temper. He is obstinate too. People can get a bad impression of him. But underneath all that he is a fine and trustworthy man. I know this for certain.'

I felt something more was coming so I remained silent.

'I'll tell you a tale to prove what I say. About fifteen years ago, David discovered that one of the workers at the Royal Armoury, a certain Geoffrey Walden, was a thief. He had to bear witness to this in court. King Henry ordered that the man be branded with a T on the left hand and that his right hand be cut off. Walden died of the punishment. David felt guilty that he'd had to testify against him.'

'But surely he knew he'd done the right thing,' I said.

'He did, but he felt sorry for the man's family so he wrote to my master and brought Walden's eldest boy to the Chelsfield armoury himself so he could have a job with us. He was a year or so older than you, I'd say, but with bright blond hair, a lovely boy and keen to learn his craft. His name was Richard but we called him Sunny on account of his locks.'

I was immediately alert. I remembered the workers at Greenwich speaking of the thief who'd died from his punishment. It had to be Geoffrey Walden. However unjustified, Walden's son could have wanted revenge against the King for his father's death. And revenge was a powerful motive.

Could Richard Walden be at Greenwich Palace?

20

I had little time to find out if I was right about Richard Walden. The pageant was tomorrow morning.

'Does Walden still work with you?' I asked.

Peter shook his head. 'It was years ago. But I remember he was a bright lad and wanted to know all aspects of an armourer's work.'

'Did he learn to engrave too?' I asked, thinking of Giles Thorpe. 'That's what I'd want to do if I was an armourer,' I added quickly.

'He picked it up at once. I believe he would have made a very talented armourer in all its aspects. But a year or so after he came to us he had his accident.'

'Accident?' I repeated. If the boy had died, my theory would die too.

'He walked into a piece of metal, red-hot from the fire. It left a horrible scar on his right arm.' He slapped the top of his own arm to show me. 'Shaped like a T, it was. Just like the branding on his father's hand. It changed him.'

Dumpling suddenly spied something tasty in a hedge and it was a few minutes before I could get him going again, much to Peter's amusement.

'How did it change him?' I asked.

Peter sighed. 'He became bitter and angry. He would pick a fight over the smallest thing. Then he marched in one day and said he was leaving. It came out of the blue.'

So Walden could still be alive. Peter had said that fifteen years ago he was a little older than me. That meant he'd be about thirty now. Roughly the same age as Giles Thorpe.

'Did he say why he was going?' I asked.

'He said he had work at an armoury in Germany.'

Thorpe often boasted of his work abroad. Had there been a glimmer of truth in his claims?

'That's a big move for such a young man,' I said.

'He didn't want to stay in the country where his father had met his unjust death,' said Peter.

I remembered that Thorpe's father was dead and his mother had invoked his memory in her letter to her son!

Peter rubbed his face and sighed. 'It was a sad business. Richard felt very bitter towards David Hartmann – even though he'd been so kind to him and got him his job while many wouldn't lift a finger to help a disgraced family. But when he started blaming

King Henry as well and saying he would have his revenge on them both one day, Master Engel told him to keep quiet. He didn't want to hear Richard speak more treason.'

'And then Richard Walden left?'

'We said our farewells and wished him good luck,' said Peter. 'And we never saw him again. I hope he prospered. He was a hard worker and he had talent. But the stain of his father's crime seemed to stay on him like the scar on his arm.'

The track narrowed and I urged Dumpling on ahead. I felt a flicker of excitement. Was the noose tightening round Thorpe's arrogant neck? Time may have passed but Peter might recognise Richard Walden even though he was no longer blond. He'd seen him more recently than David Hartmann. I just had to make sure that they met face to face before the pageant went ahead. And then I could go to Cromwell with everything I'd discovered.

I looked at the darkening dusk sky. There was so little time.

At the palace we left the horses with the stable hands. I made a note to tell Cat that I'd done the whole journey – both ways – without falling off! I didn't have to mention my tumble at the King's feet.

I led Peter towards the armoury. He exclaimed at the sight of the magnificent palace buildings that rose ahead of us, all lit with torch flames and awash with flags and pennants ready for the coming pageant.

'No sense in wasting this,' he chuckled, blowing out his lantern.

We came to the tiltyard and passed into deep shadow as we skirted the wall. I heard a sound from beyond the open tiltyard gates. For a moment I thought that someone was still having a last rehearsal.

But it was a strange, small noise and silence soon fell again. I was suddenly wary, then chided myself that I was jumping at nothing. Peter had begun to tell me a story of a splendid castle he'd seen once in Germany when there was a movement in the gloom ahead. A figure was standing in our path. Its eyes and mouth glowed with a terrible green light. The eerie light lit the whole body.

It was the ghost of the armourer.

In his hand was a large and heavy armourer's hammer. He swung it violently from side to side. Peter stood rigid, his mouth open as if he was looking into the jaws of hell.

I knew it could not be a ghost. We were facing a living man and that made it more terrifying still. It had to be Thorpe, or should I say Walden, though he'd made himself look huge and powerful. Somehow he must have known it was me at the haunted room at the armoury or recognised my face in the tavern. He had come to silence me.

I ducked the blow of the hammer and threw myself at his knees, hoping to unbalance him. He kicked me hard in the head. I managed to roll away. As I struggled to keep from slipping into unconsciousness, bright lights exploded behind my eyes. I forced myself to get to my feet, ready for the next onslaught.

But it didn't come. Through a mist of pain I could see Thorpe striding over to Peter! Groggily I fumbled about for a stick or stone – anything to use as a weapon. There was nothing. Cursing the gardeners who kept the Palace gardens so tidy, I staggered towards the two men.

Peter was strong but he was unarmed. His attacker raised his hammer. I launched myself at him, grasping him round the neck, but the hammer still swung through the air. Peter let out a cry of agony as it struck him on the shoulder. Thorpe paused only to thrust me to one side then took up the onslaught again. Peter fended off the blows but he was soon on his knees, his arms covering his head.

'Guards!' I yelled. 'Help!'

Peter's agonised shouts had turned to weak groans. I could see blood pouring from him. There was a final crunching thud of the hammer and he slumped to the ground and lay unmoving.

'Help!' I cried again.

Thorpe turned on me, the green glowing eyes burning into mine. I backed away. It was a bad move. I found myself up against the wall of the tiltyard. The hammer swung at me. I swerved away just in time. Again and again I dodged his blows, wood spraying from the wall behind me where his weapon had smashed into it. But

I was tiring and he seemed to have inhuman strength. Then I heard the most wonderful sound. Running footsteps. Someone was coming.

'Help!' I managed to croak. 'Over here. Help!'

Yeomen guard came into view, their pikes raised in front of them.

But for those few seconds I'd taken my eyes off my attacker. A pain exploded in my head and I knew no more.

21

'Jack?'

A voice was calling me from far away.

'Jack!'

Now it was right in my ear. I tried to work out what was going on. I seemed to be lying on my back. My head felt as if an anvil had been dropped on it.

'You've got to wake up now, Jack, or else!'

I began to open my eyes. The light sent fresh pain shooting through me. I closed them again.

I heard a muffled gasp and rough hands grabbed mine. I groaned as new agonies danced in my skull.

'I thought you were dead!' came Cat's voice.

'Not quite,' I croaked, forcing my eyelids apart again.

Cat was watching me, an anxious expression on her face. I looked around. I was in a tiny room full of baskets of lace and rolls of fabric, lying on a straw mattress and covered in a blanket.

'How did I get here? Where's Peter?'

'You're in the store cupboard next to the sewing room. They brought you here because I told them I'd look after you. If Peter is the man you were with, well, he's probably dead by now. He looked terrible and he wasn't moving. He was being cared for by the King's physician.'

I noted briefly that *I* wasn't worthy of the King's physician!

'Have you seen Master Cromwell?' I said.

'Not a hair,' snorted Cat. 'The King's not asked after you either. It's like you don't exist. I even tried to get to Cromwell to let him know about Michael being murdered, but of course, no one would even tell me where he was.'

I flinched as she mopped a sore place on my arm.

'Was it the ghost that attacked you last night?'

'No, it was Giles Thorpe!' I told her. 'He's the ghost. He wants vengeance on Master Hartmann and the King.' I sat up. My whole world spun and I had to stop myself from being sick. 'I must find evidence before he harms . . .'

'You're wrong,' said Cat. 'It wasn't Thorpe that attacked you.'

I stared at her blankly.

'He was in his studio when it happened. I know because I was there too. He wanted to see that wretched dress one more time so I took it to him – though it was no use in candlelight, and I told him so. And when I snooped about earlier his engraving bag was open and there was nothing that could have stabbed Samuel and Michael. Anyway, while I was there we heard the shouts and found out what had happened.'

I'd been blinded by my feelings against Thorpe. If he wasn't Walden, then who was? I couldn't take it in. My theories were crumbling to dust.

My head throbbed but I forced myself to think. His Majesty was in danger. I now knew I had to find Richard Walden, who had become an armourer. God's oath! I'd have struck myself in the forehead for being so stupid – if I hadn't thought it would make my headache worse. Peter had said that Walden went to Germany to work there. It had been fifteen years ago. He could have learnt to speak the language well enough to pass himself off as a German by now. A blond man who dyed his hair dark. I thought of the men in the armoury. It had to be one of them!

They'd all heard the Master Armourer send me to fetch Peter. I'd been wrong thinking I was the ghost's target. It was Peter. Walden couldn't risk being identified by a man who'd known him well.

I told Cat everything I'd heard about Richard Walden.

'So it's one of the armourers,' I finished. 'But all we know is, he has dark brown hair.'

'And a good ear for accents,' added Cat. 'Although I'd have sworn that every one of those men is a true German.'

'If only I could go to His Majesty and get him to put

off the pageant until I've found out who it is,' I said in desperation.

'You'd have more chance of seeing snow in Hell,' replied Cat. 'Try not to worry. You said that Cromwell knows there could be a threat at the celebrations. The place is teeming with guards. And the King's wearing full armour, don't forget. Surely there's nothing that can hurt him.'

I hoped she was right, but something was chipping away at my mind. I couldn't trust that the King was safe.

'The answer is at the armoury,' I said, wincing as my fingers found a large lump on my head. 'They'll all be busy helping people into armour up at the tiltyard. When I'm sure everyone has gone, I'm going to search that room at the end again.'

The Inner Courtyard was full of bustling courtiers, all hurrying to get a good vantage point in the tiltyard. The pageant would be starting very soon. First the jousting and then the story of St George. Cat and I were barely noticed in the hustle. Although the day was bright and cloudless I prayed that it would rain or better still thunder, sending everyone inside. I even hoped that without Peter's help the armoury hadn't finished its preparations and the Master Armourer was about to tell the King that the spectacle couldn't go on!

I tried to console myself with Cat's words. The King was surrounded by guards and protected by his new armour.

My head was thumping by the time we got to the armoury door. Slowly I pushed it open. The usually busy workshop was silent and empty. The only sound inside was the occasional crackle of wood on the dying fire.

Neither of us spoke. I took a candle from a bench and lit it in the flames. Cat followed me towards the room at the end of the long passageway. Our footsteps were eerily loud on the flagstones.

We tiptoed into the dark room. There had to be something here that would lead me to Walden's true identity.

I held up my candle and moved round the room. Suddenly a shadowy figure appeared in one corner. He too, held a candle.

'What is it?' Cat ran to my side.

With that, another figure appeared. This one wore a skirt.

Cat laughed in relief. 'We're scared of our own reflections!' she said.

She was right. A long and highly polished sheet of metal was fixed diagonally across the corner of the room. It showed us nothing but ourselves.

'How strange,' I murmured. 'What on earth could that be for?' On our last visit, we hadn't ventured to this end of the room. The 'ghost' had appeared there and frightened us off. I turned and moved slowly along the wall to investigate the other far corner. Cat stuck close behind. As I reached it I almost bumped into the edge of something hard. It was a large piece of wood on a stand that made an extra wall from floor to ceiling. It had been placed so that this corner could not be seen from the door.

'It's very odd,' said Cat. 'Like some sort of puzzle that we have to solve. But I can't think . . .'

'Got it!' I said suddenly. 'Cat, go and stand by the door and when I tell you, look at the metal mirror.'

'Why?' said Cat. 'I won't be able to see myself. It's at the wrong angle. We were well into the room before our reflections appeared.'

'This is an experiment,' I said.

I hid behind the wooden screen. I could hear Cat making her way to the door, muttering that the least I could have done was to light her way there. But I needed the candle for what I was about to do.

Cat let out a shriek. 'By all the saints in Heaven it's the ghost! Jack! Where are you, Jack?'

22

I stepped out from behind the screen. 'Here's your ghost,' I said. 'It was my reflection you saw. I held the candle under my chin so I looked—'

'Even more scary than usual!' snapped Cat. 'Don't ever do that again!'

'I'm sorry,' I said, 'but I had to prove that it's what the murderer did to us. He'd put up the wooden screen so he was hidden and fixed the metal—'

'Which he angled so his reflection could be seen and he couldn't!' Cat sounded impressed. 'But there's still one thing I don't understand. He suddenly appeared. He must have come from somewhere – and he certainly didn't run past us to get to his hiding place.'

'So there has to be a secret way in,' I said, feeling all over the cold stone wall, 'but there's no door.'

'And he didn't appear from thin air,' said Cat.

I got to my hands and knees. The floor was covered in a rough cloth. I whipped it aside.

There was a trapdoor beneath. A round handle was neatly fitted to the floor so it wasn't obvious when covered by the cloth. I pulled. The wooden door swung up with a creak. 'That was the sound we heard before the ghost appeared!' whispered Cat.

My heart was beating as if it wanted to burst out from my chest. Cat's expression went from terror to excitement and back again. We peered down at the ladder that led into the pitch dark.

'This is it,' I whispered. 'We've found Walden's lair!'

I climbed down first, then Cat handed me the candle and I lit her way.

And suddenly the hideous face with its green glowing eyes and gaping mouth was before us.

I felt a deadly shiver of cold run through me. This time I knew it was no spectre, but a real man, a living man with murder in his soul – and we had no chance of escape. Should we throw ourselves on his mercy? Could we pretend we'd stumbled on this place by mistake? A thousand thoughts raced through my head.

The spectre was eerily still. Trying to keep my hand steady, I raised the candle. Then we both saw the truth.

'It's just a helmet!' gasped Cat.

We moved slowly towards it.

The ghastly face was nothing but metal.

'It's been expertly made,' I said looking at the jagged

139

teeth on the hinged jaw. 'Only an armourer could have done it. But how did he make it glow?'

Cat pulled a small chip of stone from the rim of the helmet's eye socket. She held it in her palm where it continued to gleam with an eerie light. 'He's used witch stones!'

'What are they?' I asked. I'd learned many useful things at the abbey but we'd stayed clear of witchcraft.

'I saw witch stones at a fair once. You heat them in the fire and then they glow for days.'

'Just what you need to make a ghost seem real,' I said grimly, remembering my sleepless night after seeing it for the first time.

We left the helmet where it was and began to poke around the small room. A black cloak, no doubt the rest of the ghost outfit, lay next to some armourer's tools on a small workbench. An anvil stood in one corner. A large pile of metal scraps was stacked behind it.

Cat picked up a hammer and brought it down on the anvil. It made a deafening clang. 'That was the ghostly hammering we heard. It was just done to frighten us off.'

'The armourers reported hearing those sounds each night too,' I muttered. 'This place must be very important to our suspect. Maybe important enough for him to kill two men. Yet all we know so far is that he keeps hair dye, old notes and a ghost costume here. There must be more.'

Cat was inspecting the tools. 'These are all too big to have stabbed those poor men.'

I began carefully picking through the pile of metal. The pieces were jagged, like those I'd seen tossed into the corners of the workshops. I soon uncovered some padded material. It reminded me of the thick lining that the King had put on under his breastplate – but this was much stiffer and heavier. I held the candle closer and dropped the material in shock.

'It's saturated in blood,' I gasped.

'And look!' Cat was pointing to a dark stain on the floor. 'Do you think this is where the men were killed?'

'It looks like it,' I said. 'Walden is clearly a very clever, devious man. I'm sure he'll be there at the pageant even now, secretly waiting for his moment of triumph. But without knowing who he is, we can't stop him!'

'How about getting Cromwell to arrest all the armourers,' suggested Cat.

'Even if he agreed to listen to me, the King would never hear a word said against his armoury,' I said. 'The story of Richard Walden is not evidence enough.'

Kicking the horrible material to one side, I continued to pick through the pile.

'This is interesting.' Under the shards of metal was a complete breastplate. It had a raised circle on the distinctive pointed front. 'It's exactly the same shape as the King's,' I said, picking it up to show Cat. 'Although there are no engravings on this one.'

'What's it doing here?' asked Cat.

'Master Hartmann must have made it when he was testing out the new shape,' I decided. 'But I can't see why it's ended up in this place.'

'It looks funny,' giggled Cat. 'Everyone will think the King has eaten too many pies.' She gave a gasp. 'Don't tell him I said that!'

'It's actually very clever,' I said. 'And all Master Hartmann's design. There are two layers of steel here instead of one. They give extra protection.' I held it out towards her to show her the front. 'The King put it on to try it and I had to strike him as hard as I could on the rose with a sword.'

'Bet I can do it harder,' said Cat. Without warning, she snatched up the hammer and swung it at the raised circle. The clang almost masked another sound – a faint metallic click. From the inside of the breastplate, a blade suddenly shot towards me.

23

'God's breeches!' screeched Cat, dropping the hammer. 'What have I done?'

I was too shocked to speak. I gazed down at the thin blade sticking into my chest. Then reason slowly reasserted itself. I was still alive. Nothing hurt and there was no blood. The blade had simply pierced the padding on the front of my livery jacket. Carefully I pushed the breastplate away from me. Now I could see the whole blade, with its viciously pointed end. A blade little more than the width of one of my fingers.

'This breastplate was not made by David Hartmann,' I said. I turned to Cat. 'Thank the heavens I didn't strap it on.'

'I don't understand,' murmured Cat, still dazed.

I rested the breastplate on the floor with the knife sticking up, took the hammer and pushed on the point of the blade. It slid back inside the two layers of steel.

'It's on some kind of spring,' I explained. 'When you whacked the emblem on the front . . .'

'. . . Out it popped!'

'Just at the right place to stab a man in the belly! That's how Samuel and Michael died.' I felt cold beads of sweat break out.

'How can you be sure that's how they were killed?' asked Cat.

'Neither man put up a fight,' I said. 'They didn't stumble on Walden's plans after all. They must both have been tricked into coming down here to try on the breastplate. They wouldn't have suspected anything, because the killer was a fellow armourer.'

'It's a complicated way to kill two armourers,' said Cat. 'Why go to all the trouble of copying a breastplate? A royal breastplate at that.'

'That's exactly what we have to find out,' I said. 'Samuel and Michael were both chosen to try on the breastplate. Why those particular men?' A terrible idea was beginning to form in my mind. 'Albert said they were the biggest men in the armoury. Would you say they were as big as the King?'

Cat slowly nodded. 'You think they were chosen because of that?' She looked frightened. 'You don't mean the murderer was just testing out his breastplate on them?'

'I do,' I replied. 'I believe he intended to make sure it worked properly. When he was certain of that, he planned to engrave it and swap it for the original so that the King would wear it at the pageant!'

We gazed at each other, letting the truth sink in.

'You were right, Cat,' I said, smiling. 'With all the security, the King *is* safe today. Walden must have realised that too, and couldn't risk being found out!'

'So he didn't bother with the engraving!' said Cat fervently. 'God be praised! But I don't understand why both men had to die? The villain must have known his evil contraption worked when it killed Samuel.'

'The wounds on each were different,' I said, working it out even as I spoke. 'Perhaps Samuel took too long to bleed to death so Walden decided he'd better try a bigger knife.' I didn't go into what the doctor had told me about the artery. I didn't think Cat would appreciate the gory details. 'There's one thing I am sure of. Master Hartmann can have known nothing about this. Richard Walden must have broken into his room—'

'We know that's possible,' Cat put in. 'After all, Giles Thorpe managed it.'

'Exactly. Walden took careful note of Hartmann's breastplate design, came here at night and fashioned a replica. Then he added the blade.' I grinned at her. 'We've solved it, Cat. The King can have his pageant in safety and afterwards we'll tell Master Cromwell what we've found. He'll have to listen in the end. But for now let's see if we can find out just who Richard Walden is pretending to be.'

Cat held the candle while I picked through the rest

of the pile of discarded metal. At the bottom was something covered in a tarpaulin.

'What's this?' I muttered. 'Bring the candle closer, Cat.'

I pulled the tarpaulin aside. The flame flickered over another breastplate, the same shape as the first. But this one was elaborately engraved. And in the centre was a Tudor rose, flanked by two slain dragons.

'This looks identical to the armour David Hartmann made for the King,' I said slowly. 'It's got all the engraving.' Suddenly I was filled with foreboding.

'It must be the copy Walden was intending to use on the King,' said Cat. 'It can't be the one the Master Armourer made. I saw the King all kitted out earlier – in full armour. He paraded round the Inner Court while you were still asleep. Be careful – it'll have another deadly blade in it!'

I studied the design. 'This is no copy,' I said slowly, horror rising like vomit in my throat. 'This *is* the original.'

'How do you know?' asked Cat puzzled.

I pointed to some small marks in the curl of the dragon's tail. 'Thorpe's initials. The engraving I saw him do in secret.'

'So why isn't the King wearing this one then?' asked Cat.

A terrible picture was unfolding in my head. 'If His Majesty was wearing this one, the dragon would strike him in the centre of the breastplate . . .'

I smashed the hammer into the Tudor rose in an imitation of the dragon's tongue of fire.

'And nothing would happen.'

'So what *is* he wearing then?' said Cat, her voice full of fear.

'I don't think Walden gave up his plan. I think he *did* swap the King's breastplate for the deadly one. He made the plain one as a test and when he was sure it worked, he made another breastplate and copied the engravings. He didn't know that Thorpe had then gone back and added his initials to the design. I was the only one who saw Thorpe doing it . . . but there's only one thing wrong with that theory. Walden still had a day and a night to find out and add them, perhaps when he swapped the armour over.'

'You're wrong,' said Cat eagerly. 'He didn't have time. Don't forget that the armourers have been working nonstop since yesterday morning. Even if he noticed the initials when he swapped the breastplate, it would have taken him too long to put them on his copy.'

I dashed for the ladder. 'Come on. We have to get to the pageant!'

24

We flew along the passage. Even from here we could hear the music booming out from the tiltyard. The celebrations had begun. It took all my strength to run but I knew I had to ignore my aching head and battered body if we were to save the King.

Cat caught up with me at the workshop door.

'You've forgotten something,' she panted as I flung it open. 'The yeomen will stop you. They all know your face.'

Cat was right, of course. I needed a disguise if I was to get anywhere near the pageant. Then I had it!

'No one will see my face! Follow me.' I turned and ran back to the second storeroom. Now the rehearsals were done, the whipping boy's armour was back on its stand. I tore my livery jacket off. 'They'll just see the young St George.'

'How's this going to work?' said Cat as she tightened

the buckles on the breastplate for me. 'For a start there can't be two young St Georges in the pageant. Everyone will think they're seeing double.'

'I've thought of that,' I said. 'We're going to stop Oswyn from going on.'

'And there's another thing. As soon as you try to halt the pageant, the guards will be on you,' argued Cat. 'You'll be carted off and the whole thing will carry on as planned.'

'I intend to wait until the last minute,' I said. 'I won't do anything until the dragon appears. Then I'll stop the dragon's fire hitting the King – and take the consequences!'

I pulled the helmet over my head, biting off a groan as it pressed against all the bruises on my scalp. It felt very strange to be totally encased in metal. I feared I might have to walk like Oswyn until I took my first steps and realised that the suit fitted me perfectly. As we left the armoury I pulled down the visor so that no one could see my face. It offered only a slit of vision. The whipping boy would have been lucky to see where his royal fighting partner was, let alone hit him!

None of this mattered. Time was passing and I had to stop the dragon from dealing its deadly blow.

'Ben the stable boy told me that those on horseback for the pageant are mounting their steeds just outside the tiltyard gate,' said Cat as I made my clanking way towards the scene.

'That's no good,' I said. 'Oswyn and I will be seen

together.' The sweat was running down my face and I put up a hand to wipe it away, forgetting the helmet. My gauntlet struck the side and I heard Cat snigger.

She put her hand on my arm and steered me round something. 'I've had an idea,' she said. 'Oswyn needs a hoist to get him onto his horse. It's in the tiltyard storeroom over there. That's where he'll be. We'll waylay him.'

One of my armoured feet caught the other and I nearly toppled headlong. We were running out of time. The jousting must be over by now. I was just wondering if I should change the plan, shed all the metal and just charge into the arena when Cat gave a gasp.

'We're too late. Oswyn's already on his horse!'

This left me with one option. I would have to dodge the guards and get to the King.

I'd barely decided this when I felt Cat seize my gauntlet and pull me along.

'Where are we going?' I demanded. 'This isn't the way to the tiltyard.'

'I'm taking you a roundabout way to the storeroom,' Cat told me. 'You're going to hide in there. We'll soon have Oswyn off that horse.'

I could just make out that she was guiding me into a dark corner of the store. I dared to raise my visor. She'd hidden me behind a tall pile of wood, right next to the rope hoist.

Soon I heard her voice again – along with a horse's hooves. 'Don't argue, Oswyn,' she was saying. 'I've

150

told you, you have to come back in here to have the special saddlecloth put on.'

Cat was leading a horse in through the door. Oswyn was wobbling about on its back. He had his visor raised and I could see his weaselly face, flushed with fury. I realised that the armour he wore was more ornate than the poor whipping boy's. I hoped everyone would be too busy gawping at the grown-up St George to notice the difference.

'Get your hands off me,' Oswyn shouted. 'You've got it wrong. I would have known if I had to sit on a different saddlecloth.'

'No you wouldn't,' said Cat, as though she was talking to a small child. 'I've only just finished embroidering it – on the King's orders. If he doesn't see it under your bum when you go out there, you'll be in big trouble.'

At the mention of the King, Oswyn stopped protesting. 'You'd better hurry then,' he said sulkily.

'I won't be able to do anything until you dismount,' said Cat, hands on her hips.

'I can't,' came the muttered reply. 'It's . . . it's not easy in this armour.'

'In that case, we'll just have to think of something else,' said Cat.

She stood for a moment, her finger on her chin, looking deep in thought.

'Got it,' she exclaimed as if she'd just thought of the idea. 'We'll use the hoist! It won't take long.'

Oswyn grumbled something into his helmet. Cat led his horse under the hoist rope and turned it to face the door and away from my hiding place. Oswyn tied himself on and Cat began to pull him up. But I could see she didn't have enough strength to lift him from the saddle.

'What's the matter with you, girl?' snapped Weasel-face.

'Nothing,' panted Cat. 'You'll be sorted out in no time.' As she pulled she moved behind the horse and towards me. I knew what she wanted me to do. I quickly slipped off my gauntlets and grasped the end of the rope. We both heaved. My armour clanked loudly but luckily the sound was lost beneath the creaking of the pulley. The next minute Oswyn was dangling high over the horse. Cat secured the rope to its hook on the wall.

Her hands flew to her mouth. 'Silly me,' she giggled. 'I've forgotten to bring the saddlecloth in! Wait there, Oswyn.'

I saw Cat tap the horse on the flank as she passed. It ambled out of the storeroom after her.

'Cat Thimblebee!' shouted Oswyn. 'Bring that horse back immediately!'

I burst from the shadows. 'I'll get it,' I said, giving Weasel-face a cheerful wave. I flipped my visor down and made for the door.

'What? Who the . . . ?' spluttered Oswyn. 'Jack Briars!' He almost choked on the words. 'You've tricked me!' I heard him shriek. 'Help, someone! Get me down!'

I strode – or rather, clanked – off, trying to look confident. Several people heard Oswyn's cries and turned to look. But the air suddenly filled with the deafening blast of a royal fanfare and everyone scurried to be ready.

The spectacle of St George and the dragon had begun.

25

'**O**swyn!' The order came from Aycliffe, standing at the tiltyard gate and glaring at me. 'What in Hell's name are you doing? You'll be on in a minute.'

I didn't have time to relish the mutterings I could hear about how useless Oswyn was. Cat was holding the horse's head and beckoning. She'd put an upturned pail down for a step. Somehow I found myself on board the horse.

'Good luck,' she whispered. 'I'll be watching.' She slipped in among the crowd.

Flares had been lit inside the arena, sending out billows of coloured smoke.

'That's your cue, Oswyn,' called a voice. 'You're on.'

But the horse whinnied and skittered at the smoke. Its ears were flat against its head in terror. I could tell it was about to flee and I was powerless to stop it, no matter how hard I pulled on the reins.

Then a firm hand grasped the bridle and I heard a voice. I peered through the slit in my helmet. A girl in a large, bulging headscarf was calming my horse down. She looked at me and winked. It was Cat! She'd tied her dressmaker's apron round her head to hide her mass of red hair.

'I am now St George's long-lost sister,' she announced, 'looking after her hopeless brother.'

'Thank you,' was all I could manage.

She led the horse into the arena. Through the narrow visor I took in the crowds of courtiers sitting in the stands and the servants milling around them. The boundary of the arena was alight with more coloured flares. On one side stood a horde of yeomen guard, all dressed in armour. Men in peasant costumes stood on the other side, among the trees of the forest. I craned my neck and peered up to the top of one of the tiltyard towers. Lady Anne was there, wearing the blue dress. The crowd were drowning everything out with their enthusiastic cries. Was that for the young St George? I wondered what he should be doing now. I'd just have to try to look confident and noble until my moment came.

The moment the King was face to face with the dragon.

The peasants were beckoning to me. Their faces looked anxious. Cat led the horse over to them. I tried to remember what Oswyn had said about his part in the pageant. He had made it sound very important.

I wondered if there were words I should be saying. I waved my sword in the air in an attempt to look noble.

'Stop that.' A man in a turnip-shaped hat pulled at my stirrup. 'Don't tell me you've forgotten again. We're to stand like statues.'

'That's right, Oswyn.' A man in a monk's costume joined in. 'This is a tableau. We're not to move a muscle.'

Weasel-face had certainly magnified his role in the spectacle! The young St George was simply to be part of the background. Or perhaps Oswyn had proved so useless that Mister Aycliffe had cut that part of the pageant.

'I knew the stupid scribe would still get it wrong,' Turnip Hat muttered to the monk.

'Aye,' agreed the monk. 'Mrs Pennycod told me it should have been young Jack Briars who works with him but I heard he's in disgrace.'

'Shame. She said he would have got it right!'

Cat gave me a wink. I confess it was good to hear that someone believed in me!

The gates Cat and I had entered by had been closed. Now, as the harbingers gave a rousing trumpet blast, they were flung open again.

My horse twitched but thankfully Cat kept a tight hold on the bridle.

In rode His Majesty, resplendent in his new armour – his deadly new armour. The spectators went wild. Two rows of mounted knights followed and formed a ring round him. Women dressed as nymphs wove their way between them, throwing blossom into the air. And now the acrobats joined the spectacle. Head to toe in red with jagged pointed hats, they tumbled and darted around the arena like tongues of fire.

The King stopped for a moment to accept the adulation of his audience. His visor was up and he wore a broad smile. I wanted to shout out to him about the danger but I knew it was too soon. As Cat had pointed out – I'd just be hauled away if I acted now. King Henry dismounted and strode to the base of the tower where he took his sword from its scabbard and saluted Lady Anne.

'Do not fear, sweet maiden,' he cried. 'St George has come to rescue you from the dreadful beast that has imprisoned you so cruelly.'

A song burst forth, the singers declaring that the hero had come and would not fail under any circumstances.

Suddenly there was a flash and an explosion at the far end of the tiltyard. Cat was nearly lifted off her feet as she struggled with my horse. Thick smoke was billowing around the gateway and a terrible roaring could be heard. The crowd gasped.

Through the smoke, the dragon appeared.

It was magnificent. Now covered in scales, it seemed immense and invincible. Its eyes were blazing and green smoke issued from its nostrils. The tongue of fire, no longer just a lump of wood but shining with bright, vicious flames, darted menacingly about. The crowd cried out in fear.

'Save us, St George!' shouted the peasants around me, on cue.

'Save me!' echoed Lady Anne, waving elegantly from her tower.

The dragon roared again and His Majesty strode forward to meet it. The beast's jaws opened a little. The tongue of fire flickered inside. The crowd gasped at the sight.

I slipped from the horse – at least I swung my leg over the saddle and fell to the ground. I heaved myself up and staggered in a half run towards King Henry, brandishing my sword and shouting for him to halt. But my words were lost, muffled in my helmet.

The King wasn't smiling now. His face was red with fury.

'Get Oswyn Drage out of my way!' he bellowed. 'He's been nothing but trouble.'

The tiltyard fell silent. Everyone must have been struck dumb with shock that Oswyn could have dared to spoil the day.

I sensed rather than saw Aycliffe and the yeomen leap forwards to obey his order. I knew that if I was caught I'd be helpless to save the King. The dragon was still surrounded by thick, billowing smoke. I dived into the smoke and disappeared from view. Through the choking fog I could see the shadowy figures of the yeomen guards searching for me with their halberds. I crept out of their sight, trying not to let the creaking of my armour give me away.

If I couldn't reach the King, I'd have to stop the dragon before it delivered the fatal blow.

I heard the King's voice. 'Call off the guards! The idiot must have escaped. We will delay no longer.'

'What is to be done with him, Sire?' That was Aycliffe.

'He will be dealt with later.' The menace in his voice was unmistakable and no matter that they thought it was Oswyn now, it would be me receiving the punishment.

The dragon began to move slowly towards the King. Under the cover of the smoke I tried to grasp the heavy metal-covered tarpaulin but my gauntlets were too big and unwieldy. I tore them off, heaved up the material and clambered underneath.

It was gloomy inside, light seeping faintly in between the dragon's scales. But I could see that it was Vincent who was controlling the beast, pushing it forward with his body and operating the mouth and fire with his hands. This was lucky. Vincent had been friendly to me at the armoury. He was bound to listen to my story.

As he wound the handle at his side, the dragon's mouth opened and King Henry was visible, striding towards us.

'Vincent!' I cried.

He started and looked over his shoulder.

'Oswyn!' he gasped. 'What are you doing? You'll ruin

everything. Go away and stop being a dummkopf.'

I lifted my visor. His head jerked with shock when he saw who it was.

'Jack! Why are *you* here?'

'You mustn't strike the King with the fire,' I said urgently. 'There's a blade in his armour that will kill him.'

He stared at me for a moment and his hands relaxed on the controls. The dragon's jaws came together with a snap. If the armour hadn't been holding me up, I'd have sagged with relief.

Then he gave a chuckle. 'You're imagining things, Jack,' he said. 'I heard you had a blow to your head yesterday. I think it's addled you.'

'Come, dragon!' we heard the King command. 'Do your worst. St George is ready for you!'

'I speak the truth,' I hissed. 'You must believe me.'

Vincent shook his head. 'It would be more than my life's worth to disobey King Henry,' he said, looking worried. 'And on the word of a disgraced scribe – even a good-hearted one like you.'

He turned back, grasped the tongue of fire with one hand and wound open the mouth. I could see His Majesty, standing full square ready to receive the blow.

Vincent pulled the wooden fire back, his muscles tense as he got ready to strike.

I'd been foolish to think anyone would listen to me. I did the only thing I could. I made a grab for his arm. But encased in my armour my movements were heavy

160

and I crashed into him, knocking him off balance. The tongue of fire slipped out of its groove and toppled down at our feet.

We heard the King give a shout of disbelief as he saw the mighty jaws close again.

'I'm sorry, Vincent,' I panted. 'But I had to stop you. I went into the room in the armoury that's supposed to be haunted. But there is no ghost. The story kept everyone away while somebody was making a deadly copy of the King's armour.'

Vincent looked astonished. But my words couldn't have hit home for he snatched up the wooden tongue from the ground and fixed it firmly in its place.

'No!' I cried, wrestling with him. 'Didn't you hear what I said?'

Vincent pushed me away – so hard that I almost fell.

'Keep back, boy,' he snarled, his blue eyes cold as steel. 'You cannot stop me.'

In his anger, Vincent had spoken without a trace of a German accent.

The truth dawned. I was face to face with Richard Walden.

26

'I order you to fight!' The King's angry words came to us clearly over the roar of the crowd.

Vincent's eyes were wild. He opened the jaws and grasped the tongue of fire. King Henry stood, arms flung wide, sword in hand, ready for the dramatic blow. Vincent took aim at his unsuspecting target. In desperation I flung myself onto him. He fought to keep control of the dragon but staggered back. We fell to the ground, my steel limbs clamped round him. He rolled clear, loosening my grip. But I struggled to my knees and went on the attack. We fought desperately, crashing into the sides of the dragon and making the whole frame creak and sway. I used every ounce of my strength to overcome him, but Vincent was an armourer. He was as strong as the steel he worked with.

He broke away and suddenly he was over me, pinning

me down. He had a dagger in his hand and my face was unprotected.

I tore one arm free and pulled down my visor. The blade glanced off the metal helmet and Vincent let out a furious oath – an English oath – then jumped to his feet and ran back towards the dragon's controls. He must have reasoned that he had no time to dispatch me if he was to carry out his murderous task. I was on my feet too now, visor up again.

I had to stop him once and for all. Using my arm as a club, I swung it as hard as I could at the back of his head. There was a sickening crunch.

Vincent gave a cry and tottered against the side of the dragon. The frame shuddered and slid sideways as he crashed down, blood flowing from the wound I'd made.

He lay slumped under the dragon's mouth, unmoving.

Now there was a confusion of shouting outside and the King's commanding voice could be heard above the crowd. This was the moment I'd been dreading – the moment I had to explain to my monarch why this worthless scribe had ruined the climax of his celebrations. But it had to be done. Flapping away the smoke that was oozing under the dragon's cloth, I began to lift it.

I quickly dropped the cloth. The smoke wasn't part of the dramatic effects of the performance. The dragon was on fire! Flames were licking around its base and the air was filling with choking fumes.

Vincent's fall must have pushed the beast onto a flare!

I had time to escape – but for one thing. I wasn't going to leave even a traitorous murderer to burn alive.

The cloth above him was alight now. I dragged him away from the flames. When we were clear I shook him hard. He gave a low groan but didn't move. Stupidly I shouted for help, although I knew no one would hear.

I couldn't lift the heavy, scale-covered side of the dragon and pull out a dead weight at the same time. Then I remembered the dagger. I felt for it around Vincent's belt, praying he hadn't thrown it down in his haste. I'd never find it in the thick smoke.

My fingers closed on the hilt.

I slashed and slashed at the dragon's cloth to make an opening. But the tarpaulin was thick and tough and covered in metal scales. The smoke stung my eyes. The flames were creeping closer and I could feel their searing heat. A terrible thought was beginning to form. I might have no choice but to leave Vincent and save myself! But then at last I felt the point of the knife plunge in. I pulled downwards and heard a welcome ripping sound as the blade tore the material. Now there was a way out.

Feeling my strength sapping as I tried to breathe, I heaved Vincent through the gap and dragged him as far away from the dragon as I could.

I turned back to a horrific sight. The whole of the dragon burst into flames. The fire flashed up into the sky with a roar, raging and terrible. I staggered away from the cloud of smoke. There were screams from the stands and I heard clattering benches and trampling feet.

The tiltyard was on fire!

Figures loomed out of the smoke. Two of His Majesty's yeomen guard strode up to me.

'You're just in time,' I cried, my voice hoarse from the fumes. 'The man you want is there.'

But they took no notice of my pointing finger. Instead, without a word, they seized me by the arms and dragged me away.

'Someone must arrest Vincent!' I tried to protest as they marched me quickly through the escaping crowds and out of the burning tiltyard. 'He tried to kill the King!'

'Enough of your nonsense,' said one of the yeomen gruffly. 'You're the one who's under arrest, Oswyn Drage. Orders to be taken straight to His Majesty.'

Frightened courtiers who'd already run into the palace parted as the yeomen took me through the passageways towards the Privy Chamber. I heard mutterings. Each time, it was Oswyn's name that was on their lips. Not mine. I wondered at this. My visor was up. Surely they could see it was me and not Oswyn.

Then I remembered the grimy faces of the log boys when they'd been stoking the fires. One scribe would look much like another with soot all over his features. I had not been recognised.

I was marched through guarded door after guarded door until we came to the golden carved entrance to the King's Privy Chamber. The yeomen on duty looked scathingly down at me.

'Enter!'

A shiver ran through me at the icy command. The King was clearly in no mood to listen to my story.

27

The King was seated on his golden chair. He was still in his new armour. Aycliffe stood on his left, Cromwell on his right. Guards clustered close by, and some of the King's ministers lined the walls. Giles Thorpe was there too. How he had wormed his way in, I had no idea. As I was pushed to my knees I caught the look of utter disgust on everyone's face. A look of disgust for Oswyn Drage, the scribe who'd done nothing more than show his incompetence.

How much worse would it be when Cromwell and the King saw it was Jack Briars kneeling abjectly before them? And what could I tell them? I wondered where Vincent could be. I hoped he was still unconscious. If so, he wouldn't be able to escape.

'Take off your helmet, Drage,' ordered the King coldly. 'I have removed mine. The least you can do is give me the courtesy of taking yours off before your monarch.'

I wrenched the helmet from my head and wiped my face with my hands. I could feel sweat on my skin, and my hands were black when I lowered them.

'Jack Briars!' The exclamation burst from Mister Aycliffe. The King grasped the arms of his chair with his gloved hands, burst out of his seat and brought his fist down on the nearest table, sending the candlesticks flying. I feared his violence could be enough to activate the fatal blade inside his breastplate.

'This is beyond belief and will not be endured!' he shouted. 'It was bad enough that I thought Oswyn Drage had ruined my pageant through his incompetence but now I find it is you, Jack.'

I was barely listening to his words now. His actions were growing wilder in his fury. Surely I hadn't saved him from the dragon's deadly fire to have him die here in his chamber.

'It was not incompetence that made you act as you did, but sheer spite!' His Majesty was purple in the face now. 'You were banned from my spectacle so you sought to destroy it.'

I lifted my head. My master was looking at me with cold anger. I stared back at him, silently begging him to let me have my say. He held my gaze – and in that moment I knew he understood.

'My Liege.' Cromwell's voice was calm and quiet but it cut through the King's tirade. 'Briars has been a loyal servant until now – in many ways.'

King Henry stopped pacing. 'What are you saying, Thomas?'

'He deserves one chance, one word, for services rendered in the past.'

The King glared at Cromwell. He was going to refuse. I'd be dragged away. Who knew what fate would await me.

'Speak boy,' he growled at last. 'And mark this. Speak well or it will tell against you.'

All eyes were upon me. I imagined I saw a flash of sympathy in Yeoman Mountford's eyes. Giles Thorpe curled his lip in disdain.

'I beg Your Most Gracious Majesty,' I stumbled over the words, 'to take that breastplate off at once.'

There was a murmur of disbelief in the room.

'I am your monarch!' bellowed the King. 'I take orders from no one!'

'Jack.' My master came over to me. 'Listen to me. Stop playing the fool. I'm sure His Majesty will give you one last chance. Speak again and wisely this time.'

'One *last* chance,' muttered the King.

'If you have ever trusted me, Sire, I pray you do so now,' I said. 'The breastplate you are wearing is deadly. It was engineered to strike you dead the moment the dragon fire hit the mark.'

King Henry started in shock.

'I suggest we do as he says,' said Cromwell briskly. 'Punish him afterwards if he is lying.'

Aycliffe and Mountford ran forwards and began to unbuckle the shoulder and waist straps.

'Be careful,' I cried. 'Don't touch the Tudor rose.' I saw horror on their faces.

The two men had the breastplate at arm's length as if they were holding a viper. Everyone else stood back.

'I can see nothing wrong with it,' declared the King. 'What game is this?'

'I will show you, Your Majesty.'

I got to my feet, took my stance in front of the magnificent piece of armour and raised my metal-clad arm. It had laid Vincent out – I hoped to Heaven it would work on the breastplate. I swung it with every bit of my strength.

I had the strangest sensation, as if time had stopped. My makeshift hammer seemed to take an age as it passed through the air. The thought ran through my head. *What if I'm wrong?*

Then my arm smashed against the Tudor rose.

A knife shot out. Long, vicious, fatal.

28

A heavy silence followed as all stared horrified at the blade.

Aycliffe and Mountford lowered the breastplate to the floor and stepped back. I saw Thorpe swaying on his feet with shock.

'How did you know, Jack?' asked the King in a low voice.

I could see the same question on everyone's face. Without giving away my secret work for Cromwell, I had to explain how I'd stumbled upon this terrible instrument of death – and how I'd guessed what it signified.

'I was bored!' I blurted out. 'Some days ago Your Majesty kindly offered me a tour of the armoury but there was no time. After that I was forbidden to go near the pageant so I went exploring there instead. Sire, I hope you will understand that the Royal Armoury is so magnificent that I could not help myself. Please forgive me.'

'Go on,' said King Henry sternly.

I told him of my grim discoveries in the hidden cellar.

'As these breastplates were so like your own, Your Majesty, and as I found that one hid a blade, I reasoned that Your Majesty was likely in deadly danger.'

'How very lucky for me that you are so nosy, Jack,' said the King simply.

He knew that I was far more than just a nosy scribe. I guessed there would be many questions in private later, but the full truth of my actions could not be told in front of others.

'We will swiftly conclude this matter,' he commanded. 'Fetch David Hartmann. He shall answer for this.'

I felt a chill of horror. Would Vincent still have his revenge on the Master Armourer?

Not if I could help it.

'If it please you, Sire,' I ventured. 'I humbly suggest you speak to Vincent Lang, the armourer who was operating the dragon at the pageant. He . . . may know something.' I held Cromwell's gaze again after I'd spoken. He gave a tiny nod.

'It would be wise, my Liege,' he counselled.

'Fetch him!' snapped the King. 'Fetch them both!' Guards marched away to carry out the order.

'I always knew Hartmann was a villain,' said Giles

Thorpe. The King silenced him with a glare.

The only sound in the chamber was the drumming of the royal gloves on the arm of the chair.

The door swung open and David Hartmann was brought in, a guard on either side. He looked sick with fright. Behind him stumbled Vincent, pale, dazed and appearing puzzled at his summons, his bloodstained cap in his hands. He was back to playing the innocent. Someone was with him, holding a bowl of water, and a wet cloth to the back of his head where I'd struck him. His nurse looked round eagerly, her bright eyes taking everything in. I should have known that Cat would find a way to see what was happening.

'Stop there,' said the guard at the door, barring her way with his halberd.

'I'm needed,' she told him importantly. 'If you don't let me in this poor man will bleed all over His Majesty's fine carpet. And then he'll be in terrible trouble.'

Spoiling the King's carpets would be the least of Vincent's problems – if I could prove his guilt.

King Henry waved her in. Cat sank into a deep curtsey, then led Vincent over to stand behind David Hartmann who was kneeling at the King's feet.

'What can you tell me about this, Hartmann?' King Henry rose and kicked the breastplate with his armoured foot.

The Master Armourer stared at the knife sticking out from his creation. His eyes were wide and he seemed to be gasping for breath.

173

'Answer me!' bellowed the King.

'I don't understand, Your Majesty,' said Hartmann. 'It is my breastplate but I know nothing about that . . .' He pointed a shaking finger at the knife.

'You were the only one who worked on this piece,' snarled the King. 'You are lying!'

'Your Majesty, I swear on my life—'

'Which, I warrant, will shortly be over,' King Henry cut in. 'Step forward, Vincent Lang.'

Cat supported Vincent as he obeyed the royal command.

'Your master has tried to kill me,' said His Majesty, 'yet he denies his treason. Jack Briars claims you may know something of this unholy business.'

Now was my chance to accuse Vincent. But as I began to speak, the King put up a hand to stop me.

'I will hear his testimony from his own mouth,' he announced.

Vincent swayed a little despite his gallant prop. 'I had no idea that there was any problem, Your Majesty,' he said, his voice weak, his foreign accent strong. He looked at me. There was not a trace of the Englishman Richard Walden, just an honest German armourer. 'Then this boy came into the dragon and told me not to strike the breastplate. I tried to move the dragon away at once but I fell and was knocked senseless.' He blinked hard. 'This breastplate is Master Hartmann's work alone. He would let no one else near it. None of us could have guessed the terrible truth.'

Vincent sounded completely convincing. I had to think quickly. A terrible fate awaited the Master Armourer if I couldn't clear his name and identify the real traitor.

'My Liege,' I began. 'That is not the whole of the story . . .'

I hesitated. It was useless accusing Vincent of his crime without proof. I alone knew what had happened at the pageant and he would certainly deny it. It was his word against mine.

'There will be time for the details later, Jack Briars,' said the King firmly. 'I wish to conclude this matter swiftly. I have many guests I need to attend to.'

He turned to Vincent, thanking him for his help and promising him a handsome reward for saving his sovereign's life! There was a ghost of a smile on the traitor's lips. He thought he'd won.

There was only one tiny thread of hope. I knew of someone who might recognise Vincent as Richard Walden. I stepped quietly over to Cromwell.

'You do not seem satisfied with the outcome, Jack,' murmured my master.

'Hartmann is innocent of this crime,' I whispered. 'Vincent Lang is not who he appears to be. And I believe that Peter Keller can tell us who he is.'

A strange look came over Cromwell's face.

'That is not possible,' he said gravely. 'Peter Keller died this morning.'

29

Cromwell's words slowly sunk in. The spy within me refused to let me feel any grief at the man's death. I had lost my witness. How could I prove Vincent's guilt now?

The King rose. 'David Hartmann, you stand accused of the crime of high treason. I can scarcely believe it of my trusted Master Armourer of so many years. What have you to say?'

'I am innocent, my Liege,' cried the trembling man. 'I beg you to hear me. The breastplate was designed to afford the greatest protection to my King, not to harm him. Your Majesty wore it and requested it to be struck at the armoury.' He looked round wildly. 'Master Cromwell saw that test. And Jack – you carried it out.'

'That proves nothing!' thundered the King. 'You added the mechanism afterwards. Admit your heinous deed or it will go very badly for you.'

I knew that it would make no difference whether Hartmann confessed or not. The thought of his fate sent stabs of icy horror into me. Horror mingled with pity for this innocent man who had done his duty by testifying against a thief and then tried to help his family.

Suddenly I had the answer.

'I beg leave to speak, Sire.' I kept my head bowed low as I said the words, dreading the angry refusal that would surely come.

But it was Cromwell's calm tones that broke the silence. 'I am sure your prisoner will think it wise to confess in due course, Your Majesty. Meanwhile Jack Briars may be able help us get to the truth.'

I raised my head. 'My Liege, please allow me to relate the tale of a certain Richard Walden. I heard it from Peter Keller, God rest his soul, as we travelled to Greenwich.' I cast a glance at Vincent's face. His expression did not change. But the Master Armourer started at the name.

'What in Heaven's name has this Richard Walden to do with the matter?' snapped the King. 'Is this really necessary, Thomas?'

'I believe so, Sire,' said Cromwell.

I related the story that Peter Keller had told me. As I spoke, David Hartmann grew more and more agitated. Vincent Lang stood impassively, as if the tale was of little interest to him. The King looked as though he was about to burst with outrage.

'Where is Walden?' he bellowed when I'd finished. 'I command that he be brought to me!'

'He is here,' I said. I walked up to Vincent. 'This is Richard Walden.'

The armourer merely looked puzzled. 'You are a good, brave lad, Jack, and I am ever grateful that you rescued me from the blaze. But with all that has happened to you I fear you have lost your wits.'

'Your proof, Jack?' asked Cromwell quietly.

'Keller said that Richard Walden bears a burn mark on his arm.'

'All armourers have old burn scars,' said Vincent airily. 'It is a hazard of the job.' He rolled up his sleeves and held out his forearms. They were crisscrossed with silvery marks.

'The burn is high on the right arm,' I said desperately. 'It is in the shape of a letter T.'

Vincent ignored me. He turned and made a deep bow to the King. 'I beg leave to go, Sire,' he said. 'The armour must be stored away again and we are short-handed.'

'Bare your arm immediately,' ordered King Henry.

'I don't wish to waste your precious time, Your Majesty,' said Vincent. Beads of sweat began to trickle down his brow. 'I have no other marks.'

'Then prove it, man,' snapped the King.

For the first time I saw a flash of fear in Vincent's eyes. He tried to pull away as Aycliffe seized his right arm and ripped his sleeve open.

At the top of the arm was a deep scar, silvery and brown. It was in the shape of a letter T.

'Your name is Richard Walden,' I said to Vincent. 'You hold His Majesty and Master Hartmann responsible for your father's death and planned a terrible revenge on them. It was you who made the breastplate with the hidden knife.'

Vincent gave a cry of disbelief. 'I do not understand,' he said, his German accent stronger than ever. 'I am Vincent Lang from Hamburg. An honest armourer.'

'You disguised yourself in order to work at Greenwich palace,' I continued. 'You were a little older than me with bright blond hair when Master Hartmann kindly got you a job at Chelsfield and took you there himself. So you must have dyed it in order that he shouldn't recognise you when you came to work at the Royal Armoury.'

'I would never have recognised him!' said David Hartmann, hardly seeming to believe what was being revealed. 'I had no idea, Your Majesty . . .'

'You are mad, Jack Briars!' shouted Vincent. 'I have always had dark hair.'

Cat whipped a clean cloth from her apron pocket and dunked it in her basin. 'Look out, Vincent. You're bleeding again.' She clung to his shirt and scrubbed hard at the top of his head.

'Get off,' he pushed her aside. 'I can't be bleeding. I wasn't injured there.'

Cat looked at the cloth in mock surprise. 'Lord love

179

us, you're quite right. This isn't blood.' She held it out for us all to see. The linen was stained brown. 'It's hair dye, Your Gracious Majesty.'

30

Vincent gave a roar of anger and leapt for the door. Aycliffe was on him in an instant, a knife at his throat.

'Don't be foolish, Walden,' said Cromwell quietly. 'The passageway is full of yeomen guard. It is better for you to confess now than wait for His Majesty's men in the Tower to persuade you.'

Aycliffe lowered the knife but kept a firm grip on his prisoner.

'Henry Tudor!' Vincent spat at the King. The German accent had disappeared and his eyes were mad. 'My father died because of you and the Master Armourer. David Hartmann could have kept his mouth shut but he chose to bear witness against him. And you decreed the punishment which killed him. So I decided you should die as well. I planned for years. I honed my skills in Germany, came to Greenwich and bided my time, making sure I was known as a trustworthy man, fit to serve the King of England. Little did you know I cursed you every waking moment! You escaped my first attempts on your life. Then your pageant gave me the perfect opportunity to have my revenge on you and David Hartmann together. And it would have worked if it hadn't been for this boy.'

He pointed an accusing finger at me.

'No one suspected a thing until Jack Briars came along. Samuel was flattered into thinking Master Hartmann had specially chosen him to try on the King's armour because he was the same height. But the wretched man took too long to die. So I had to repeat my test with Michael and a wider blade.'

'You're a devil!' exclaimed Cat. 'They were good men. So was Peter Keller – killed because you thought he might know who you really were!'

'And they will be avenged,' bellowed the King. 'We are finished with this wretch. Seize him.'

Aycliffe called the guards in. They took Vincent by the arms.

'But *I* have not finished,' screamed Vincent, spittle dribbling from his mouth. 'My ghost was a triumph. The tale was easy to spread. Each night it gave me the freedom to carry out my plans in secret – and if anyone dared to enter my lair they saw something so terrible that they never came again. After fashioning my special breastplate, and exchanging it for the original, I only had to wait for the glorious moment when I could make the deadly thrust. I came so close to victory . . .'

He was still ranting as they dragged him off.

'Rise, Master Hartmann.' The King extended a hand to his Master Armourer.

Weak with relief, Hartmann stumbled to his feet.

'I am heartily glad of your innocence,' said the King. 'You are ever my faithful servant. Now you may go.'

We all knew he would get no apology. The King was never wrong!

Hartmann bowed and walked out unsteadily.

His Majesty dismissed his ministers.

Giles Thorpe hung back, approached the King and gave him an elaborate bow. 'Your Majesty, I believe you asked for my painting of St George to be hung in the Great Hall for your guests to admire. Shall I ask my assistants to see to it?'

I couldn't believe the nerve of the man.

Nor could the King. 'You think I would have that monstrosity hang there to taunt me?' he yelled. 'You go too far, Thorpe. Get you gone from the palace. I never wish to see your face again.'

The artist turned white. 'But I have not been paid—' he began. Then he saw the murderous look on the King's face and scuttled out.

The King stormed to a window and grasped the sill in anger. The smoke from the distant tiltyard coiled into the air. 'I shall make sure that Richard Walden dies more slowly than his victims,' he muttered. He turned to Cromwell. 'I will be the laughing stock of Europe.'

'Not at all, Sire,' said Cromwell. 'Walden is not the only one who can make up a story to fit a purpose! We will spread a tale of our own so that all believe King Henry braved the mighty flames, climbed the tiltyard tower and rescued Lady Anne from certain death. Who can say otherwise? I am certain Lady Anne will remember it like that.'

'See to it,' said the King. 'I am sick of the matter.' He went to leave then turned. 'Jack Briars, I thank you for your actions today and am aware that you did more than you could share publicly. I will hear it all later. Meanwhile I have not forgotten that you spurned my pageant. What have you to say about that?'

'Sire, forgive me,' I said. 'I did not spurn it. There was a misunderstanding with another scribe.'

'Another scribe?' said the King thoughtfully. 'I must make sure that the right scribe is rewarded for saving my life. See to that too, Thomas.'

His Majesty swept away, surrounded by his guards.

'I might have guessed that you would persevere with your investigation no matter what I ordered,' said Cromwell. 'In truth, I'm heartily glad you did. I have been a fool to doubt you, Jack.'

'I don't know how you could have done it,' said Cat, 'begging your pardon, sir.'

'It won't happen again,' said Cromwell. He tried to look solemn but he couldn't hide the trace of a smile.

'You would never permit it, Mistress Thimblebee.'

'Indeed I wouldn't, sir,' said Cat vehemently. 'And by the way, if Thorpe doesn't get paid, his mother is going to have to dig his grave – or so I heard. Just thought I'd mention it.'

'So you have been involved in this business too?' said Cromwell. 'I might have guessed that as well.'

'I couldn't possibly say, sir,' answered Cat.

Cromwell gave her a bow and followed the King.

'He forgot about the reward,' snorted Cat. 'Go after him.'

'I've had my reward,' I said. 'I've still got my job – both of them.'

'Well I've got a reward for you too,' said Cat. 'The guests were going to have a magnificent feast after the pageant. If we hurry there'll be loads of food left over in the Great Hall.'

'Lead me to it,' I said. 'I can take the armour off afterwards.'

We headed off down the passage.

Cat suddenly stopped and gave a laugh. 'Am I seeing double?' she squawked.

Another figure in armour was limping towards us.

'I've been looking for you, Briars.' It was Oswyn. He had his helmet under his arm and his weaselly face was livid. 'I've been hanging from that hoist for hours. And everyone's been blaming me for spoiling the pageant and burning the tiltyard down. I'm off to tell the King that it was you. I'm not going to be punished for your crimes.'

'Don't worry,' I said breezily. 'His Majesty already knows it was me.'

'So you're well and truly off the hook, Oswyn,' cackled Cat.

Cat had got the last word as usual. But it was worth it for the look on Oswyn's face!

THE WALK OF DEATH

1

I dipped my quill in the inkwell. This was going to be the most important letter I'd ever written in my life. More important than the hundreds of documents I'd copied in my work as a royal scribe. More important even than King Henry's letters to His Holiness the Pope.

A sound outside made me pause. It was the regular thud of a hammer on wood. My hand began to tremble. I knew what it meant. They were building a scaffold. A traitor was going to be executed tomorrow.

And that traitor was me.

Despite the cold of my damp cell, I broke out in a sweat. I wiped my forehead with a stinking cuff. I'd been given no change of shirt and hardly a scrap of bread since I'd been thrown into my cell in the Tower of London. The paper and quill were my last request. My plea to Thomas Cromwell for clemency. The

King's spy master had always said that my secret work for him could be deadly. I was learning the terrible truth of his warning.

I turned to my letter. My hand shook so violently that drops of ink splattered onto the page. I threw down the quill in despair.

I'd been in many a dangerous situation in my secret work. But now I struggled to remember how to keep the icy fear in my belly from overwhelming me.

I paced the few steps from wall to wall, my feet beating horrible time with the regular banging beneath my window. Tomorrow I would be walking out to my death.

Be calm, I told myself. That was easier said than done. I tried to force my brain to think straight. I thought of my friends, and of my godfather, Brother Matthew. If all had been well, how would I have related this strange tale?

By starting at the beginning.

2

It all began the day that the King went missing from Hampton Court Palace. Early that morning I was on the bank of the River Thames, fighting as though my life depended on it.

The sword flashed towards me faster than a falcon. I managed to get my own blade up and block the blow. The force nearly had it spinning from my hand but I clung on and dodged out of range. I lunged, pretending I was making a rash move, but then retreated quickly so that my attacker flailed his sword in thin air. His Majesty King Henry had taught me the manoeuvre himself.

'Well done, Jack,' said my opponent, pausing for a moment. 'You are light on your feet and becoming skilled in swordsmanship.'

'I aim to become as skilful as you and Master Cromwell,' I answered.

'Master Cromwell is far more expert than I,' said Aycliffe. 'He learned to fight in the wars abroad.'

I had a sudden yearning to do as my master had done – to travel across the water and visit strange countries, to see people and places I would only ever hear about in stories.

'You learn fast, Jack. You will be a formidable opponent one day. But can you counter this?'

Robert Aycliffe suddenly came at me again and I found myself pressed against the river wall. I was trapped. If Aycliffe had been a real adversary I'd have been run through.

'Hold hard.' The voice was quiet and calm but we both turned, my lesson forgotten. Thomas Cromwell stood there. I swallowed down a gulp of surprise at his expression. His hooded eyes and plump face, normally so impassive, showed signs of worry.

'I need you both,' he said simply.

He didn't need me to copy a letter for him, of that much I was sure. To everyone else at Court I was a skinny twelve-year-old scribe, excited to be working at Hampton Court for the first time, and my opponent, Robert Aycliffe, was a young man of good family who was training to be a lawyer. Only the two of us standing there on the riverbank knew of our secret work in the service of our monarch and that Thomas Cromwell was our spy master. Well, there was one other who knew but she wasn't there.

My sword fighting lessons were by way of a reward

from King Henry for my services to him in the past. Although I was a foundling brought up in an abbey with no idea of my family, I was being taught how to fight like a young man of high birth.

'What is wrong?' Aycliffe asked Master Cromwell in a low voice.

Cromwell glanced about him to ensure that no one else was in earshot.

'His Majesty is missing.'

There was a beat while Aycliffe and I took in the terrible announcement.

'Missing?' echoed Aycliffe. 'But how . . . ? He was full of cheer at the banquet last night. He was delighted to be here at Hampton Court. What villainy is this?'

'We do not yet know,' said Cromwell. 'His gentlemen saw him to his privy bedchamber at midnight. The King said he would read a while and sent them all on errands to ensure that he had some peace. He gave instructions that if the door to the inner chamber was closed, he had put himself to bed. When they returned the door was indeed closed.'

'But His Majesty never puts himself to bed,' gasped Aycliffe. 'What were they thinking?'

'They were obeying their sovereign lord,' answered Cromwell.

'Surely some of his gentlemen sleep on the floor in his chamber,' I said.

'That is also correct, Jack,' said Cromwell evenly. 'Unless he decrees otherwise. Which of his men would dare argue with him? I'd certainly not do so.'

We heard shouts and saw flashes of red uniform as a swarm of yeomen guard appeared, running along the banks as they made their desperate search.

I hardly dared ask my next question. 'Do you think he's been taken away by force?'

'There is no sign of it, God be praised,' said Cromwell. 'But his enemies are many – and some are cunning.'

'With your permission, sir, shall I go to his chambers,' asked Aycliffe, 'and see if there is any answer to be had there?'

'You won't have to!' I burst out.

They looked at me, astonished at my boldness. I said no more but pointed to a small boat approaching the Water Gate, the main river entrance to the palace. Three men sat in it. The one who plied the oars had brawny arms and wore a tattered cap. He made easy work of the rowing. The second held a halberd and I wondered if he was a constable of the law. The third was a large man, dressed in a plain, ragged jerkin and breeches, with a rough cloak slung over his shoulders. But there was something about his bearing that told me that this was the royal figure of our monarch.

'God's wounds!' I heard Aycliffe mutter under his breath, as we hurried to the landing stage in front of the Water Gate. The yeomen guard came running.

Grim-faced, the constable stepped from the boat, moored it and indicated with a short jab of his thumb that the King should follow. His Majesty bounded out, and went to push past the man. He found his way blocked by the halberd. I waited for the explosion of rage, but King Henry merely grinned and winked at me!

The other man leapt on to the landing stage to stop their prisoner escaping.

'I wish to speak to Thomas Cromwell,' said the constable importantly.

'I am Cromwell,' said my master.

'This vagabond was arrested last night in the village of East Molesey and put in the lock-up for the night,' the constable replied crossly. 'He is clearly a madman because he insists he is the King of England. We brought him here for your yeomen to do what they will with him.'

'Throw him in the river,' said the boatman with relish.

'If I may make so bold as to ask a question,' Cromwell said to the King, 'what have you been about, my Liege?'

It took a few seconds for his words to sink in. The constable and his man turned whiter than snow. The constable began to gobble like a turkey.

'But . . . he behaved like . . .' He gave up and collapsed to his knees, his nose almost touching the King's muddy boots. 'Forgive me, Your Majesty.'

His comrade followed suit.

The King held up a hand to the approaching guards.

'I have had an adventure, good Thomas,' he declared. He stood tall and majestic despite his rough clothing.

'An adventure?' echoed my master. His tone was polite but I was sure I didn't imagine the edge to it.

The King's eyes twinkled. 'I took myself to East Molesey,' he said, grinning round at us all like a small child hoping for praise. 'I wished to see how well my constables and their men keep my subjects safe – but I did not wish to be recognised as their monarch. Hence the disguise which, I'm sure you will agree, served me well! So well that I was arrested by the constable here for loitering and locked up under the care of his deputy.'

The two men cringed and bowed their heads even further.

'I spent the night in the lock-up,' the King went on. 'I could not persuade these fellows of my identity. And now' – he rubbed his hands together eagerly – 'I am eager to break my fast.'

He waved to his guards who swarmed forwards to protect him.

'And these men?' asked Cromwell. 'What is to be done with them?'

The King had set off through the gate into the palace grounds. He turned, hands on hips, staring thoughtfully at the two poor souls. They cowered before him, dreading their punishment.

3

'**R**eward them of course,' the King said at last. 'They have performed their duties in an exemplary fashion.'

I thought the constable was going to faint on the spot. 'A gift of some shillings now and see they receive a goodly wage for their work each year. And it occurs to me that the lock-up should receive funding from the royal purse to ensure that there is some bread for the prisoners – and wood to heat the cell!'

He marched off with his escort.

'I thank you for keeping our gracious sovereign safe,' my master said to the two gibbering men. 'Mr Aycliffe will give you your reward and then you may return to your duties.'

Robert Aycliffe dutifully plunged a hand into the purse on his belt and handed some silver coins to the constable and his deputy. He knew as well as I did that the King would not think to reimburse him. They pocketed the coins and rowed away – very quickly!

As the guards dispersed a distant clock struck nine.

'We must go to our duties too,' said Cromwell. 'Now that the King's "adventure" is over I find I have no need of your investigative skills after all, Jack.'

I bowed and hurried along the bank and round the palace walls towards the gatehouse that led into the Base Court. I passed the brightly striped tents that had been put up on the green in front of the palace. King Henry had decided that the hunting would be better here at Hampton Court and his whole vast household had travelled up river only two days ago.

The palace was large but there was never enough room for all the courtiers. Some were lodged on the other side of the river in East Molesey, and the rest in the tents, grouped together close to one of the walls separating the palace from the river. The tent dwellers were mostly young men. His Majesty favoured courtiers who offered good companionship and these gentlemen were always available to hunt or play bowls or whatever the King wanted. Some of them were out on the green now, doing some archery practice.

'Well, well,' said a familiar voice. 'His Majesty has become as adventurous as you, Jack!'

I turned to see one of the yeomen guard striding along behind me. I had met Nicholas Mountford when I first came to work for the King. It was an unusual meeting. Mistaking me for a vagabond he chased me all over Whitehall Palace – inside and out – and he had never let me forget it.

'His Majesty has a good way to go to catch up with me,' I replied. 'I have yet to see him on the roof.'

The giant yeoman roared with laughter. 'You've a ready wit and a lively spirit,' he chuckled. 'But something puzzles me. Why is it you're always to be found where there's something interesting going on?'

A sudden worry started to gnaw at me. As far as the Court knew, I'd merely happened to be present to offer my help a few times when the King's life was in danger. Did the yeoman suspect there was more to my work than scribing?

'Just luck,' I said carelessly. 'I was having one of my sword fighting lessons with Mister Aycliffe when the boat arrived.'

'I'd better keep an eye on you, Jack,' said Mountford. 'You'll be after my job if I'm not careful.'

I bade him farewell and went through the gatehouse that towered over me. The Sergeant Porter gave a nod at my royal livery. I crossed the square Base Court and took the wooden staircase to the scribes' room on the first floor.

I paused outside the closed door. A morning of dull copying lay before me and I'd had no breakfast! I loved my secret work for Master Cromwell. My scribing duties were a neccssary cover for that but they were exceedingly boring. A tiny guilty feeling flared up. I would never want any harm to come to the King – that was treason – but for a moment on the riverbank, I'd thought Cromwell would have a use for his spies and that a more intriguing day would lie ahead.

I pushed away my treacherous thoughts and went into the chamber. Mark Helston glanced up from the document he was copying. He leaned forward over the table.

'You were out early, Jack,' he whispered. 'I won't ask why. It must have been important for you to miss breakfast.'

Mark was always a good friend, though rather timid. He never asked questions but had covered for me in the past when my secret work had taken me away from my scribes' table.

I pointed out of the window to the river. 'I was down there, fighting Mister Aycliffe,' I said.

Mark started in horror at this.

'And you will never guess what happened.'

Mark's eyes grew wide as I related the King's adventure. Oswyn Drage pretended to be busy with some letter or other but I could tell he was earwigging every word.

'His Majesty should take more care,' muttered Mark. His hand flew to his mouth. 'I'm not criticising him, of course,' he added nervously.

'Watch your words, Helston,' hissed Oswyn. His narrowed eyes and sharp nose made him look more weaselly than usual. 'It sounded dangerously like criticism to me.'

Mark froze like a rabbit cornered by a fox.

'On the contrary, Oswyn,' I said firmly. 'Mark is showing great concern for King Henry.'

Weasel-face scowled. 'The likes of you shouldn't be discussing the King's affairs, Briars,' he spat. 'But then in my opinion, a foundling brought up in a humble abbey should not have been permitted to set foot in the King's palace – even less work in the same office as someone as important as me. I'll have you know the Drage family can trace its line back to the Normans.'

I was about to remark that they'd probably been weasels for the Norman hounds to hunt when the door opened and Mr Scrope, the Chief Scribe, came in carrying a trencher of bread and cheese. He gave us a brief nod and plonked himself down in his chair to eat.

My stomach growled and I fervently wished I hadn't missed my breakfast. Lunch seemed an age away. Mr Scrope eventually finished his plateful and picked up a piece of paper.

'There's an errand to be run,' he announced. 'Someone must take this order to the Sergeant of the Wine Cellar. It will inform him that the King has a new favourite burgundy and so a supply must be ensured.'

The thought of the long, boring morning ahead spurred me into action.

'I'll go,' I said, rising quickly from my seat.

As this was my first time at Hampton Court I'd been longing to explore.

I took the list. Mark rummaged in his livery jacket

and produced a crumpled map. 'I made this when I first came to Hampton Court three years ago and was terrified of getting lost,' he whispered. He traced a route for me from our office, across the Base Court and into the courtyard behind the King's Chambers of State.

'Don't go up that staircase,' he said, pointing. 'That leads to the King's Watching Chamber. It will be full of important people. This passage here is one of the routes to the kitchens and the wine cellar is down there too,' he finished.

'The kitchens,' I said with interest. 'Maybe there'll be food going spare.'

We usually took our meals in the Great Hall after the courtiers had finished. But King Henry had the builders in. The Great Hall was being transformed into a place worthy of a royal banquet. So us servants were having to congregate in the serving place outside the kitchens and eat our meals standing up at the hatches.

'I hope for your sake there is some breakfast left,' said Mark. 'Missing meals is so dangerous, Jack. I heard of a boy who missed meals and he became so thin he slipped through a crack in the grate and into the sewer.'

Oswyn opened his mouth, no doubt to remark that I belonged in the sewer. I made for the door before he could say a word.

The Base Court was bustling now with servants going to and fro between the workshops opposite our office. Courtiers were strolling among them and getting in the way. I headed diagonally across towards the main palace buildings as Mark had shown me.

I passed the stairway that led up to the King's State Chambers and his chapel.

The noise of hammering was very loud. King Henry was in such a hurry for his grand new chamber that the workmen were working day and night.

Remembering Mark's map, I hurried down a long passageway full of more servants scuttling in and out of the many doorways. The smell of roasting meat from the kitchens made my stomach snarl like a hungry dragon. Lunch was being prepared. The lure of food proved almost too strong, but duty reared its ugly head and I decided I'd better get my errand out of the way first.

I didn't have to be a spy to work out which door led to the cellar. The god of wine and a host of drunken nymphs were carved onto it.

I pushed the door. It swung open on well-oiled hinges. Huge barrels stretched away in long lines under a low vaulted ceiling. I'd expected it to be busy, full of men in aprons sorting out the wine and ale for the Court, but it was strangely quiet. I was halfway down the stone steps when I heard low voices. I was about to call out to announce my presence but something in their tone made me stop, senses alert.

The voices were coming from the other end of the cellar. I crept along between the barrels. The place looked empty but I could still hear the muttered talk.

Then I spotted an open door in the far wall. More steps led down to a deeper chamber beyond. The faint flicker of a candle told me that the speakers must be down there. As I stopped at the door my foot caught a small stack of crates and I only just grabbed them before they clattered down the steps. I waited. The voices were suddenly silent, but no one called out to challenge me. After a while they continued their conversation. I listened hard.

'So you have not got the information I require.' The accent was Welsh and the speaker sounded like a courtier. 'Why not?'

'It has been difficult.' The second speaker spoke in a hushed, nervous tone.

'Difficult? You assured me you have connections with the highest at the palace.'

'I cannot talk here,' came the reply. 'Let us go into my office.'

'There's no time for that,' said the first speaker impatiently.

Somewhere outside I heard shouts and a clattering of barrels being shifted. The nervous speaker must have heard it too. 'But we cannot speak freely here,' he whimpered. 'The men could be in from the yard at any minute.' He continued, this time loudly. 'I am sorry, sir. Your . . . *wine order* will be ready as soon as I can manage it.'

This was clearly a man who worked in the wine cellars.

'No one is coming in,' growled the Welshman. 'Your excuse is not good enough! I need it urgently. Remember what happened to the last man who disappointed me.'

'Let me explain,' pleaded the other in a choked voice. His companion must have had him by the throat! 'But not here. I beg you . . .'

'Then we must meet later. Where you will be satisfied that no one will overhear us.'

'Where will be safe enough?' The other man was truly frightened now. I wondered what fate the last one had met.

'You will come to the tennis court at noon. I will ensure that we have the court to ourselves. You will explain yourself to me – as we play a match.'

'Play?' spluttered his companion. 'I am no courtier. I have never played—'

'Then by Lucifer's horns, it's about time you did. Be there promptly. I must go now. You have delayed me enough. Meet me by the twisted oak outside the court. Not a minute after the chimes of noon.'

I heard a far door slam shut as he left. There was a pause, filled only by the frightened breathing of the cellar man. Then his footsteps hurrying towards me. I couldn't be found loitering. I turned to rush back to the main door and dislodged the stack of crates. This time I was too slow to save them and myself. Together we crashed to the floor.

'Who's there?' The voice came out in a squeal of

fright. A portly fellow in a velvet coat and cap puffed up the steps. He ran his hands through his grey hair, making it stand on end. He started as he saw me surrounded by the fallen crates.

'I'm so sorry!' I said. 'I didn't mean to alarm you.'

'Who are you?' he asked. His hands trembled as I helped him stack the crates. 'Have you . . . er . . . have you been waiting long?'

'Not at all,' I said breezily. 'I've only just got here. I didn't see the pile. I'm Jack Briars, one of the royal scribes. I have a message to deliver but I had no idea where the cellars were. Hampton Court is so big and I've never worked here before. That's why I was in such a hurry. I'm going to be in terrible trouble for taking so long with this errand.' I watched the man's face. He gradually relaxed, believing I'd heard nothing of his conversation. I chattered on. 'Mister Scrope always sends me to deliver messages – even though it takes me ages to find my way about.' I pulled the message from my livery jacket. 'It's for Mister Finch, the Sergeant of the Cellar.'

The man held out a hand. 'That's me,' he said.

I handed him the message. He cast a brief eye over it and nodded. 'Thank you, Jack Briars. I will deal with this at once. You may go.'

I hurried off, my head buzzing with what I'd heard.

What was the information that the Welshman was so keen to receive? A man who threatened an unpleasant fate for those who failed him. It certainly wasn't a simple matter of a wine order. My pulse quickened. No underhand goings-on at Court could be ignored in case they threatened the safety of His Majesty. I'd hoped for intrigue – and now I'd found it.

Little did the two men know that when they met at noon they would not have the tennis court to themselves. I would be there to hear every detail of their talk.

4

I should have gone straight to Master Cromwell. But I didn't. I feared that he might tell me that I was not required in this investigation. I feared he'd say that his other operatives would deal with it. I reasoned that if I waited and then reported both the meetings to him he might decide that he couldn't do without me.

My stomach led me to the kitchen serving hatches. They were open but I couldn't see any food on offer. Breakfast had been cleared away and lunch wouldn't be ready for the servants until after the Court had eaten. I stuck my head through the nearest hatch. The Great Kitchen lay before me, full of steaming pans and busy servants. A huge fire added to the heat. Something delicious was being turned on a spit. It was all I could do not to clamber through the opening to grab a hunk of it.

A man chopping onions on a long bench saw me and grinned.

'Here's a friend of yours, Mrs Pennycod,' he called.

A small figure bustled into view, wiping her hands on her apron.

'Jackanapes!' she cried.

The elderly pastry cook came over and slipped me a scrap of bread, but not before she'd wrapped it round a sliver of the roasting meat.

'Thank you, Mrs Pennycod,' I said. 'Shame I'm too early for one of your delicious pies.'

'They should be delicious,' the man chopping onions called over. 'She's had enough practice. I bet she made pies for William the Conqueror.'

'Rufus is being too cheeky for his own good,' said Mrs Pennycod with a grin. She snatched up a ladle and pretended to threaten him with it. 'Anyway, where's my favourite boy off to this morning?'

'I've just been taking a message to the Sergeant of the Wine Cellar,' I explained.

'To Mister Finch?' Mrs Pennycod almost spat the words. 'That man! He comes in here and struts about boasting about how important he is and how he's in the confidence of all the King's ministers.'

'I think it's a lot of hot air,' Rufus piped up. 'I've not seen one courtier treat him as an equal.'

'So he isn't a man with many friends,' I said, hoping to hear more.

'If you ask me he knows no one likes him,' said Mrs Pennycod. 'And that can sour a person – like lemon juice sours cream.'

'He's sour all right,' said Rufus. 'There's never a smile on his face – and since we came to Hampton Court he's been right snappy with us all.'

'I hope he was polite to you, Jack.' The pastry cook's hand tightened on her ladle and I wondered what would happen if she thought he'd insulted me!

'He took the message and I left,' I replied. 'He did say thank you.'

'Just as well for him!' said Mrs Pennycod vehemently.

'I must get back,' I said. 'Thanks for the bread and meat. I didn't have time for breakfast so it was very welcome.'

Mrs Pennycod looked stricken. 'God-a-mercy!' she exclaimed. 'You must be half dead with hunger.' She scurried about the kitchen and pressed two carrots and an apple into my hand. 'It's carp pie at lunch so come along early.'

I thanked her for the advice and set off, munching gratefully as I stored away the new information I'd gleaned about Finch. It was only when I was halfway up the stairs to the scribes' office that I remembered I had to be at the tennis court before noon. I'd be missing the carp pie!

Once back at my table I kept my head down and began my copying task, wondering how I was going to manage to slip off to the secret meeting. If Mister Scrope kept a record of all my different excuses for leaving the office, he'd have a book full! But for once, luck was on my side. As the time drew near I saw that the Chief Scribe was having one of his naps. I hurried off before he could wake up.

I wasn't sure where the tennis court was, but the men had said they'd meet at the twisted oak. I'd spotted that tree when we first arrived at Hampton Court. It was a good tree to climb, as I'd said to Mark. He, of course, warned me about a boy who tried to climb a tree, got caught by the seat of his breeches and hung there for three days while magpies pecked his bum.

I took a route that led me out into the palace grounds, skirted round the back of the workshops and headed towards the Home Park. The oak was hard to miss. It was huge with strong, twisting branches. I was just making my way along on the side of a tall hedge which hid me from the base of the oak, when I sensed I was being followed. It wasn't much, just the faint crack of a twig, but it was enough for me to beware. I slipped into an arched shelter in the hedge, behind a marble urn. I decided it must be nothing, that the two men I'd overheard couldn't have known my intentions. But even so, the Sergeant of the Wine Cellar might be suspicious if he spotted the clumsy scribe from earlier, so close to his meeting place.

There was a rustle of leaves and a muffled curse. I shrank further back into the shadows, waiting for my pursuer to appear. To my surprise a small figure came into view. A small figure with red hair tumbling out of her cap. I was being tailed by someone I was very well acquainted with. Cat Thimblebee. The only other

211

person at Court who knew of my secret job – and not because I'd told her! Somehow she always wormed her way in to my missions. But this time she'd just be in the way.

As she passed I leapt out behind her and clapped my hand over her mouth.

'Great Heavens!' came the muffled cry.

'Keep quiet and I'll let you go,' I muttered.

My prisoner nodded. I took my hand away. She turned slowly. The minute she realised who her captor was, she swung her hand to give me a clout. I ducked.

'What do you think you're doing, Jack?' exclaimed Cat, furiously straightening her seamstress apron.

'I could ask you the same thing,' I whispered.

'Me? Well, I was sitting in our workshop, in the middle of hemming a cloak for Mistress Blanchard when I saw you come scurrying across the Base Court,' said Cat. 'I thought you were a bit early for lunch but then you went off round the back of the workshops. I deduced you were going somewhere important because I'm clever like that.'

'I *am* going somewhere important,' I hissed. 'And you're holding me up.' I began to walk off.

'Anyway . . .' Cat wasn't giving up. She trotted along after me. 'How did you guess I was following you?'

'You're not as good at tailing as you think,' I threw over my shoulder. I stopped at the end of the hedge and glanced at the tree. No one was there. I now saw the plastered building that stood on its own against the palace garden wall. It was high with small windows close to the roof. A paved path led to its door. This had to be the tennis court.

'I'm guessing that you have to get in there secretly,' said Cat. 'There's another way in where no one will spot you – but I'm sure a great investigator like you doesn't need me to tell you that. I'll be getting back to work. I can see where I'm not wanted.'

She began to flounce off, knowing perfectly well she'd won.

I grabbed her arm. 'Don't go.'

Cat raised an eyebrow.

'All right, all right,' I said. 'I have to spy on two tennis players. One is Mister Finch . . .'

'That fat old windbag!' exclaimed Cat. 'Surely he's not playing tennis.'

'It's an excuse for a secret meeting,' I explained.

'Who's the other one?' asked Cat.

'That's what I want to find out,' I said. 'And what their secret business is. Which way do we go?'

'Follow me,' said Cat. To my surprise, she dragged me through the hedge. We fought our way among twigs and branches until we came to a small clearing. Spitting out leaves, I found we were at the rear of the building, in front of a small, plain door.

'This is where the servants come in,' explained Cat.

She eased the door open. 'There shouldn't be anyone playing at this time of day,' she said confidently. 'The courtiers will be at lunch and the tennis court

213

attendants usually take theirs at the same time so they can be at the players' beck and call in the afternoon.'

We crept in. I'd seen a tennis court on board the King's ship but this was much bigger. The rectangular court was well lit by the high windows and bounded on three sides by walls which bore the marks of tennis balls. The fourth side was a viewing gallery. Any spectators were kept safe from missiles by a strong mesh. A net also stretched across the middle of the court. We had the place to ourselves.

We crept along the corridor next to the court, past boxes of tennis rackets and balls and into the viewing gallery. There was nowhere useful to hide. No helpful nook or cranny for two spies to conceal themselves.

'Hurry up, man.' It was the Welshman's voice. They were coming.

5

Cat and I stared at each other in panic. I had hoped to be well hidden before the two men arrived. The seats for the spectators were slatted and only the royal chair in the centre was cushioned. We'd be seen in a heartbeat if we dived under any of them.

Then Cat grabbed my sleeve and pointed. There was a large hamper at one end of the net. We scampered across the wooden floor and threw the lid open. Inside was a mishmash of balls, broken rackets and a spare net rolled in a tight scroll. We forced our way in, shifting everything aside. I pulled the lid down and we burrowed under a feeble covering of rackets. I prayed their meeting would not last long. Cat's elbow was digging into my guts.

My face was pressed up against the rough wicker. A broken bit of basket gave me a view of only one side of the court. Finch came into my sight. He removed his doublet and gloves and threw them onto a bench at the side. Then he took up a racket, holding it as if it was going to bite him. I tried to catch a glimpse of his opponent, whose voice I could hear. But I couldn't move without the basket making alarming noises.

'You are sure no one saw you come here?' That was the Welshman.

'I am sure, sir. I was very careful.'

There was a twang and in the next instant a ball thudded into Finch's stomach. He doubled up, wheezing for breath.

'I'm sorry.' The voice was mocking. 'Weren't you ready? No matter. Just look as if you're playing in case anyone comes in. Don't try to return my shots. I always win, no matter what. Now, explain yourself. It is vital I have those figures so that things can proceed to plan. Why haven't you got them?'

'I couldn't get access.'

'You had just one task and you've failed,' spat the Welshman.

'God's oath!' cried Finch, jumping to one side as a ball flew past him. 'It's impossible to do as you ask. Believe me I have tried to find a way.'

'I gave you the job because you swore you had the trust of important men.' His companion was almost shouting now. 'You led me to believe you'd be able to access state documents. Was that all a lie?'

I could have answered the Welshman. Few men had access to state documents and I was willing to swear that the Sergeant of the Wine Cellar wasn't one of them. It had just been a boast, like those he'd made to the kitchen staff.

'I'm sure I didn't quite say that,' Finch gabbled. 'You must understand that I've been very busy. And it's not easy . . .'

'You lily-livered fool.' The tone was low and menacing now. 'I will not tolerate this! I thought you were with me. But I am beginning to doubt it.'

'I am with you,' said Finch. He turned away and wiped the sweat from his forehead, but not before I'd seen the panic in his eyes.

'Time is running out,' said his opponent. 'Everything is coming together swiftly now. Even at this late stage, I am persuading more to my side. And each man has shown me more loyalty than you have.' There was a chilling menace in his voice. 'A failure of loyalty could jeopardise this whole enterprise. I cannot have that.'

Finch stood uncertainly for a moment, as if he wanted to run from the place. Then he steeled himself and turned back to face his fearsome opponent. 'There is news of Nathaniel.'

'What is it?'

'I have heard word that he is sick.'

'Sick? What do you mean? Speak, man. How sick?'

'I . . . I don't know the details. But I think it is serious.'

Now there was silence, broken only by the Welshman stamping about the court.

'If . . . he should die then your plans will surely come to nought,' whimpered Finch.

'By Lucifer's horns, nothing is going to stand in my way.' The man hissed the words with venom. 'I have come so far.' I willed him to say more.

He must have hit another ball at Finch for the foolish man suddenly decided to try and play it. He ran up to the net, swung wildly, lost his balance and came crashing down on our hamper.

Cat let out a muffled yelp. Luckily Finch was complaining too loudly to hear. The basket swayed alarmingly as he struggled to his feet. We saw his podgy hands clutching at the wicker. Finally, with a great harumph, he staggered back onto the court.

'My racket!' we heard him exclaim wheezily. 'It's broken. I'm afraid I won't be able to play any more.' He sounded very obviously relieved at the accident.

'Get another one,' snapped his opponent. 'There are plenty in the boxes out there.'

The Welshman could not be refused. Finch soon came scurrying back.

His opponent tutted. 'And don't leave the broken one on the court. It goes in that basket.'

Cat stiffened beside me. There was only one basket – the one we were hiding in.

The Sergeant of the Wine Cellar lumbered towards us.

As he lifted the lid, the Welshman spoke. 'You've wasted enough of my time. Back to business. You will have the figures by tomorrow evening!'

Finch tossed the pieces into the basket without glancing down. We breathed again as he dropped the lid. 'By tomorrow evening?' He stood twisting his new racket uneasily in his hands.

'If that's not too inconvenient!' snapped his opponent.

We heard another ball being slogged with force. I saw it whizz over Finch's head and slam into the wall behind. Footsteps echoed as the Welshman stormed out. The Sergeant of the Wine Cellar stood uncertainly for a moment, then he picked up his doublet and walked slowly away, as if he had the weight of the world on his shoulders.

For a moment Cat and I didn't move. After a while she dug me painfully in the ribs. 'Are we going to spend all day in here?' she grumbled.

I listened hard for any movement. There was none. We eased ourselves out of the basket and rubbed our cramped limbs. Cat picked up one of the discarded tennis balls.

'This is as hard as a cannonball,' she said. 'Mister Finch was lucky. He could have been killed when it hit him!'

'I don't think luck came into it,' I answered. 'Those were just scare tactics. The Welshman needs Finch alive. He's planning something serious and I have to find out more. What could these figures be that he wants to steal?'

'They must be important,' said Cat.

'Were you able to see who he was?' I asked.

'Not with your foot in my face.'

'He had the voice of a courtier,' I said thoughtfully. 'He's from Wales and he plays tennis well. Oh, and his temper is short.'

We headed for the servants' door. I pushed it open tentatively and stepped outside when I saw that all was clear.

'I'll track him down for you,' Cat offered, as if it was a simple matter.

'With your tracking skills?' I laughed, expecting her to make a rude retort. Instead I heard the door slam shut behind me. I wondered if I'd gone too far with my teasing. I pushed on the door but Cat was leaning on it from the other side.

I was about to call to her not to be so silly when I heard a voice.

'Come here, girl!' It was Mister Finch. 'Immediately.'

6

My pulse started racing. The Sergeant of the Wine Cellar hadn't left after all. Had he heard our talk?

'Me, sir?' Cat answered promptly. 'Mister Wiltshire sent me not one minute ago. He wanted me to check whether the royal cushion in the gallery could do with mending.'

There was a pause.

'Can I help you with anything, sir?' Cat went on. I was impressed by her bravado. 'Only, Mister Wiltshire was anxious that I hurry back.'

'I dropped a glove here,' came Finch's voice. 'You will look for it.'

There was a long silence, then I heard a few muffled bumps. What was he doing to Cat? I grasped the door handle ready to fly to her rescue.

'Here it is, sir,' said Cat chirpily. 'It was under the bench.'

I heard a muttered thank you as his footsteps moved away. And then Cat was through the door, her eyes wide.

'That was close,' she gasped. 'I just saved the day. So in return you can let me in on our mission.'

Bitter experience had taught me that there was no point trying to keep it to myself. As we headed back to the workshops, I related everything that had happened that morning. She chuckled at the story of the King and his adventure. But her face was grave by the time I'd finished.

'It stinks like a mouldy kipper,' she said. 'That Welshman is a nasty piece of work. So what do we know?'

'The Sergeant is meant to be getting some state documents for him,' I said. 'And a lot of people are involved – although the Welshman is definitely in charge.'

'And he got all hot and bothered, saying that time is running out,' said Cat. 'So something must be happening soon. Oh, and don't forget there's a sick man called Nathaniel.'

'It's not much to go on,' I said. 'But it all sounds very sinister.'

'So you'll be after my help,' retorted the irritating girl. 'I'm going to keep my ears open and find out who this Welsh courtier is. His accent will soon give him away.'

'There's likely to be more than one Welshman here,'

I said. 'How will you work out which is the one we're after?'

'I'll have to listen to them all, won't I!'

As she scampered away to the sewing room I had a sudden vision of Cat lining up all those with a Welsh accent and getting them to recite the rules of tennis.

Something very nasty was stirring at Hampton Court. I had to report to my master. I had an idea where he might be. When the King wasn't sporting with his new young companions, he was supervising the improvements to his palace. Mark had told me that His Majesty had insisted Cromwell be at his side for this.

I came to the Great Hall. Loud banging and shouting stopped me in my tracks. Woodcarvers were sitting on the floor, creating intricate designs on large pieces of oak. Wooden scaffolding towers soared up to the ceiling. Carpenters swarmed over them like ants. I couldn't help gazing in astonishment at a huge vaulted beam being lifted slowly into position. And in the centre of the Great Hall stood the King. He was resplendent now in a velvet coat and hat, gold chains and sparkling rings. It was hard to believe he'd been the vagabond locked up overnight in East Molesey. He watched the proceedings like a hawk, but not in silence. He was shouting a constant stream of orders. The workers appeared very nervous under their monarch's sharp gaze – but no one dared tell him to go away and let them get on with it. The foreman, who was trying to direct his men from the ground, probably wanted to do just that!

The King was surrounded by yeomen guards and courtiers, and among them I spotted Master Cromwell. I drew closer and hovered, hoping that my master would see me and excuse himself so that I could speak to him. But as I watched, I saw that he was concentrating on the work going on above as much as the King, offering a calm word now and then. I would have no hope of attracting his attention.

'Stop there . . . no, not *there* . . . to the left . . . now to the right,' the King was bellowing. 'To the right! *My* right, you fools! God's wounds, I have imbeciles working for me!'

His Majesty paced the room. The poor woodcarvers hurriedly stopped their work, jumped up and bowed every time he passed them.

The carpenters above were all staring down in confusion at their foreman.

The King had spotted something else. 'I wanted apostles carved into the beams,' he bellowed. 'Not grinning gargoyles.'

Master Cromwell passed through the crowd of courtiers and walked up to the King.

'What is it?' snapped His Majesty.

'My Liege,' said Cromwell calmly. 'I am loath to take you from this important work, but you must prepare for the Privy Council. They meet in an hour.'

The King glared at his half-finished ceiling and

nodded. 'Very well, Thomas, we will go,' he said at last. He swept off to the door opposite, my master following. 'I warn you all, if this is not completed soon I shall personally . . .'

I made my way back to the office. Mister Scrope hadn't got back from stuffing his face yet.

'Didn't see you at lunch, Briars,' was Oswyn's opening shot.

'That would most likely be because I wasn't there,' I said, outwardly calm, but waiting for the next barbed remark. I didn't have to wait long.

'You were hiding, weren't you?'

A thrill of horror raced through me. Surely Weasel-face hadn't seen what I was up to at the tennis court.

7

I kept my expression blank.

'Was I?' I said casually. 'Why would I do that?' I saw that Mark was twitching with nervousness so I winked at him as if this was just the usual game. But in truth I dreaded Oswyn's reply. I would have a lot of explaining to do if my recent actions came to the ears of Mister Finch and his companion.

Oswyn leaned back in his chair and put his feet on the table. 'Well, you're always trying to get out of working,' he drawled. 'You probably ran out of excuses to leave the office so you thought you'd lie low somewhere for a while.'

The horror subsided. He had no idea where I'd been.

'And yet I've come back,' I countered.

'I expect you thought, "Oh deary me, if I stay out too long I'll get the sack and Oswyn's brother will take my place".' He slammed his feet down on the floor and jabbed a finger at me. 'And one of these days that's what's going to happen.'

Before I could reply we heard the click of the door latch. Oswyn quickly snatched up his quill and we all bent our heads to our work. To my surprise it was not Mister Scrope returning but Master Cromwell who stood in the doorway.

'Jack Briars,' he said. 'I will see you in my office. I have some copying to be done.'

The door closed again. I rose and turned to Oswyn. 'It would appear I've found another excuse to shirk,' I said, smiling apologetically. Weasel-face threw a venomous look at me as I left. He could never understand why Cromwell always chose me to do his private scribing.

For a plump man, Master Cromwell could move quickly and I didn't catch up with him until we got to the door of his room. Mark had told me that his usual office at Hampton Court was near the King's apartments but for now my master had wisely distanced himself from the building noise as much as possible.

I followed him in, wondering why I'd been summoned and thankful that I'd have the chance to report my discoveries to him.

I was always amazed that, whichever palace we were at, Cromwell's room was the same – small, dark and mysterious, lined with cupboards and solid, padlocked chests. A single candle stood on his heavy oak table.

I pulled the door shut. My master was in no hurry to

speak. He sat at his desk, pressed his fingers together and gazed steadily at me.

'Well, Jack?'

I was flustered. 'Sir?'

'You have something you wish to say.'

I found myself staring open-mouthed at him. 'How did you know?'

'I saw you in the Great Hall,' he said. 'You had a twitchiness about you. I've seen it before.'

I was crestfallen. 'Am I so obvious, sir?' I asked.

'Only to me.' He seemed amused. 'No one else would have seen anything but a nosy scribe admiring the splendours of the King's renovations and listening to his . . . suggestions. Now speak.'

'I have overheard something troubling.' I relayed the conversation in the wine cellar. My master would be swiftly taking in and assessing every detail as I spoke. But he gave no outward sign of it. However, when I explained that the men had arranged to meet at the tennis court, he suddenly interrupted.

'It is well past noon now,' he said abruptly. 'And yet you did not come to inform me of this second meeting. We might have missed something important.'

'I am sorry, sir,' I blustered. 'There was scarcely time and I guessed that you would ask me to monitor that meeting. So I did.'

Was there a brief look of relief on his face at this? I wasn't sure, for my master never gave much away.

'So, Jack Briars, let me be certain I have this right.' His tone made my stomach give a lurch that was nothing to do with hunger. 'You have worked for me for just a few months and yet you know better than I do how to conduct an investigation?'

'I was hasty, sir,' I said humbly. 'I realise now that you might have preferred one of your more experienced men to be at the tennis court.'

'Indeed I *might*. Finish your account.'

Leaving Cat out of the story, I described how I'd hidden with the broken rackets and balls in the wicker basket and listened to the meeting on the court. I often had cause to be thankful to my godfather, Brother Matthew, who'd trained both my memory and my powers of observation – or nosiness as he called it. I believe I remembered almost every word of the secret conversation.

When I was done, my master rose and walked slowly to the window.

'There is a group of young men that the King has recently gathered round him,' he said as he gazed out. 'You will have noticed the tents they are housed in. His Majesty is pleased to spend a good deal of time with these men. They are a little wild, which appeals to his adventurous spirit – as demonstrated by his exploration of the East Molesey lock-up last night. They sport and hunt together as if the King were their age. From what I can gather, His Majesty outdoes them all at every turn.'

I was certain he was right. No one beat the King at anything if they wanted to stay in favour.

'However,' my master continued, 'of late my people have heard hints of careless talk among them. There are one or two men who may not be showing the loyalty they should to our sovereign. I cannot ignore the fact that it might be connected with what you have discovered.' Cromwell turned back from the window. 'Anyone who wants access to state documents without permission is most unlikely to have His Majesty's interests at heart. There could be some plot afoot that must be stamped out before it gathers speed and threatens the security of the King. It is important that we track down anyone involved and find out just what they are involved in. In truth Jack, I am surprised you have not already done it!'

I bowed my head, stung by his sarcasm.

'As for this Nathaniel who is sick, I will get my men to search him out. I will instruct them to be even more vigilant as they go among the courtiers. I will also make sure that security is increased in the places where state documents are held. And as for you, Jack . . .'

My pulse quickened. I was willing to wager that I would be taking no further part in the business thanks to my rash actions. I shuddered to think what he might do if he knew that Cat was already off investigating.

'. . . I will give you one more chance to show that your – let us call it boyish enthusiasm – will not lead you astray again. It sounds as if the Welshman is a leader in whatever is being planned. The sooner we have his name, the better. Get it and report back immediately.'

'I will not let you down, sir.'

'Be sure that you do not,' he said sternly. 'You should have come to me as soon as you heard the talk in the wine cellar. You were fortunate that you were not discovered at the tennis court. However, I will let you off the hook this time, for two reasons. The first, you have gleaned valuable information without being caught.'

'And the second?' I dared to ask.

'None of my other operatives would have fitted in that basket!'

8

I'd only just left Cromwell's room and was bounding down the staircase to find Cat when she found me.

'Guess what, Jack!' she hissed, stopping me and resting her linen basket on the banister. 'I've done your snooping for you and I didn't even have to listen for accents. You've only got the last little details to deal with now, thanks to me.'

I was astonished. We'd not parted long ago yet she'd already found out the name of Finch's companion.

'Well?' I said.

Cat launched into her tale. Grateful though I was for her help, I often wished she would come to the point more quickly. 'I got back to the sewing room and Mister Wiltshire asked me to deliver some mending straight away. This is my chance, I thought, so I set off with my basket. Then I bumped into John Carter in the knot garden. Or was it the kitchen garden? Well,

232

anyway, I remember he was in one of the gardens because he kept waving his trowel around. So I claimed I had a shirt to deliver and I'd forgotten the name of the gentleman and I was scared I'd get into trouble. That was a clever excuse, don't you think?'

In the excitement of her success, Cat was speaking more and more loudly.

'Shhh,' I warned. 'Master Cromwell is in his chamber. I can't have him thinking you're in on this. The moment you tell me the name, I'm going back to him. Although he might think I've been practising witchcraft to have got it so quickly.'

As I spoke, we heard a door open above. I turned to see my master walking down to us. Cat gave a polite curtsey.

'Mistress Thimblebee,' he said. 'I would ask a favour of you.'

'I am always at your service, sir,' answered Cat promptly.

'So I understand,' said Master Cromwell without a flicker of a smile. 'On many occasions.'

'How can I help you now, sir?' asked Cat, puffing herself up importantly.

'Try to keep Jack in check,' answered Cromwell.

Cat broke into a triumphant grin as he passed. 'I will, sir,' she called. 'Don't you worry about that, sir.'

'Carry on with your story,' I said, trying to hide my irritation.

'Not sure I need to now,' chirped Cat. 'Looks like I'm in charge.'

'Master Cromwell was just joking,' I said through gritted teeth.

'I'm not so sure . . . anyway, I said to John Carter I had to find a young Welshman. He said that there are five Welshmen among the young men who are staying in the tents. He said they arrived with the others in a great band not so long ago, and they're always doing something dangerous, shooting arrows all over the place, charging about on horses and—'

'And which one is *our* Welshman?' I interrupted.

'Oh, I don't know that yet!' said Cat breezily.

I was incredulous. 'And that's your "last little detail"?'

'Not at all,' said Cat. 'I narrowed it down to two.'

'How?'

'I went to see Tom who cleans the tennis court. I told him the story about the mended shirt. And he told me that only two of the Welshmen play tennis!'

I was forced to admit this was clever.

'So I came to find you,' Cat went on eagerly. 'The only thing we have to do now is discover which two of the five Welshmen are the two that play tennis and then which of the two who play tennis is the man we're seeking.' She stopped, out of breath from her long sentence.

'That won't be as easy as you seem to think,' I

said. 'I can't exactly ask who was having the secret conversation on the tennis court with Finch. I guess I'll just have to track them both down and try to listen to their voices.'

'I'll come along,' put in Cat. 'I heard him too and I can remember exactly what his voice was like. "By Lucifer's horns!"' she exclaimed in a very poor imitation of the Welshman.

I ignored this. 'Did John Carter say which tents the Welsh courtiers are in?'

'They have them together in a circle in the centre of the camp,' said Cat. 'And they should be in them at this moment as the King was supposed to have a Council meeting but he's upped and cancelled it so he can play bowls and there was a terrible rush as everyone went to get ready.' She stood there smugly waiting for me to congratulate her. I wasn't going to give her that pleasure. Her head wouldn't have fitted inside her cap!

'I'd better get the information now before they leave for their game!' I replied. 'Master Cromwell won't be pleased if he has to wait all day.'

'Hold your horses,' exclaimed Cat. 'You can't do it.'

'Why not?' I asked impatiently.

'Scribes don't usually go knocking on tents and striking up conversations about tennis.'

She was right.

'On the other hand, I still have that mended shirt and funnily enough I *still* can't remember the name of the gentleman it belongs to.' Cat patted my arm and took up her basket. 'Leave it to me.'

'Certainly not,' I said. 'I'll come with you. I can stay out of sight and see my prey without him seeing me.'

We passed through the outer gate. A groom was leading a horse towards the stables. Cat gave a sigh.

'I wish I could go riding whenever I wanted,' she said wistfully. 'Not that I want to go on a hunt and kill things like the courtiers do but I love being on a horse, going as fast as the wind.' She lowered her voice. 'I imagine you'll be too busy with your swordplay to want a riding lesson. It's a shame as the Home Park has some good spots for secret galloping.'

It was tempting to say no – especially if she was going to make me gallop – but it was important that I learn to ride. I'd claimed that I could, when Master Cromwell first took me on, so I had to make sure the lie became truth. Cat Thimblebee was an amazing horsewoman but however hard she tried to show me what to do, I still looked like a sack of turnips in the saddle. At least, she took delight in telling me that I did.

'Yes please,' I said reluctantly. 'Whenever you can arrange it.'

'I think I can fit you in tonight at seven,' said Cat, as if she had a queue of pupils instead of just me. 'When the King and that rabble of his are getting ready for their feast. No one will be wanting their horses then so the stables will be quiet.'

'Agreed.'

'Make sure you come,' she added, serious now. 'It's not so easy to "borrow" a horse here at Hampton Court. I haven't made friends with the new stable lads yet. I can't hang around if you're late.'

'I'll be there,' I said.

Armed with the linen shirt, Cat picked her way among the tent pegs and guy ropes. I followed at a distance, as if I was searching for someone.

Courtiers yelled and servants ran between the striped canvasses as everyone rushed to be ready for His Majesty's game of bowls. Cat wasn't going to be very popular if she held up the players.

There were five tents in a group. Even without that information I'd have known our prey was staying in one of them as they all flew jaunty flags bearing red Welsh dragons. I lurked beside a pile of archery targets, pretending I wasn't sure which way to go, while Cat stepped up to the first tent.

'Coo-ee! Anyone at home?' she called.

The tent flap opened and a servant hurried out.

'Yes?' he demanded. He sounded harassed.

'I'm returning this shirt to your master,' said Cat. 'He tore it playing tennis.'

'Not *my* master,' said the man. 'He's never played the game in his life.'

'My mistake,' said Cat breezily. She moved on to the next tent. The flap was open and a courtier sat inside. Cat carried on past and I saw why. The man had his leg bandaged and strapped to a wooden splint. The bandages were dirty and had obviously been on for some time. He couldn't have been playing tennis.

The third tent flap was closed.

'Hello-o,' called Cat. 'Delivery from the sewing room.'

No one answered. Cat called again, waited for a moment then moved on. I tiptoed along behind the tents opposite to keep an eye on her progress, but had to duck out of sight of a passing courtier. By the time he'd gone, Cat was by my side, shaking her head.

'No luck,' she said. 'None of them that I spoke to fit the bill. I found the other player but he hasn't had a game since we came to Hampton Court. It must be the one who's away from his tent.'

There was nothing to be done. I could hardly creep about outside it until our man returned. Cat nudged me.

A servant was walking up to the tent that Cat had thought was empty. He opened the flap and went in.

Cat gave an angry gasp. 'There *is* a gentleman in there! I saw him. And he didn't bother to answer when I called. I'll flush him out.'

Without another word, she went skipping up to the tent. With a sudden dramatic cry, she tripped over one of the guy ropes. Her foot pulled the peg clean out of the ground, making the tent rock violently. She did an elaborate tumble and landed on her bum. The clothes in her basket went flying.

I watched the side of the tent start to sag.

'By Lucifer's horns!' came an angry roar. 'What is the meaning of this?'

We'd found our scheming Welshman.

9

A young courtier stormed out of the tent. He was tall and athletic and dressed for sport in a short tunic and boots. His servant sauntered out after him. The courtier looked down his arrogant nose at Cat, tutting in irritation as she gathered up the strewn linen. The servant forced the loose tent peg back into the ground. Cat helpfully handed him the flapping guy rope to hook over it.

'I'm so sorry,' she bleated. 'My mother always said my clumsiness would be the death of me.'

'It will be if you're not more careful.' There was a veiled threat in the words.

'I'll be off.' Cat's cheery voice showed no fear. I was impressed. 'I just have to deliver your shirt that I mended. After you fell over playing tennis.'

She flapped a shirt from her basket.

'That is not mine,' snapped the man.

'Are you sure, your worshipfulness?' said Cat. The man pressed his lips together in an angry line but she didn't give him a chance to answer. 'Aren't you Alfred Compton?' she persisted. 'Though I might have heard wrong.'

'You must be very deaf if you think Parry sounds anything like Compton!' sneered the Welshman. 'Enough of this. Get out of my sight.'

Clever Cat. Now we had his name.

'Of course, Mister Parry, your honourableness,' she said. 'Forgive me for having disturbed you.'

She ran – making sure she barged clumsily into one or two more tents, no doubt in case Parry was watching her go.

I kept out of sight until Parry had vanished back into his tent. I didn't want him to see my face – not yet, anyway. A bold plan was forming in my head. With it I was sure I'd be able find out valuable information about the man and his intentions. First I would have to see Master Cromwell. I prayed he wasn't with the King again.

Master Cromwell was with the King again. I waited at the carved gold door to His Majesty's apartments where a guard told me that the monarch was inside and wasn't happy about the new windows in his bedchamber. I heard the royal voice before he emerged red in the face and shouting, followed by a retinue of frightened men. My master was among them, the only one who appeared composed.

He caught my eye and drew close to the King.

'Might I remind Your Majesty about your game of bowls?' he said. 'What better way to forget all this upheaval for a few hours.'

'More enticing than a meeting of my Council!' said the King, suddenly cheerful. 'I warrant I'll win.'

We all bowed as His Majesty hurried off. Cromwell led me away to the Great Hall.

'Since I last saw you there have been no developments,' he said in a low voice. The shouts and hammering of the workmen meant we couldn't be overheard. 'However hard my men have tried they have been unable to discover who Nathaniel is, nor have they heard any more talk. Whoever is leading this unsavoury business is no fool. He is covering his tracks too well. I hope you have something for me.'

'We – that's to say, I – have discovered who the Welshman is. He is called Parry.'

'Parry?' said my master thoughtfully. 'That will be David Parry, one of the King's new companions. He works for the Master of the Horse. Sir Nicholas Carew has found him indispensable. You are certain you have the right man?'

I nodded. 'I recognised his voice immediately.'

'He is well liked at Court,' said Cromwell. 'But I am guessing you've seen a different side of him.'

'I have, sir,' I said. 'He is a clever, calculating man who rules by fear.'

Cromwell nodded. 'Those involved with him would be too scared to be anything but loyal.' He rubbed his jaw. 'Even so, this is good. We have someone to concentrate our efforts on.'

I feared that my master would now say that the investigation was so serious that his more senior operatives would take over. I decided to get in first. 'Sir, I believe I can find out more about Parry. I should like to have your permission to act on a plan I have.'

'Why you?' asked Cromwell sharply.

I had to be careful. My master had warned me not to take matters into my own hands.

'Because I am a mere scribe,' I said. 'Like all servants, I am invisible at Court. We fear that the man could be hatching some plot against His Majesty. If I can give Parry the impression that I have no loyalty to you or to the King he may take me into his confidence. He boasted that he is still recruiting. If I am careful he will accept me and suspect nothing.'

'You might be getting close to something very dangerous,' said my master.

'I've never shied away from danger,' I said. 'It's part of my job.'

'That is certainly true. You realise of course that I will not be able to speak up for you should you be discovered. And if Parry gets wind of your true allegiance you could be in the greatest peril.'

My master had made it clear to me from the very beginning that a spy would be disowned if he was unmasked. If I was caught playing the part of a traitor, I could expect nothing less than death. Even my master might not have the power to save me.

I swallowed hard and nodded. 'I am willing to take the risk, sir. It may be the only way to uncover what is going on.'

Cromwell was silent for a long time. 'Very well. Then I will ensure that you come to his notice. There is a feast tonight for His Majesty and his companions. I will be present.'

I was astonished. My master would never willingly attend one of those rowdy occasions. He saw my mouth drop open.

'Yes, Jack,' he said sourly. 'I was not intending to be there, but now I must. When the feast is underway you will bring me a letter that you have copied.'

'A letter, sir? What will it say?'

'The content is not important. Copy something you find in the office. When you have handed it over, you will play along with whatever happens. I trust to your acting skills.'

'Can I know more?' I asked, intrigued.

But Cromwell suddenly turned on his heel and walked away. 'Make sure Mister Scrope gets my message immediately,' he called over his shoulder.

I soon saw why. Behind me, two woodcarvers had come to work on some nearby panelling.

I'd have to wait until the feast to find out what my master had in store for me.

10

Oswyn was first out of his chair that evening.

'Supper time,' he said. 'We're to snatch what we can while the Court is at the feast.'

Mister Scrope beat him to the door. But Mark waited for me.

'You go on ahead,' I said. 'I want to catch up with my copying.'

'I'm glad to see you're taking your job seriously for once,' sneered Oswyn from the doorway.

'I won't see you after supper,' said Mark. 'I'm heading to Cheapside. Master Cromwell has given me permission to visit my mother and stay the night. She gets lonely since my father died. Don't do too much writing after the light fades or you'll damage your sight. I heard of a boy who worked by candlelight every night and his eyes fell out!'

I assured him I'd be fine, wished him a safe journey

and found myself alone. With no one to make excuses to, I picked up a letter addressed to the Chief Clerk of the Spicery and copied it as Cromwell had instructed, using my best secretary hand. Then I headed off to see my master.

As I drew closer to the Great Hall I saw that the brightly painted passageway was decorated with tapestries that I hadn't seen before. Cat had told me that tapestries were often taken from palace to palace when the Court moved but these were new to me. The largest one showed gods and goddesses on gleaming horses in a dramatic hunt scene. Cat would not have liked to see what the dogs had caught. One of the horses had an evil gleam in its eye. It looked very like Diablo – the black stallion that the King no longer rode – a devil horse that Cat made me ride for my lessons in spite of my protests. And that reminded me that I was meant to be having a riding lesson tonight. Cat was going to be furious with me! Even if I'd remembered I couldn't have done anything about it. Work always came first. I gritted my teeth and carried on.

There were two yeomen guard at the entrance, tall and imposing with sharp halberds held at their side.

'I have something to deliver to Master Cromwell.' I waved the folded letter.

They nodded and let me pass.

The Great Hall had been transformed. The scaffolding towers and carpenters' tables had been pushed to one side and covered in rich velvet drapes and some of the floor had been uncovered to show the new green and white tiles which gave grandeur to the place. The feast was in full swing. The guests were crammed onto benches, barely able to move their elbows but all managing to raise their goblets to their mouths. The mood was cheerful and noisy and servants went hurriedly from guest to guest. I scanned the room quickly. Parry was sitting at the end of one of the long tables, surrounded by men just like him, lively and athletic. I recognised some of them from my visit to the Welsh tents.

At the top of the room was the royal table. His Majesty sat in the centre with Charles Brandon, his brother-in-law. The two men were talking about the King's success in the afternoon's game of bowls. Their enthusiasm made their speech so loud that I heard it over the rest of the hubbub. Lady Anne Boleyn, the King's love, sat smiling happily, enjoying their tale. King Henry then went on to speak of his night-time adventure. Lady Anne's smile wobbled at the thought of the danger her lord had put himself in.

I was knocked aside by a late arrival. It was Finch. He hastened over to the royal table and bowed low, uttering garbled apologies. His Majesty waved him away, barely listening, and went on with his story so Finch turned and made for the far corner. He was sweating and flustered. Parry glanced up as he passed and I saw Finch shake his head. Parry clenched his fists, his knuckles turning white. So for all his boasting, the man had failed again in his secret task. Had he come up against Cromwell's increased security?

My master sat at the end of the King's table. He was listening to the chatter about him but he did not join in.

I bowed to the King and made for Cromwell, dodging the servants with their trays full of delicious-smelling food. He saw my approach, excused himself and walked towards me. We met just behind where Parry sat chatting to his companions.

'Yes, Briars?'

'The letter you asked for, sir.' I held it out.

He read it and his face darkened. 'What is the meaning of this?' he demanded in a low, cold tone. He flapped the paper, almost striking me on the nose with it.

My master had instructed me to play along with whatever happened. I needed no acting skills to show my complete astonishment.

'You really are the most stupid boy,' he went on relentlessly. 'It was a simple copying task and yet you've got it wrong. I don't know where I find the patience to put up with such idiocy. You are no brighter than a donkey in a field.'

Out of the corner of my eye, I saw a slight movement at the table. David Parry was silent now, his head tilted. I was certain he was listening to our talk. Now I understood Cromwell's game. He had deliberately engineered the scene to take place within Parry's hearing.

'I'll write the letter again, sir,' I said sullenly.

'You think I want to see your face back here tonight? One of my most trusted scribes – and this is how you work. You are being disloyal not just to me, but to our King. You had better pray he does not get to hear about this.'

'I'm sorry, sir,' I bleated, staring at the floor.

'Sorry you say? You deserve a beating. Now get from my sight. I will speak to you tomorrow.'

He swept off. Although I was sure that Cromwell was acting, it seemed so real that I could almost believe I'd failed him.

I glimpsed Parry's expression. While his drunken companions mocked me, he watched me slyly as if considering what he'd just heard. I flashed a mutinous look at my master's back which I made sure Parry saw.

'You'll be sorry,' I muttered.

As I slunk out of the door I bumped into Oswyn. At least, he bumped into me, and laughed as I staggered against the wall. His weaselly features were alight with pleasure.

'How lucky I was passing,' he hissed in my ear. 'I heard it all. You're slipping, Jack. You were always the golden boy with your fine handwriting. Always called upon when Master Cromwell was after a scribe. Well, you've let him down this time. I wonder what will happen now.'

'So do I, Oswyn,' I said, making sure I sounded scared. But in truth my pulse was racing. I was willing to wager that my path would cross with Parry's again soon.

11

The next morning Oswyn wasted no time in telling Mark all about my humiliation of the night before. As he described the scene in every detail, Mark grew paler and paler at the thought of the trouble I was in. Mark had been in a happy mood after seeing his mother and I was angry with Oswyn for spoiling that. But I was forced to keep up the pretence that I was seriously out of favour with Thomas Cromwell. In truth I'd never wanted to punch Oswyn's sneering weasel face more than at that moment.

'It was one stupid mistake,' I said sulkily. 'Master Cromwell must have been in a very ill humour to take it so badly.'

'It could have happened to anybody.' Mark was desperately trying to defend me.

'But it happened to Jack.' Oswyn didn't stop crowing until Mister Scrope came in and started devouring

250

the pasty and beer he'd brought with him.

'Get on with your work,' the Chief Scribe ordered between mouthfuls. 'We have so much to do. Especially you, Jack. I've heard about last night. You'd better be extra careful today. Master Cromwell has complained that your work isn't up to standard. He's told me I must check on you. He hasn't time now, he said. He'll be shutting himself away and catching up with his work today – His Majesty has given him leave. I will report to him tomorrow. As if I didn't have enough to do without worrying about my scribes,' he grumbled into his tankard.

A knock came at the door.

'Maybe Master Cromwell has changed his mind and come to check on you himself,' whispered Oswyn smugly.

Playing my part to perfection, I put on a frightened expression and turned to my work.

Mister Scrope hurriedly took up some papers in an effort to show how busy he was. 'Enter,' he called.

To my surprise the person who entered was not Master Cromwell. It was David Parry! I tried to remain calm but felt sure I knew why he was there. He hadn't wasted much time in seeking me out.

'Good morning, sir.' Mister Scrope rose to greet him and bowed in his usual grovelling way. 'How can I help you?'

Parry got straight to the point. 'I have some accounts to be copied,' he said. 'Some business with my estate in Wales. My own scribe is back at my house in Abergavenny. I will choose one of your boys. It will mean some extra pennies for him.'

'We are very busy—' began Mister Scrope.

'And there will be something in it for his master . . .'

Mister Scrope's eyes lit up immediately. 'Take your pick, sir,' he said in a toadying manner. 'We can easily spare one.' The mere sniff of extra money had made him forget that we had a great pile of work to complete. 'And I am certain they will all do their best.' He glared at me.

Parry strode about the room, scrutinising our writing. Mark quailed, probably dreading he'd be chosen.

'May I offer you my services, sir?' said Weasel-face. 'I am Oswyn Drage, the senior scribe here, and by far the most experienced.'

'Then you'll do,' said Parry.

I hope I hid my astonishment. I'd been so sure he was going to choose me. But I'd underestimated the cunning of the man. He peered closely at Oswyn's work and then at mine.

'Hold hard,' he said at last. He put a heavy hand on my shoulder. 'I'll take you instead. Your script will be perfect for what I have in mind.'

Oswyn turned purple but did his best not to let his temper burst out. 'Sir,' he spluttered, 'Jack Briars was publicly berated at the feast last night for his careless work – by Master Cromwell!'

Mister Parry looked at me as if he'd forgotten the

252

incident. I was willing to wager the crown jewels that he hadn't.

'Ah yes, I think I call it to mind,' he said casually. 'In that case, Jack Briars won't expect to lighten my purse until he's proved himself. Which I am sure he will.'

Mister Scrope frantically nodded his agreement.

'Did you wish to give me the accounts here, sir?' I asked.

'I would not want to disturb your fellow scribes,' said Parry. 'Come with me to my lodgings. I am in one of the tents on the river bank.'

I picked up a penner and quill and followed him out of the door, enjoying Oswyn's expression of indignation as I went.

I scampered along behind him as he strode through the gatehouse and over to the tents. My plan had worked – so far. Cromwell had got me to Parry's attention and Parry had taken the bait. Now I'd act the disgruntled scribe who could be tempted into treachery. I'd have to use all my skills. If I was too eager he would smell a rat. It was up to him to make the first move.

The inside of his tent held a truckle bed with a fur cover, two trunks, a table and a couple of chairs. The floor was covered with tarpaulin and a brazier full of glowing logs kept the April chill away. Parry threw himself into his chair and gestured to me to pull the other up to the table. His servant paid us no attention. He was a large man with brawny arms and broad shoulders who whistled under his breath as he lazily cleaned his master's hunting boots.

I quickly trimmed a quill and took the lid off the inkwell. 'What would you like me to do, sir?' I asked eagerly.

'You're keen to start,' Parry said with an amused smile.

'I am, sir,' I replied. 'I'm a hard worker and I want to prove it to you.'

'Is that so?' He stared at me. 'Your master didn't think so last night, as I recall.'

'I caught Master Cromwell at a bad moment,' I muttered.

'Are you saying there was nothing wrong with your work?' asked Parry.

'There must have been,' I admitted. 'Though I couldn't see it.'

'You are being very loyal, Jack,' said Parry, sympathetically. 'It is to your credit.'

He said no more but rifled through a pile of papers. He chose one and put it down in front of me, next to a blank piece of paper. The list showed the wages earned by his servants last year at his house in Wales.

'I shall be sending this to my steward,' said Parry. 'You will make a copy for me.'

I began. For a while Parry said nothing.

'Look at the money I give my workers,' he said suddenly, pointing to the column of figures. 'I pay well, don't you think? I'll warrant my scribe at home earns more than you do here.'

An innocent remark? I doubted it. He was trying to ensnare me. I chose my words carefully.

'I can see you are very generous to your staff, sir,' I said. I risked saying more. 'I would happily work for you – if the opportunity arose.'

The Welshman gave a slow smile. 'And leave your position at Court?' he asked mildly. 'Most boys would give their right hand to work for the magnificent King Henry. Why would you give that up?'

'I didn't mean anything by it, sir.' I put my head down and scratched away at the list.

No more was said until I'd finished. Parry took my copy and checked it.

'Very good,' he said. 'You could teach my scribe a thing or two.' He handed me a letter. 'And now I need a record of this.'

I took a clean sheet of paper and began to write. The letter was to a man who bred deerhounds. Parry wished to buy some for the King's hunting pack.

I worked in silence. The only sound was the scratching of my quill. When it was done, Parry took his own quill and signed it.

'I am most surprised that Master Cromwell found anything to criticise in your work, Jack,' he said. 'He has been unfair – do you not agree? You may speak freely.'

'I can't, sir.'

'It will go no further.'

His expression was encouraging and sympathetic.

'Well, in truth, sir . . .' I made myself hesitate as if still scared. Then I gulped hard and went on in a rush. 'In truth, sir, I want to tell Master Cromwell to jump in the Thames.'

'Just Master Cromwell?'

'No, because he's acting under orders, isn't he?' I said sulkily. 'And we all know who from. We can't question royal orders.' I screwed my face into the most mutinous expression I could. 'It isn't fair. We all work very hard and for nothing most of the time.'

I held his gaze. 'I wish he was still in that lock-up!' I declared. The dreadful words almost burned my mouth.

David Parry suddenly lurched forwards and slammed a hand down on the table. 'By Lucifer's horns! That is dangerous talk, Jack Briars.'

12

I felt a stab of fear. Had this dangerous man suspected my intentions? Had he tricked me into speaking treachery in order to get me arrested and out of his way? Parry slowly sat back in his chair.

'I hope I didn't scare you, Jack,' he said. His friendly manner was back as quickly as it had gone. But I sensed a dark threat under the smile and understood Finch's fear of him. 'You should be more careful whom you speak to on these matters.'

'I am sorry, sir,' I burbled.

'However on this occasion you are lucky.' Parry shrugged. 'Lucky to have spoken in front of a man who agrees with your views. So, Jack, I'm guessing you would like to see some . . . changes around here, yes?'

I nodded dumbly.

'It might surprise you to hear that you're not the

only one. Many are – let's say, dissatisfied with the one that you didn't name.'

I suddenly felt very vulnerable. But I had to shake that off. I had come to insinuate myself into Parry's confidence and I wasn't going to back out now.

'Change is coming. I'm sure you'd like that as much as I would, Jack.'

'Indeed, sir.'

'Well then, stick with me, for I have a plan.'

'What is it?' I asked like an eager child hoping for a present.

The smile disappeared in a flash. 'Let us get one thing straight,' said Parry. 'You will ask no questions. If you agree to help me, then I will help you. There are many here involved in our enterprise and each of my loyal followers will reap rich rewards when we achieve our aims.'

Loyal followers! The words jarred in my head. There could be no loyal followers in a conspiracy against the crown.

He went on. 'The wages of a scribe – even one of mine – will seem very small beer compared with what you and my other followers will receive.'

'I am with you heart and soul,' I whispered, my hand on my chest.

'That is easy to say,' said Parry. 'First you will have to prove yourself worthy. As for our other business. I said I would pay you for your work.' He tossed me a penny. 'That is for you, not your greedy Mister Scrope.'

I caught the coin. 'Thank you,' I said, wondering how I could get more information about Parry's plan. The man was clever. He was giving little away. 'How else can I help you?' I asked.

Parry stroked his beard thoughtfully. 'There is something,' he said. 'Something that should have been sorted out by now. But it's a delicate matter. Indeed it could be thought a little dangerous.'

'Tell me,' I burst out eagerly. 'You've shown more faith in me than anyone else here. I'm at your service.'

'Let me warn you that what I am about to say cannot be repeated. I will deny everything if you do and a favoured courtier of King Henry will always be believed over a disgraced scribe.'

'A disgraced scribe with nothing to lose,' I added fervently.

'Indeed.' Parry's cruel dark eyes bored right into my head. 'And yet it is your work for Master Cromwell that makes you very useful to me.'

A stab of horror ran through me. He surely didn't mean my spying. I kept my face calm and looked back at him inquisitively.

'My work?' I ventured.

'Your work,' repeated Parry with some impatience. 'I hope I am not dealing with the dolt that Cromwell believes you to be. You scribe for the great man, is that not so?'

I nodded. I was safe from his suspicions – for the moment at least.

'Then he will suspect nothing if you are found alone in his office?'

'No, sir,' I assured him. 'I am often there.'

Parry stood for a minute as if considering his next move. 'I am guessing he has a document showing the numbers of loyal men of England that he could muster to form an army in times of trouble,' he said. 'I want to see that muster list.'

His words chilled me like a shower of hail. This must be the state document that Finch had failed to get. Parry wanted to gauge the strength of the royal defences! There could surely be only one reason. He was planning an attack on the King!

I found myself struggling to stay in character as loyal servant to a traitor. Every bone in my body fought against it.

I realised Parry was staring hard at me. 'What is the matter?' he said suspiciously. He grasped my jacket and pushed his face into mine. 'I hope I don't have to doubt your commitment to our cause.'

'Not at all, sir.' He released me. 'Indeed,' I quavered, 'I was thinking how honoured I am to be involved, and how wonderful my future will be.'

'Then you will find out at what time Master Cromwell will be away from his chamber and you will get that document and bring it to me before I go to dine this evening.'

I would not be carrying out Parry's order. I would certainly go to Master Cromwell's office, but only to report to him what I'd discovered. He would know the next step to take.

'I will get it, sir,' I said. Then I allowed some doubt to show on my face. 'But if Master Cromwell has such a document, he might well notice if it vanishes.'

'Not if you are careful,' said Parry.

I could see that he wasn't a man to discuss his orders. He expected others to worry about the detail.

'There's just one more thing, Jack Briars. The task will serve as a test of your loyalty to me.'

'I will be true, sir.'

'I can't be sure of that. From this moment on, therefore, you will be constantly watched. I will be told where you go, what you do and whom you speak to. If I find you false your life will be worth no more than a fly's.'

13

I snatched up the penner and left. As I hurried between the tents and into the Base Court, my mind was racing. Parry was ordering me to commit treason – there was no softening the word.

What I'd just learned had shaken me. Parry was planning an attack on the King – and it didn't sound as if he intended to use a single assassin. He was demanding to know the strength of the King's defences so I guessed he was planning to use fighters of his own in an uprising, an armed attack against the crown!

But Parry had said I would be followed. With someone on my tail I could not get to Cromwell to ask him how I should proceed.

The only answer was to send him a written message. But who could be charged with such a message? I couldn't give it to Mark. Although he would ask no questions, he was too nervous to approach Master

Cromwell. And I couldn't trust Mister Scrope or Oswyn not to read it.

I made a show of dropping the penner. As I bent to pick up the spilled contents, I glanced around hastily as if embarrassed that my clumsiness had been seen. The place was bustling, as always. Courtiers, servants, yeomen guard, all about their business. It was impossible to catch whoever was on my tail. Any of these people could have been a spy for Parry and watching my every move. And then I spotted Parry's servant. He was in conversation with the Sergeant Porter. Was that just coincidence? Surely if he was the one following me, he would take more care not to be seen.

I needed to give myself time to think out what to do next. I went back to the scribes' room. I had no doubt that the door would be under observation and my shadow would follow me again if I left.

'Was Mister Parry happy with your work?' asked Scrope hopefully as I entered.

'I think so,' I said, holding up my penny.

'And where's mine?' he asked.

'I'm sure Mister Parry wants to give it to you himself,' I answered.

Muttering, Scrope moved his chair nearer the fire. I doubted he'd ever see his pay. Mark gave me a quick smile while Oswyn scowled fit to burst.

I bent over some accounts from Cat's master, Mister Wiltshire – well, he was Cat's master in name only.

No one was in charge of Mistress Thimblebee! And thinking of Cat gave me an answer. She was the ideal person to deliver a message to Cromwell for me.

A good solution with one obvious drawback. I couldn't openly hand over a note and ask her to take it to him. Somehow I had to slip the message to her secretly.

I began my task of copying out Mister Wiltshire's accounts. Then, when I was sure everyone was busy, I took a small piece of paper and leaned heavily on one arm so that my work was hidden. It occurred to me that putting my note to Cromwell down in ink was very dangerous. If Parry read it, I'd be dead before I could draw breath.

There was no time to do a code. I wrote quickly.

I am being followed and cannot speak to you. P wants me to take the muster list to him. I await your instructions.

Hearing the hurried scratching of my quill nib, Oswyn's head shot up. 'I hope you're doing your best handwriting, Briars,' he said loudly. 'Perhaps Mister Scrope had better check what you've done so far.'

Luckily Weasel-face turned to make sure the Chief Scribe had heard him. As soon as his beady eyes were off me, I blotted the note and pulled the copied accounts on top of it. Mister Scrope heaved himself out of his chair.

'That was a waste of time, Oswyn,' he complained as he inspected my neat rows. 'I'm not going to check it again until he's finished. He hasn't done much but it's good enough.'

'I've been working very slowly to make it perfect,' I explained in an angelic tone.

From then on, it was as if Oswyn was scrutinising every stroke of my quill. He sensed that something was going on. I itched to hide the note in my jacket but I knew that if he saw me, he'd do everything in his power to get hold of it. He didn't even make his usual trips to the jakes. I finally came to the end of my accounts. I was going to have to take my work to Mister Scrope and I wasn't sure I could scoop up the hidden note without being seen. There was only one thing for it.

'Mark,' I said casually. 'Pass me that box behind you. It's got the latest bills for the threads used mending the tapestries. There's something I have to check.'

Mark heaved the large box from its pile in the corner and placed it on the table. I pulled it towards me until I was hidden from Oswyn's sight. I slid my note out and into my jacket in one smooth action. Then I made a great show of rifling through the papers in the box and referring to the accounts I'd written, before returning the box to its place and handing the accounts to Mister Scrope.

My relief was short-lived. My next problem was more difficult. How to get the note to Cat. If I could smuggle it into her hands, hopefully she'd guess what must be done with it.

At last Mister Scrope dismissed us for lunch. As I put my quill down I snagged the point on my cuff, tugging until it tore a small hole.

I followed Mark down the stairs and when we reached the Base Court, I showed him the ripped, ink-stained cuff, holding it up so that any pursuer could see it. 'Look at this tear,' I said. 'I'd better go and get it mended first. I'll see you at the serving hatches.'

Mark nodded. 'Thank goodness you didn't stab yourself, Jack. I heard of a boy who skewered himself to his desk with his quill!'

I agreed that I'd escaped death by a whisker. I was cutting across the court when someone grabbed me by the shoulder. I wheeled round, ready to face my unknown follower.

14

Oswyn was glaring at me.

'Sneaking off again, Briars?' he demanded suspiciously. 'That's not the way to the serving hatches.' He held my shoulder in a firm grasp.

'I'm going to the sewing room, Oswyn,' I said breezily. 'Do come if you want.'

Oswyn's eyes narrowed. 'I might just do that,' he said. I cursed inwardly. If he started shouting to all and sundry that I was up to something, Parry would surely get to hear of it and consider me more of a liability than a help. I didn't want to think about my fate if that happened. I already knew too much.

Fortunately a young courtier called to him. 'Will we see you tonight at the card game, Drage?'

Weasel-face pushed me away.

'You certainly will,' he said in a loud, jolly voice.

'I warrant you wish you had friends in high places, Briars,' he added in an undertone.

I ignored him and made my escape. I wondered just how jealous he would be if he discovered I was secretly working for the King's most important minister.

My skin prickled as I walked towards the sewing room. I soon found out why. Parry's servant was sauntering along behind me. This time it couldn't possibly be a coincidence. Parry had been as good as his word.

The moment I poked my head round the sewing room door I could see that Cat wasn't there.

Several men were seated on the floor, busy mending piles of shirts and breeches. Thanks to Cat I was acquainted with them all. They nodded to me.

'Can I help?' asked a cheerful young Frenchman called Emile. He was perched on a stool and hemming a large bed coverlet.

I couldn't back out now. I told him about the problem cuff.

'Mon Dieu, that was careless!' he commented.

I scanned the sewing room as he made the repair. 'At least Mistress Thimblebee isn't here to scold me,' I said, hoping someone would mention where she was.

'She is certainly fierce, that one!' laughed Emile. 'I will be as quick as I can, because she could be back any minute. On the other hand she might be out for many hours. Monsieur Wiltshire he sends her on the errands when the ladies want special work done, as she is the only girl, you know.'

My cuff was soon done. I handed him the penny that David Parry had given me. Outside, Parry's servant was sitting by a small fountain in the middle of the courtyard. He doffed his cap in my direction. To anyone else it would have passed as a friendly gesture but it filled me with dread.

I saw no sign of Cat as I made my way to the serving hatches in the Great Kitchen to collect my lunch, and no sign of her as I returned to work. Back at my table I racked my brains to think of a way I could leave the office to find her.

'Mister Scrope,' I blurted out in desperation. 'I've just remembered – Master Cromwell gave me an errand.'

Mark looked surprised and Oswyn's keen eyes bored into me. I'd made an error. I was out of favour with Cromwell. He'd be unlikely to trust me with any task.

'It's the statues,' I blundered on, inventing wildly all the time. 'Around the palace. The King's young friends have been playing all manner of games in the passages.' I lowered my voice. 'And some while very drunk.' I paused. 'Master Cromwell wants me to make an inventory of any damage before the King notices. I think it's a sort of punishment for my poor work last night.'

Oswyn's eyes narrowed so I gave Mark a gentle kick under the table. He jumped.

'That's right. I remember too,' he said feebly.

'Off you go then,' sighed Mister Scrope.

I must have walked miles around the palace, clutching my parchment and penner. I saw a thousand golden Zeuses, bejewelled cyclopses and silver cherubs – but no Cat. I made a great show of inspecting each statue and occasionally writing things down. I hadn't forgotten my shadow. And he hadn't forgotten me. I came round a corner to see him sitting on the plinth of a marble angel. He winked at me and got up to follow.

This time I smiled back, hiding my desperation to find Cat. And then, as I made my weary way along a crowded passageway I suddenly spotted a mass of bright red curls bobbing along towards me. It was Cat, carrying a big basket of sewing. I slipped my hand inside my jacket and palmed the note. As she saw me her face darkened with fury. She hadn't forgotten my missed riding lesson.

She turned on her heel and stalked off the other way!

15

What was I to do? If I chased after her, then Parry's man would know something was going on.

I'd just have to head her off. I still hadn't had a chance to explore all of Hampton Court, but I managed to call to mind Mark's map. I quickened my pace, glancing to left and right as if checking the vases on the plinths that I passed. Cat had been moving slowly, under the weight of her basket. I calculated that at this pace I had time to get in front of her. I turned the next corner and there she was. The mass of people between us meant that she hadn't seen me.

In the press of the crowd I dodged around a large servant carrying a pitcher and knocked Cat's basket from her hands. Then I staggered back as if she'd barrelled into me.

'What the . . . !' she exclaimed angrily.

'Mistress Thimblebee,' I shouted. 'You are the most clumsy clotpole.'

We both bent at the same time to pick up the basket, our heads knocking together hard. I heard passers-by laughing. Cat certainly wasn't. Her eyes flashed angrily. As she whisked up the basket I made to help, slipping the note under her fingers as I did so.

'I have *urgent* business for Master Cromwell and you're delaying me.' I held her gaze for an instant.

She stared back, then rammed me in the belly with her basket. 'Call me clumsy, would you?' she screeched. 'Get out of my path.'

I watched her go, remembering to shake my fist for the benefit of my watcher. I hoped and prayed that this was an act and that she would get the message to Cromwell.

The statues were of no further use so I headed back to the scribes' room. I took my place at the table and began to copy out a bill for candles. It was long. You could have lit the road from Hampton Court to Cornwall with the candles used by the palace in one week alone. But I barely took note of what I was writing. My thoughts rushed round like leaves in a whirlwind. Had Cat been so angry that she'd thrown the note away? And if not, would she understand my words and work out what I wanted her to do?

I had to trust Cat. She was resourceful. But now my mind flew to Cromwell's gloomy office. In my imagination he was sitting at his table, my message already in his hands. A worm of worry told me I'd been foolish to involve myself with the dangerous David Parry. It whispered in my ear that I'd got in too deep, so deep that I would be branded a traitor. My master himself had warned me that I was taking a hazardous step. I banished the thought. I forced myself to believe that even now he'd be working out what to do for the best. And somehow, he would get a message to me.

The afternoon dragged on. No message came from Cromwell. The brawny servant would be hovering about outside the office, waiting for me to do Parry's bidding. I had no choice but to go to my master's room. Then at least my pursuer would believe I was after the muster list. I would have to linger outside and wait until Cromwell left. I'd decide what action to take when I got inside. The one thing I could *not* do was to give the list to David Parry. But what would happen when I didn't appear with it? The ruthless Welshman had already threatened to kill me if I was disloyal. His servant probably had orders to dispatch me if I failed this important task.

Snatching up my statue inventory, I pushed back my chair.

'I forgot to check the passageways by the Watching Chamber,' I said, making my voice rise in panic. That was easy enough! 'It'll be the first place the King spots any damaged cherubs.'

My panic was infectious. 'Go!' gasped Mister Scrope.

As I ran down the stairs, I heard hoof beats outside

273

on the cobbles. I looked through the window to see a figure in a plain black cloak on a chestnut horse. I knew the horse – and I knew its rider. It was Thomas Cromwell. He was leaving the palace! I only just stopped myself from calling out to him.

I had no notion if he'd received my message. A sound at the top of the stairs made me spin round. Parry's servant stood there. He'd been staring out of a window too. He gave me a grin and a thumbs up. It came to me that he too had seen Cromwell leave, so I had no excuse not to go into my master's office now. But the way he made his fist was a cold reminder that I mustn't fall out of line.

I knocked on the door of Cromwell's office, my inventory of broken statues flapping in my hand. I lifted the latch and went inside. The candle had been snuffed out but a little afternoon light filtered in from the small window and the remains of a fire gave a low glow.

I closed the door, placed the inventory on his table and scanned the room, putting myself in the place of a traitor trying to find the muster list.

A large chest stood against the far wall. Two others, equally solid, were on either side of the fireplace. Smaller boxes were stacked on the many shelves, each one no doubt full of important papers. Even if I'd been on Parry's side, I'd have stood little chance of finding what he wanted.

I found myself pacing up and down, pondering my

next move. I had never felt so helpless. One thing was certain. I could not take the list to Parry. I wondered feverishly if I should write a false list that might satisfy him for the time being. I even considered escaping through the window and trying to find my master. But that would be foolhardy.

If only Cromwell had sent a message back to me. I was sure he would have done if he'd got my note. One of his spies could have slipped a piece of paper into my hand. A line or two to tell me what I should do.

It was possible that my master had considered it too dangerous. I tried to think how I'd have acted if I was in his shoes. If he'd received my message he would guess that I'd have to come to his office.

And then I had it. If he did guess I'd come here, then this is where he would leave a note! It was a long shot but it was my only hope. I began to hunt around. Master Cromwell was highly methodical. Nothing was ever out of place, no documents scattered over his table, no discarded letters thrown in a corner – in fact, nowhere to hide a piece of paper in plain sight.

I walked round the room, my gaze sweeping over the shelves and boxes. No note was tucked neatly between them. I sat in his chair and ran my fingers under the table top for hidden compartments or drawers. Nothing. But as I was getting up again, I noticed the corner of a paper wedged between the cushion and the wood of his seat. It seemed to have fallen but my master would surely have cleared it away before he left

– unless he'd meant it to be found. I pulled it out. It was a small folded letter, the wax seal imprinted with the ornate ring he wore. There was no name on it, just a smudge of charcoal in one corner. Cromwell was too particular to put a seal to a letter with a smudge on it. I took it to the window and examined it from all sides. Then I peered closely at the charcoal mark. In the faint sunlight I saw that it was actually a drawing. A tiny sketch of a bush. A bush with thorns. A briar bush.

16

Cat had got the message to him after all, and Master Cromwell had left the note for me. I was almost dizzy with relief.

I broke the letter's seal and read it intently. At first it appeared that Cromwell had lost his reason and was writing about a field with three large trees to the north of Ipswich!

Then I kicked myself for being a slow-witted dolt. Of course it was in code. The chest against the far wall was in the north aspect of the room. And it had three crests on its studded lid. I ran to it. It was locked with a large, stout padlock.

I studied the coded note again. There was a drawing of a sword at the bottom. But Cromwell didn't keep a sword in the office. I was to look for a blade of a different sort. The only blades in the room were in Cromwell's box of quill-trimming knives on his table.

I carefully sorted through the box. Nothing there. I lifted it up. Wedged into the underside was a key.

The clunk of the padlock opening was too loud in the quiet room and the creak of the lid was even louder. I feared that someone might hear and come in, knowing that the room should be empty.

The chest was full of papers. On top was a separate scroll tied with embroidered velvet ribbon and gold tassels. Cromwell would not usually bind his papers up so elaborately. He must have done that to draw my attention to it. My heartbeat quickened. I untied the scroll and thumbed through the papers. They were certificates from the Commissioners of every part of the country listing the men and weapons at His Majesty's disposal.

The certificates promised archers, light horsemen and billmen. Robert Aycliffe had once told me that billmen were foot soldiers who wielded long poles with vicious hooks on the end. The dates were recent. I guessed that the King had ordered this information because of threats from Spain. The country was unhappy that the King of England wanted to divorce Queen Katherine, his Spanish wife, and marry Anne Boleyn.

I stared at the numbers for a while. Aycliffe had also told me that England would be well protected if any foreign power tried to invade. These numbers must mean that the King could muster a very large army. But I couldn't believe that my master wanted me to give this important information to David Parry. In any case, Parry had asked only for a list of figures so he must have heard there was a document summarising that information.

I couldn't see it.

The last parchment was much larger than the others. On it was a list of counties and the numbers of men promised by each one. A summary of the figures. Just what Parry had ordered.

Still I hesitated. I turned to the list again. My master was too cunning to give Parry exactly what he needed. What was I missing? I went back to the certificates, found the one sent from the county of Surrey and totted up the figures. Then I checked my calculation against the list I was to give to Parry. On the list the number was much lower than the true figure! I tried again with Berkshire and found the same.

At last I understood! According to the list, the country was not nearly as well defended as the certificates promised. Master Cromwell had found a way to make Parry believe that he would meet a poor resistance in his uprising. He was spinning a clever web to lure him in. And Cromwell had left the original certificates with the list so that I would see the real figures and realise what he'd done. I stowed the document inside my shirt.

Now I guessed why Master Cromwell had left the palace. He knew an uprising was planned. He must be sending out trusted riders to muster the troops from the closest counties. He couldn't do this at the palace for fear Parry would get to hear of it.

I retied and replaced the bundle of papers, adding Cromwell's coded letter, and closed and locked the chest. I was replacing the key where I'd found it when there came a fierce rapping at the door.

17

The door slowly opened. I just had time to jump away from the box.

Nicholas Mountford stood in the entrance. He gave a start when he saw me. Then his expression became stern.

'Jack! What are you doing here? It's no use waiting for Master Cromwell. He's been called home to Austin Friars.'

In my scramble of thoughts, I noted that the door was still ajar. If I spoke loudly enough, my shadow would be able to hear our words. I snatched up my scribbles about the statues.

'I was ordered to deliver this inventory for my master. I wanted to impress him with my hard work after . . . well I wanted to impress him so I came to give him this in person.' I shrugged. 'I expected him to be here. He must have left in a hurry.'

'He said there was a fuss over some building works,' said Mountford. 'He'll be back in the morning I should imagine. I thought you'd have heard.'

So that was the excuse Cromwell had made when he'd galloped off. It was good one – most people were aware that he was always improving his grand house – just like the King.

'He didn't say,' I offered feebly.

Mountford stood impassively watching me fumble as I placed my inventory back on the desk.

'Still, it'll be the first thing he sees when he gets back.'

'You're sailing close to the wind, Jack.' There was a warning in the guard's voice as he spoke. 'You've got a lot of talent but I'm beginning to wonder where it might lead you. By all accounts your work isn't up to scratch, you've fallen out of favour with Cromwell and now I find you in his room. You'll have to come up with a better excuse than inventories.' He scrutinised my face. 'Why are you so nervous?'

I had to think quickly. I pretended to be embarrassed. 'How did you know I was in here?' I asked, playing for time. 'Did you see me come in?'

'No,' replied Mountford. 'A log boy reported that there were strange clunks and creaks coming from inside this room. He knew Master Cromwell was gone so he feared there was a ghost in here. I find no ghost but a guilty-looking scribe! What were you doing that made so much noise? You'd best be honest now.'

282

'The truth is,' I stuttered, 'I wondered what it would be like to be Master Cromwell so I walked up and down trying to feel important. Then I . . . well, I sat at his desk. I – er – I accidentally knocked his candlestick onto the floor. I don't think I damaged it. You won't tell anyone, will you?'

Could I see doubt on Mountford's face? If he didn't believe me he might arrest me on the spot – and find the muster list tucked inside my shirt! When Master Cromwell returned, he would be able to say nothing in my defence, even though the document was false. I prayed my acting skills hadn't let me down. After what seemed like an hour, Mountford's stern expression softened. He burst out laughing.

'It wouldn't surprise me if you really were in that seat one day, Jack Briars.' He tapped his nose. 'If that's all it was, I won't spread it about.'

He held the door open for me.

'Thank you,' I said faintly as I left. 'It won't happen again.'

It was only when I was well clear of Cromwell's room that my breathing steadied. I'd got away with it! I wondered what Cromwell would think when he saw my made-up inventory on his desk.

I headed quickly for the tents. I could hear the church bells in East Molesey ringing for evening prayers. Parry would be getting ready for his meal. I was just in time.

The canvas flap of his tent was open. As soon as I entered, his servant appeared behind me. I tried not to show my shock. I hadn't seen him since I left Master Cromwell's office. He could be secretive when he wanted to be. He tied the flap shut.

Parry was pulling on a rich silk doublet over his shirt. He snatched my list without a word and read it through, his forehead creased in concentration. Then he opened the lid of one of his trunks and pulled out a map. He spread it out on the table and traced a route with his finger. He nodded and at one point gave a grunt of satisfaction. The figures pleased him.

'You have done well,' he said finally, as he rolled up the map. He handed me a coin. It was a silver sixpence and I felt sick at having to take it. 'I think you will prove useful to me.'

I nodded eagerly. 'I am at your service, sir.'

'Put this back where you found it. But before you go, here is your next task.' He gazed at me, his eyes cold. 'Remember, I trust no man. There will still be eyes on you.'

His servant cracked his knuckles together. The noise ripped through the tent.

'There is to be a gathering for cards later this evening,' Parry went on.

I knew this must be what Oswyn was going to. 'How can I help?' I asked, dreading his reply. Whatever it was, I'd have to find a way of complying.

'I won't be able to attend until much later. I shall be preparing for the hunt that is to take place tomorrow. I need you to pass on a message about the hunt to each man.'

This puzzled me. It was a simple and innocent job after the treacherous task I'd just completed.

'I want you there all evening,' Parry went on. 'It'll be easier to keep a watch on you so you will volunteer to serve the gentlemen.'

'But I have proved now that I am loyal, sir,' I protested. 'I've put myself in great danger to fetch you the list.'

'I'm sure you are loyal,' said Parry smoothly. 'And Garth will continue to help you stay that way.'

I cast a quick glance at the hulking servant. I imagined he could break my back with one blow.

'This is the message you are to convey,' said Parry. '"The King has decreed that the hunt will be in the North Park tomorrow at dawn. Wishing you all success". Now repeat it back to me.'

'I will let them know that the hunt is in the North Park at dawn tomorrow and wish them—'

'Not good enough,' snapped Parry. 'You will say the exact words.'

Surprised at his insistence, I did so.

He appeared satisfied and dismissed me with a wave of the hand.

I made my way back to Cromwell's office to return the muster list. Something troubled me. The message I'd just been given sounded a reasonable thing for the man who organised the hunt to say to his fellow riders. But it wasn't just the information I had to pass to the hunters. I was to use the exact words. My mind wandered back to my old home at the abbey. My godfather, Brother Matthew, and I had a number of code words and phrases that we used as warnings. 'Bad weather ahead' signalled that the abbot was on his way. And 'the sky is clear' meant the abbot had gone from the monastery and we had some peace for a few hours!

I was certain that the men involved in Parry's plan would hear a message hidden in those words. But what was it? How could I find out before it was too late?

18

I presented myself at the serving hatches at seven o'clock. Garth slunk about in the background, pinching sweetmeats when no one was looking. I joined a line of men in aprons and took a tray full of empty goblets. I trudged after the other servers through the palace gardens to a large tent set up by the Water Gate. The tent was full of male courtiers of all ages, taking seats at tables and enjoying banter with their fellows.

'Is the King coming?' I whispered to the servant in front of me.

'No,' he whispered back. 'He's gone to dine in Kingston with more noble company than this.'

In His Majesty's absence the guests could relax. They fell upon the drinks as if they hadn't taken a drop all day, making the lively mood lift even higher. I deposited my goblets and was handed a heavy pitcher of ale which I lugged round and attempted to serve without spilling any. I was turning to fetch some more when I nearly bumped into Oswyn. I'd been wondering where he was.

'What are you doing here?' he gasped.

As we stared at each other, I noted his strange expression. He wasn't angry. If anything he was embarrassed.

'Drage! We're waiting for you.' Someone summoned him to a nearby seat.

I left him to it and went to refill my pitcher.

I could see Garth in the corner. He was staring at me, an insolent grin on his face. I wondered if all Parry's conspirators had shadows assigned to them.

I set about delivering the message exactly as I'd been instructed. It occurred to me that Parry could just as easily have got his servant to do it. Then I reasoned that I'd barely heard the man speak. Perhaps his skill was his strength and memorising messages was beyond him. This cheered me a little.

I came to the table where Oswyn was sitting.

'The game is Gleek,' announced a rotund chap in a purple doublet. He held up a deck of cards. 'Sixpence a point.'

I was surprised that Oswyn had the money to join in such pastimes. But then I saw that he wasn't being dealt a hand of cards like the other three at the table. A shot of intense pleasure ran through me. Weasel-face had given us to believe he was going to be playing cards with the courtiers. Instead he was merely holding the money pot for them! Perhaps the players didn't trust each other with their coins. Oswyn always boasted about how important his family was but here he was as much the servant as me. I couldn't wait to tell Mark. Oswyn glanced up and saw me hovering.

'Go away,' he snarled. 'The gentlemen don't want the likes of you lurking.'

God's bodkin in a basket! Weasel-face was asking for a thumping. But I ignored him and went round the players at his table, passing on the message. I watched closely for their reactions but these men were either very good actors or innocent courtiers eager to go hunting. I would trust none of them but it gave me a tiny glimmer of hope that not everyone was involved in Parry's treachery.

'Now begone,' snapped Oswyn.

I moved on to the next group.

I gave them all Parry's message and approached the table where Finch sat. This brought me near to Garth. He had something behind his back. When he thought no one could see, he took a huge swig from a goblet. The furtiveness of his action convinced me that the man had not been given permission to drink.

Finch was the only one who reacted differently to my message. He suppressed a gasp and his eyes goggled. He kept glancing round towards the entrance to the tent as if expecting – or rather, dreading – someone's arrival. I was sure he gave a small squeak of fear when David Parry eventually turned up.

Parry went round the room replying to the friendly greetings from his fellows. Cromwell had told me he was a popular figure at Court.

'David!' someone hailed him. 'Will you ride ahead with the King again tomorrow?'

'Aye,' said another. 'It was hard to keep up last time. And I believe you pleased His Majesty very much.'

'I wish I could join you,' Parry answered with a smile. 'But I have something else to do that will please His Majesty even more. I am off in the morning to inspect some new deerhounds for him.'

I knew that pleasing the King was the last thing on Parry's mind. I wondered where he was really off to.

Parry was standing apart now, next to a tall man with a grizzled beard. His red velvet coat and hat were of fine quality. I was sure I recognised him. I racked my brains and got the answer – Walter Warrendon. I had the feeling he was a particularly important courtier. I took a jug of ale and walked slowly past them. Parry and Warrendon were speaking in low voices but I heard the name Nathaniel mentioned. I slowed to a snail's pace, hoping they wouldn't notice me hovering.

'We won't let it stop us,' murmured Parry.

'But what if he dies?' muttered Warrendon.

I suddenly remembered something more about Warrendon. He had recently been appointed to His Majesty's Council. Like an expert fisherman, Parry had hooked one of the men closest to the King. I fought down a wave of horror. How many more had he got dangling on the end of his line?

'We will deal with his death if it happens.' Parry broke off as someone waved them both to a table where a game was about to start.

Warrendon moved to join them but Parry touched his arm. I was convinced I heard the words 'meeting tonight' and saw Warrendon give a slight nod.

'Ah,' said Parry, sitting and accepting a hand of cards. 'The fates are smiling down on me.'

I went round the table, playing my role of willing servant. As I filled the tankards time after time, my mind was full of the words I'd heard Parry murmur to Warrendon. When David Parry set off for his clandestine gathering, I would follow. But in my eagerness I'd forgotten Garth. I wouldn't get very far with him on my tail. I picked up a flagon of Mad Dog Ale – a potent brew – and went over to him.

'Thirsty work,' I whispered, holding up the flagon.

He winked and held out his pot. I filled it to the brim.

I refilled it quite a few more times as the evening went on – when he wasn't looking.

Armed with a fresh jug of ale, I found myself back at Oswyn's table. Oswyn greeted me with a mocking smile. I kept my face blank, fighting down the urge to tip the drink over his head. However, Oswyn wanted to play a little game. As I poured, he moved his tankard slightly so that some splashed onto the table.

'You're spilling it!' he said haughtily. 'Even this menial role is too good for you, it seems.' He spoke so loudly that most of the room could hear. 'You should go back to the gutter where you belong.' He turned to the card players as if they were his friends. 'I cannot fathom how Briars is tolerated in the company of gentlemen,' he drawled. 'He's nothing but a foundling, tossed away by his drab of a mother and dragged up by some simpleminded monk.'

He gave a sneering grin to all at his table but most of the players didn't pay him any attention. The tips of his ears went red. If he hadn't been such an odious weasel, I'd have felt sorry for him.

I carried on with my duties. I noted that Parry was watching me, a thoughtful expression on his face. Little did Weasel-face realise that he'd done me a favour with his insults. They would reinforce Parry's belief that my life at the palace was an unhappy one.

Garth was gently swaying in the corner, eyes half closed. I sneaked some more of the strong brew into his pot. By the time the card game was coming to an end, the man was so drunk he wouldn't have been able to walk a step, let alone follow me.

Many of the card players had gone before David Parry got to his feet. He looked as if he was leaving but I feared that he would first check that Garth was doing his job. He only had to walk to the other end of the tent to see his servant slumped in a corner.

But Parry was in a hurry. He gave a glance round.

It was quick, and to the unsuspecting eye, casual. I sensed he was about to leave and didn't want anyone following him. The next minute he was gone. I hid my tray under a table and slipped out after him.

19

Parry strode out of the tent, wrapping himself in his cloak. The flickering flames of the torches were well spaced and he was easy to spot as he crossed the gardens. He stopped suddenly and checked around. I ducked behind a bush. Satisfied that no one had seen him, he seized one of the torches and listened by a door in the wall. The guards would be patrolling here but most were on the riverbank, waiting for the King to return home. When he was satisfied that there was no guard nearby he opened it and slipped out. As soon as the door latch clicked shut I hurried up to it and listened. I heard nothing on the other side. I eased open the latch, hoping Parry was out of earshot.

I could see him going into the Home Park.

I followed the faint light into the parkland. Now I was being led away from the lighted windows of the palace. The darkness was deeper and it was all I could do not to trip on the long grass. Peering ahead, I made out the black shapes of trees and Parry's tall cloaked form as he headed away. If it hadn't been for his lantern I would have become hopelessly lost.

When we'd walked for a good while through a wild, wooded area Parry came to a stop near a thick cluster of trees. His light showed a tangle of bushes round their trunks. I crept closer.

I heard his low voice saying one word. 'Victory.'

Another voice answered. 'Enter, friend.'

So 'victory' must have been a password. Parry had arrived at the secret meeting. To my surprise he pushed his way through a bush and disappeared into the thicket. I crept up to where I'd seen him but all I found was a wall of tough brambles. Where had he gone? He must have been torn to shreds by the thorns. I felt about, biting my lip as I ripped my hand on the sharp spikes. Then I discovered a small piece of wood close to the ground. The brambles were fixed to a wooden frame. This was a gateway, cleverly disguised. I couldn't see any sign of a light. The bushes and trees were too thick.

The place had been set up so that no one would suspect it was there. I was sure this was Parry's doing. The man wasn't taking any chances.

I circled round the thicket, trying to get closer without being seen. I moved slowly and silently. The thicket was small, but dense, giving me no way through. Eventually I found a tree that I could climb. An easy task in the day, no doubt, but now I could only feel for hand and footholds on a tree that was slick from a recent rain shower. The night was cold for a skinny scribe with no warm cloak. I gradually got myself to a good height and edged along a branch, hoping I'd be able to spy on the meeting below.

Two round owl eyes suddenly stared into mine. A talon flashed out and I nearly fell as I lurched back. The owl took off, screeching angrily. I waited, stock still, my heart hammering, but heard no shouts of alarm from below. The owl's cry must have hidden my scrabblings. I pulled myself further along the branch and peered down.

The centre of the bushes had been cut away to form a hiding place. Four cloaked figures stood in a circle around a lantern hanging on a low branch. Its faint light showed they all wore black masks. It was an eerie sight. They were like demons communing with the devil.

From what I guessed of their plans, that image wasn't far short of the truth.

'Why did we have to cover our faces?' asked one. The only way I could be sure who was speaking was the cloud of breath from under the mask. As far as I could make out from my lofty perch, the speaker was taller than the others. I recognised his voice from the gambling. It was Walter Warrendon.

'One of us present is not known to you.' Parry's voice

was unmistakeable. 'And it is better that you remain unknown to him for the moment.'

The masks looked round at each other but no more was said on this. Parry was clearly their leader.

'Why have you brought us here?' asked another of the group. He was a stout man and the anxious tones were unmistakeable. This was Finch. 'It's not safe,' he wittered on. 'The guards are out in force tonight. If we're discovered we'll be on the end of their halberds in an instant.'

Parry stepped up to him. 'Are you saying you don't trust my judgement?' he snarled.

Finch took a step back. 'No . . . of course not.'

'We cannot afford to have weakness in our ranks,' said Parry coldly. 'What have I told you about the yeomen guard?'

'That you have recruited a number of them—' jabbered Finch.

'And that they will vouch for us if we are discovered,' finished Parry. 'Understand?'

There was a mumble of agreement. The thought that some of the King's loyal guard could be traitors made my guts twist with horror. I shifted carefully on my branch. The cold was turning my fingers numb. It was getting harder to hold on.

'It would be helpful for us to have their names.' This was Warrendon again. 'And the names of the other courtiers who are with us. Why so secretive?'

'The less you know, the less you can give away if

you are caught,' Parry snapped at him. 'Only I know all those who make up our faithful band. It is better that way.'

I had to admire the man. This was just how Thomas Cromwell ran his team of spies!

'Victory,' came an urgent whisper from beyond the brambles.

'Enter, friend,' said Parry.

A figure burst into the circle. 'I have grave news,' he said.

20

Ididn't recognise the voice of the newcomer. I could see a beard under his mask – and something else. As he moved, the light showed his skin was badly scarred with pock marks. He had survived smallpox. I didn't think anyone like that had been at the gambling so it didn't help me identify him. I stored it in my memory.

'Spit it out, man,' said Parry.

'Nathaniel has worsened. He is sinking fast.'

'Our cause is lost,' wailed Finch.

'By Lucifer's horns, I will not hear such defeatist talk,' spat Parry. 'Our cause does not depend on Nathaniel alone. Besides, I have a candidate in mind should he die.' He jabbed Finch in the stomach, making him stumble backwards. 'Have you got the muster numbers for me?'

'I tried,' wailed Finch. 'But Cromwell stayed in his office all day.'

'Liar,' snarled Parry. 'You have failed me. Luckily I have obtained the figures and they are low. Thanks to my careful planning there is little chance of a rising against us – and even if there were it would be easy to overcome.'

'Wonderful,' blustered Finch.

'You have wasted enough of my time. Now to business.' Parry turned to the man who stood silently next to him.

The man pulled off his mask. He still wore his hood and I couldn't see his face.

'Gentlemen,' said Parry as smoothly as if he was at a social gathering. 'May I present Otto. He leads our army. All proven fighters and with the promise of a good payment after the event so they are eager to work for us.'

Mercenaries! Men who would fight for any cause as long as there was gold in it for them. No wonder Parry wanted his own supporters masked! Otto clearly had no loyalty to the cause. If he identified them he could betray them all – as long as the price was right.

Otto paid the others no attention. 'We are ready,' he said to Parry. His accent was not English.

'Then we should wait no longer!' Warrendon had spoken. 'Why not give the order to march this very minute?'

'And ruin all my endeavours?' snapped Parry. 'You fool!'

'But the more we hesitate, the more likely we are to be found out.'

'Are you questioning my planning?' Parry growled the words.

Warrendon stepped back nervously. David Parry had him in thrall as well, despite his high position on the King's Council.

'Yes, of course, but are you sure the men are well hidden?' Warrendon blustered on as if trying to get back some dignity. 'The sight of an army would be sure to alert a local watchman or constable.'

'We are hidden in plain sight,' said Otto, his tone unchanging. 'At the place you ordered us to be. All who see us will think we are merely craftsmen at a spring fair – a very big fair.'

A faint mutter of relief went round the group.

'Excellent,' said Parry, rubbing his hands together. 'I and my followers will be gathered at a location close by. When you receive my signal, you will immediately march to join us. By then we will have caught our prey. And that will of course be accomplished in a few hours.' He swung round to face Warrendon. 'You are ready to receive it, I trust. It is essential we keep it alive – for the time being.'

Warrendon nodded back.

'I will meet you there later in the morning,' added Parry.

'Catch our prey! So that's what the message meant!' blustered Finch. 'I mean, I knew it, of course. You'd said that when we heard the words "wishing you all success", our enterprise was underway. But I don't hunt. What should I do?'

There was silence for a moment. 'What should you do?' said Parry, his tone cold. 'I'll tell you. Be at work early, before any of your men. Make sure you are seen by the kitchen servants as you go. Then you will have an alibi and can't be linked to what takes place.'

'Oh thank you, thank you!' Finch sagged and at last stopped talking.

I mulled over everything I'd heard. The hunt was somehow important in their plans and that was in a few hours. Was that when Parry intended to capture this prey? But every hunter hoped to do that, so why had he bothered to mention it this time? And why would they not be killing it straight away? Something about the way he'd laid a slight emphasis on the word worried me. Before I could think more about it, I heard Parry speak again.

'Everything is in hand. Our glorious endeavour cannot fail. I shall have victory.'

'Please God,' murmured Finch.

'There is no doubt of it,' retorted Parry. 'I always win. Now we must disperse. The hunt leaves at dawn. With our unsuspecting prey at its head.'

His words sank in like terrible weights dragging me down. King Henry would lead the hunt as he always did, riding as fast and as hard as he could. He must be the prey that Parry had spoken of. Parry had been even more clever that I thought. By the time his secret army marched, the King would already be in his power.

I forced myself to wait for them to leave the hidden clearing. If Parry discovered me now, I wouldn't be going anywhere. But as soon as they left I'd be heading for the palace to raise the alarm and stop the hunt. Master Cromwell had gone and I couldn't trust the terrible information to a yeoman guard. I didn't know which of them were on Parry's side. I couldn't even be sure of Nicholas Mountford. My only hope was Robert Aycliffe. It was vital I get to him before Garth woke up and tracked me down.

I was attacked by a screeching fury of feathers.

21

The owl was back. I must have been lurking too close to its nest. I clung desperately to my branch. Talons like sharp knives slashed at me and when the bird wasn't sinking its beak into my flesh, it screeched like a banshee. It was hard not to add my own squeals to the unearthly noise.

I put up a hand to fend it off – and began to slip. Suddenly I was dangling by one arm from the branch. The owl pecked furiously at my fingers. I bit my lip hard to stop myself crying out in pain and fear.

'Who's there?' quavered Finch.

The men were staring up into the tree. My only hope was to hang there perfectly still and hope they couldn't see me in the dark. It was a very slim hope! My wounded hand was slowly losing its grip.

Above the owl's angry cries, I heard Parry's laugh. 'Some rodent is putting up a good fight.'

If it had been possible to feel relief when being attacked by a furious bird, I would have felt it then. Parry and his unholy band made their way through the brambles and off into the darkness.

I hauled myself back up onto the branch, which was doubly difficult with a face full of flying feathers. Once there I hunched low, giving my attacker only my back to savage. Playing dead turned out to be a good move. After a few more vicious swipes, it must have decided it had killed me. It flapped off.

I shuffled back along the branch and climbed down.

All was silent. There was no helpful moon, and no glimmer of any lanterns. It was impossible to find my bearings. I tried to remember which way I'd come. I searched for the bramble gate Parry had used, thinking I might be able to trace my route back from there. It was too well hidden. I was wasting time. I moved as fast as I could, stumbling and tripping, but I had no more vision than a blind man. I fell headlong into long wet grass. As I got to my feet, my fumbling fingers found nothing in front of me. I crept forward on hands and knees and touched cold water. I'd nearly toppled into one of the ponds in the Home Park.

I followed the bank along and then in the distance, I saw flickering lights. I stopped and tried to make sense of them. Were they moving towards me? After what seemed an eternity, I decided they were keeping still. Hoping that they were the torches in the palace grounds, I made for them.

As I drew near at last, it became patently clear that what I'd thought was an array of lights were in fact only two. They shone across the water of the lake and I'd been fooled by the rippling reflections. I came to a small village with a church and a few houses. And on the horizon the black sky held a faint line of grey. It wasn't dawn yet but I now knew that my stumbling route had led me east. This must be Hampton Wick. I'd been heading the wrong way. And with every false step I was losing my chance to stop the hunt.

Cursing under my breath, I turned and ran, stumbling, along the lake's edge.

The eastern sky was glowing by the time I left the trees and could see the palace ahead. A confusion of shouts and laughter filled the air. The hunt was getting ready to set off.

I forced my tired legs to pick up the pace. The hunt servants were bringing a pack of eager deerhounds around the outer walls and past the tennis court to the mounted horses that stood waiting. One rider in the centre was unmistakable. Tall and majestic on his stallion sat the King. Beside him stood David Parry. He'd come to see the hunt safely off. Garth was nowhere in sight. The King was leaning down to Parry, sharing some joke, completely unaware of the danger he was in. Aycliffe was just swinging into the saddle of his mount.

I raced across the open parkland, not caring who saw me now. But I wasn't fast enough. With a great cry from the young men and a peel from the hunting horns, they were away, the dogs baying fit to drown them all out.

In a moment of madness I thought of taking a horse from the stables and going after them. But even Cat and Diablo wouldn't have stood a chance of catching up. A wave of helplessness washed over me and I struggled to keep my thoughts from scrambling. Parry's men were going to capture King Henry and nothing could stop them.

Then I remembered Finch – the weak link in Parry's chain. While I could do nothing else, I might be able to persuade him to share any information he had. He would surely know where the King was being taken. When I found out I would track down my master – no matter what it took.

At least locating Finch would be easy. Parry had instructed him to be at work early. I headed off for the wine cellar, hoping that Garth was still sleeping off his drink. I couldn't see him but I remembered he could make himself invisible when he wanted to.

I couldn't let fear of the hulking servant stop me if I was to learn more of Parry's plot.

22

I'd barely reached the Clock Court when I heard an urgent whisper.

'Jack!'

It was Cat. She beckoned to me and disappeared down a narrow passage. I stumbled after her, my lack of sleep making my legs heavy.

She led me out into a small yard. There was no one about. I wasn't surprised – the place stank. A heap of fish guts and vegetable peelings lay rotting in the corner.

'I've been searching everywhere for you!' she exclaimed crossly. 'What's going on? First you leave me hanging around the stables and then you stick notes into my hand. Lucky for you I'm clever so I understood what you wanted.'

As quickly as I could I told her what I knew of Parry's plans.

Her hand flew to her mouth when she realised the dreadful danger the King was in. 'And no one knows but you?' she gasped. 'What about Master Cromwell?'

'I have no idea when he'll be back.'

'Let's go to the Captain of the Guard then,' said Cat desperately.

'I've already explained, we can't be sure who's involved. If the wrong person gets to hear that I'm investigating, my chances of helping the King will be over . . .' I drew a finger across my throat.

'That's true,' breathed Cat.

'And even if I spoke to someone loyal to the King, why would anyone believe a mere scribe? As Parry made very clear, it would be my word against his.'

'But we can't just stand here doing nothing!' exclaimed Cat, flapping her apron in frustration.

'I'm not going to do nothing,' I said. 'I'm off to see Finch. He's acting like a man at the end of his tether. I'm hoping to get him to talk.'

Cat led me down an alley and out into the Base Court to avoid the crush of servants already going about their work.

'We can get to the wine cellar this way,' she explained. 'Not so many people to see us.'

I scanned the crowd for Garth. I prayed he hadn't woken by some miracle and come after me. I couldn't see him anywhere.

'How are you going to get Finch to talk?' asked Cat as we headed towards the door with the wine god on it.

309

'We're not exactly yeomen guard – or torturers. Why would he let anything out?'

'That's true,' I said. 'It would be better to trick him while he's so bound up in his own fears. Last night Parry said that he'd be joining his followers later. I'll explain that Parry sent me and that his plan has succeeded earlier than expected and that he wants Finch to join him at – then I'll say I've forgotten the name of the place and hope he'll "remind" me where it is.' I looked at her with sudden hope. 'If I find out the name and I can't track down Master Cromwell, will you take me to the place on one of the horses?'

'Of course!' said Cat. 'We'll go on Diablo.'

I almost protested at the thought of the devil horse but thought better of it. The sooner we got there the better – and Diablo could go like the wind.

I led the way between the large barrels. The silence felt eerie. I tried to tell myself that it was only because Finch's men weren't at work yet but it didn't help.

'Hello?' I called. 'Mister Finch?' My voice echoed round the cellar.

Nothing. Cat glanced at me.

'Perhaps he's still in his bedchamber,' she whispered.

'He won't be,' I whispered back. 'I bet he's here somewhere. He wouldn't dare disobey Parry. Maybe his nerves have got the better of him and he's hiding.'

We searched between the barrels but there was no sign of the Sergeant of the Wine Cellar. A slight noise had me whirling round but nothing stirred.

'Probably the wine fermenting,' muttered Cat. 'Well, I hope so.'

I peered down the stairs of the deeper cellar where I'd first overheard Parry and Finch. It was dark as night down there, so I took a candle from one of the wall sconces.

Cat was behind me. 'I don't like the look of that,' she said in a low voice. 'It's got a nasty atmosphere.'

'You stay up here then,' I replied. 'I've got to find Finch. He could be hiding in the dark.'

But when I set off down the steps I could feel her tiptoeing after me, clutching the back of my jacket.

As soon as she'd got to the bottom step, Cat immediately flattened herself against the nearest wall. 'Now nothing can creep up without me seeing it first.'

I didn't point out that in the feeble candlelight she'd have little chance of seeing anything till it was on top of her!

'He's not here,' she whispered before I'd had a chance to search round. 'Let's come back later.'

'You're not scared, are you?' I whispered back.

'Of course not. We're just wasting time, that's all.'

I swept the candle round the cellar, between the rows of barrels.

And then I found Finch. He was slumped in a far corner, his head lolling sideways. For one mad moment, I wondered if he was asleep, but as I held the candle nearer I saw the huge wet stain on his chest. I put the candle down, reached out and touched it. It was blood. There was a dark pool around him.

'He's here,' I gasped. 'He's dead.'

'Mary, Mother of God,' breathed Cat.

Finch had been stabbed through the heart. I could guess who'd ordered that murder. Finch had been a millstone around Parry's neck. So Parry had told him to get to work early – to meet his killer.

There was a gasp from the steps and a figure appeared, silhouetted by the lights of the cellar behind.

'Murderer!' it cried. 'You're a murderer!'

I recognised the accusing voice. It was Oswyn Drage.

23

I felt a moment of sheer dread. Oswyn would be delighted to get me arrested for murder. And here I was, found with a dead body, and stained in the victim's blood!

I stumbled through the dark cellar towards him. I passed Cat's shadowy outline against the wall. Oswyn hadn't seen her. I willed her not to move.

As I ran up the steps, Oswyn slapped his hands against the sides of the open doorframe, blocking my way out.

'I've been right about you all along, Jack Briars,' he drawled. 'You're a bad lot. But this time you've been stupid. As soon as I saw you hadn't been to bed last night I knew there was something going on. So I made it my business to find you out. And it looks like I have.'

'It's not what you think, Oswyn,' I began.

'You can't wriggle out of this one,' crowed Weasel-face. 'I can even see the scratches where he tried to fight you off.'

I cursed last night's brambles – and the owl.

'Let me explain,' I said, hating myself for having to plead with him.

'No need.' Weasel-face wasn't bothering to hide his delight at his discovery. 'You can explain to the guards instead.' He turned to shout for help.

My tired brain began to scramble. Only one clear thought jumped out at me. If I was accused of murder there'd be nothing I could do to save the King. No one would listen to me.

I swung a mighty punch at the back of Oswyn's head. He hit the flagstones with a sickening thud. My knuckles throbbed but it was the most satisfying pain I'd ever felt.

Cat raced up to join me. She poked the lifeless Oswyn with her toe. 'He's out cold,' she said. 'But he'll be yelling the place down as soon as he wakes up.'

'Run,' I ordered her. 'You mustn't be seen with me.'

'But what will you do?' asked Cat. Her voice was hoarse with fear.

Oswyn gave a groan.

'I'll be off as soon as you're out of sight!' I told her. 'Go!'

Cat ran.

Oswyn staggered to his feet and lurched to the door. He began yelling for help at the top of his lungs. I heard guards' feet pounding along the passage towards the

314

wine cellar. That escape route was now blocked. I'd have to go back to the deeper chamber and leave that way. I had to get away from the palace.

Suddenly someone clamped his hand over my mouth and dragged me backwards through the cellar. I was bundled up some steps. A door slammed shut.

Not a word was spoken. My captor held me in an iron grip. I was safe from the yeoman guards but was I safe from danger? My spy instincts took over. I swiftly took in what I could see of the small room. There was a narrow door in the corner, opposite to where we'd come in. I had an escape route.

Then I heard the guards. And Weasel-face.

'Jack Briars is a murderer,' he was screeching. 'He's killed Mister Finch and he tried to kill me. I fought him off but he had a knife . . . and a sword . . . I heard him run away!'

Footsteps thundered through the cellar. There were shouts as the guards discovered Finch.

'You two, take the body away,' came an order. 'The rest of you, find Jack Briars.'

At last silence fell again.

The man holding me swung me round. I was peering up into Parry's face. He looked furious.

'What in hell's name do you think you're doing here?' he demanded, shaking me violently.

'I don't understand!' I burbled. I remembered I wasn't supposed to know that Finch was one of Parry's men. I prayed he hadn't been there when Cat and I came in.

If he'd heard our conversation, the game would be up.

His evident shock at seeing me gave me a little hope. I would need to invent a good reason for going to the cellar so early. I acted breathless with fear to give myself time to think.

'Yesterday Mister Scrope told me to . . . ask the Sergeant of the Wine Cellar something . . . Do you know him? It's Mister Finch . . .'

'I do,' said Parry. 'We are standing in his office. Go on.'

'Well, I didn't have time last night so I thought I'd better do it this morning. And . . . and . . . Oswyn Drage came to the wine cellar too. I bet he was trying to get into Mister Scrope's good books and make me look bad. When I got there, I found Mister Finch dead – and then Oswyn found me with his body and he accused me of killing him.'

'We know that's not true, don't we,' said Parry.

'I'm glad you believe me, sir,' I answered.

'It's not a case of believing you, Jack,' Parry went on. 'It's a question of fact. I had Finch killed, you see. He was working for me – until he became unreliable.'

'But thanks to Oswyn, everyone will think I did it,' I gasped.

'I see your problem,' the Welshman said smoothly. He put an arm round my shoulder. 'I must help you. Let me think how that can be done.'

If I stayed with Parry there was a chance I could find the King.

'I have an idea, sir,' I said. 'When I stole the muster list I guessed that you have men ready to march against the King. And that message I delivered last night about the hunt – something's going to happen today, isn't it? If you're joining those men, let me come too! I would gladly fight alongside them.'

'Indeed, that would be a solution. But supposing you were arrested before I could get you away? Suppose someone got wind of your connection with me? You might be persuaded to blurt out everything that you know about my plans.'

'I would never do that, sir!' I insisted.

'It is all very well to say that now,' said Parry. 'What if you were in excruciating pain? I have a much better idea.' His tone was calm and friendly. 'You've drawn too much attention to yourself.' And with one swift movement he seized me round the neck. I felt a cold knife at my throat. 'Dead scribes tell no tales.'

I tried to think of something that would persuade him to keep me alive. But I didn't dare move. The blade was fatally close.

24

'**P**arry!'
The narrow door at the back of the office was flung open and a man burst in. 'Your servant said I'd find you here ... What's going on?' He stopped in horror as he took in the scene.

I stared at him, willing him with my eyes to rescue me. And then hope died. I could see scars under his beard. This was the pock-marked man from the secret meeting. He'd be more likely to help Parry finish me off.

'Keep your voice down, Wright!' demanded Parry in an angry undertone. The knife cut into my skin. I couldn't stop myself giving a whimper of fear. 'What are you doing here?'

'Nathaniel has died,' gasped the man.

Hardly a moment could have passed but time felt very heavy.

318

And then the knife had gone from my throat.

Parry spun me round. 'Well, Jack Briars,' he said, speaking to me as if I was a dear friend. 'It's your lucky day. I do have a use for you after all. And for that, we must get you to safety.'

For one moment, my life had been about to end. It was a dizzying experience. I hoped I would never go through it again.

'You go on ahead, Wright,' ordered Parry. 'We will follow shortly.'

I could not imagine why news of Nathaniel's death should have saved my life. How long would I be safe for? What use could I be to Parry? I tried to focus on the fact that I was going to get my wish and leave the palace. I would have to forget that I was wanted for murder, and deal instead with the more important mission – finding the King and rescuing him.

Without any further explanation, Parry opened the narrow door. He kept a firm grip on my arm as we slipped out. We hurried down dark passageways. When anyone came by Parry quickly got us hidden in shadows or alcoves. He was as good as a spy. I found myself curiously glad that he was familiar with the quiet ways round the palace. I was relying on this dangerous traitor to keep me from certain arrest!

The camp was empty. All the young men had gone on the hunt. We made it to Parry's tent.

'Garth!' he bellowed.

The servant appeared. I was tired and scared and

hungry but I'd warrant I still looked better than he did. He stumbled in, paler than whey. His eyes were screwed up against the daylight and he flinched at every noise. The potent brews of last night were not agreeing with him. I took some satisfaction from his discomfort.

Parry slapped him hard in the face. 'How did this boy get to the wine cellar without you knowing?' he snapped.

'I was behind him right up until the last,' mumbled Garth. 'He just ran very quickly.' He glared at me as if challenging me to contradict him.

'I was in a great hurry to get to Mister Finch and deliver my message,' I said. And I did not mistake the relief in the servant's eyes. He'd probably forget about my help in an instant but there was a slight chance he'd remember. If I was heading for a nest of vipers, it wouldn't hurt to have one that didn't strike at me instantly.

Parry seemed satisfied with this. He glanced around the tent. 'Have you finished packing?' he snapped at his servant.

Garth hurriedly threw the last few things into saddlebags – as fast as his sore head would let him.

And then we were leaving. Garth bustled off, trying to impress his master, no doubt, and was soon back riding a horse and leading another.

Parry gave me a shove. 'Get up behind Garth and hold on.'

Parry swung onto his horse and led the way.

And so I left Hampton Court Palace, clinging to the back of Parry's servant. I tried to take in where we were going. But my knowledge of the country was very poor and I couldn't put names to any of the small villages we passed. We rode along the river away from London but then cut across fields. By the position of the morning sun I knew we were riding north-west. But even with my well-trained memory I had no chance of remembering the route over countryside with no landmarks but trees and fields that were all the same.

Parry galloped in front of us as if we weren't there. It felt as if we'd been riding for hours when at last he spoke.

'We can slow our pace and spare the horses,' he called over his shoulder. 'I can't see any sign of pursuit. No one expects the murderous scribe to have the wit to escape.'

His words struck me hard. That's how I would be viewed now. I thought of poor Mark and Mrs Pennycod. They'd been true friends. They'd feel I'd betrayed their trust. This was the cold reality of being a spy.

Garth reined the horse in and we proceeded along at a trot.

'Where are we going?' I dared to ask him. My words came out in a choppy whisper as my whole body shook from the ride.

'To Mister Warrendon's house,' he whispered back.

'Where's that?'

'No idea,' grunted the servant. 'I just follow Mister Parry.'

So we were going to where the mercenary's army was hiding. Eventually we came to an old manor house. It lay in grounds encircled by a moat. The grounds were full of servants. At least, they were dressed as servants but their behaviour was that of guards. Armed guards. We'd hardly ridden in over the bridge when we were commanded to halt.

'I am David Parry,' said Parry. 'You will let me pass.'

The men stood aside without a word. We rode up to the front door. We had barely dismounted – or fallen off in my case – when Warrendon came running.

'You heard about Nathaniel?' he asked. He looked as if panic was threatening to overtake him.

'Of course,' said Parry. 'But there is no cause for alarm.' He pointed at me. 'I have brought our replacement.'

'A palace servant?' Warrendon was incredulous. 'Who's going to believe—'

'Silence!' snapped Parry. 'He knows no details yet. Really, Warrendon, you doubt me at every turn.'

His words filled me with horror. What new part was I to play in this dreadful business?

Warrendon struggled to pull himself together. 'I would never doubt you,' he said at last. 'You have hatched the perfect plot. Our prey must surely be taken by now. Otto's men are waiting not a mile from here. You have but to give the word.'

They were ready for their terrible endeavour. But where did I fit in?

'Has Nathaniel been removed from his bedchamber?' asked Parry.

Warrendon nodded.

'Then it's Jack's room now,' said Parry.

He pushed me into the house, through the Great Hall and up a wide, ornate wooden staircase. Then up another smaller flight and down a long passageway to the very end.

Parry threw open the door and ushered me inside. The chamber was large and light. It was on the corner of the house and had windows on two sides. There was a table, a chair and a real bed with a canopy and curtains. That was where Nathaniel had breathed his last. The thought of it chilled me. A large, ornately carved box stood at the end of it. A fire burned in the grate. These were luxuries that I had never had, yet I wished with all my heart that they weren't mine now.

'When you said you wanted to work for me, you thought you'd prefer it to your job at Court,' said Parry.

'That's right, sir,' I said. 'And now I'd prefer anything to being hanged for a murder I didn't commit.'

'Well it is going to be better than your wildest dreams!'

He watched me with a gloating smile.

I had no idea what he had in mind for me. He was planning to lead an army against the crown and I was no soldier.

'Am I to be your scribe?' I asked. I didn't believe this for a moment but I wanted him to stop playing games and tell me.

He laughed. 'No, Jack Briars. I have it in mind to make you King of England!'

25

'I don't understand,' I spluttered. 'We have a king—' I stopped myself. I was meant to be on Parry's side. 'Much as I hate his very guts.'

'Henry Tudor is no true king,' spat Parry. 'Our so-called monarch cares nothing for his country but only for his own pleasure. I have long itched to grasp the reins of power from our so-called King and his toadying Council and bring this country back to greatness. Then I would gather an army such as the world has never seen. All would be in awe of England. And now the time has come. But I cannot do it myself. I cannot claim the throne of England – much as I would like to. The Parry family is known to have no royal blood and cannot pretend to. This is where you come in, Jack.'

So that was why he'd kept me alive. The sickly Nathaniel was to have played this part. I was just a convenient stand-in. A wave of sickness twisted my stomach at the thought of my new role in this hellish business.

'I have no claim to the throne either!' I protested.

Parry laughed coldly. 'I think you will find that you do. Let me explain. Have you heard of the Princes in the Tower?'

I nodded. It was a story told to frighten children into good behaviour. 'It happened about fifty years ago,' I said. 'King Richard Crookback imprisoned his nephews in the Tower of London. It's believed he smothered them in their sleep because they were the sons of King Edward the fourth and rightful heirs to the crown, not him.'

I remembered the time when I was a small boy, and the abbot had threatened to do that to me. For weeks afterwards I found it difficult to sleep.

'It did Richard no good,' Parry went on. 'He was killed in battle by Henry Tudor – the present King's father – and his army. But there have always been rumours that the princes escaped and went abroad. That is a convenient rumour for my purpose. I will be presenting the country with you – the grandson of the elder brother, Prince Edward, and therefore the true king.'

'But I'm not royal. I'm a nobody.'

'And being a nobody makes you perfect for the part.' He leaned against the wall and regarded me. 'Like poor Nathaniel, you have no family so when we say how you were born abroad and then hidden in the abbey to keep you safe, it will seem perfectly reasonable. I will make sure there are people who'll swear to that.'

My thoughts flew back to the gambling and Parry's expression when Oswyn had taunted me with being a foundling. I would make a perfect substitute for the sickly Nathaniel.

I forced myself to play along. I was supposed to be pleased with the news. I thrust my chin up and strutted about. 'My blood could truly be royal,' I said in awe.

'It is not,' sneered Parry. 'I have invented a family history for you to suit my purpose. And it will suit you to play along. You will wear fine things and dine on fine food.'

'I like the sound of that life,' I said. I had to force out the hateful words.

'I am sure you do,' said Parry. 'And in public I will bow and scrape and do homage to my young king along with your other subjects.' He thrust his face close to mine and I saw the terrifying lust for power in his eyes. 'It will be you crowned at Westminster Abbey tomorrow but you would do well to remember who is in control.'

'I will indeed, sir,' I said. 'It will be reward enough to live like a king.'

Parry nodded slowly. 'Good. Very good. Now change out of that livery. You will find clothes in the chest. You're about the same size as Nathaniel so I'm sure they will fit.' He moved to the door and turned. 'You'll be pleased to hear that Garth will be close by – for your protection.'

I knew what that meant. Garth would be there to make sure I didn't get any ideas about escaping. And I doubted that the servant was grateful enough to me to let me flee.

Parry left.

A terrible weariness washed over me. After my night without sleep I wanted nothing more than to throw myself on the bed and close my eyes to the world.

In a daze I dumbly obeyed Parry's instructions. Even the plainest of the clothes were better than I'd ever worn in my life. They were heavy on my back, heavy with treachery. I longed to suddenly wake and find out that this had all been a nightmare. But that wasn't going to happen. I was deeply mired in the most horrible plot – and now I found myself at the very centre of it. King of England. The words thudded loudly in my head. I could see no way to stop the march of fate.

I tried to cling to my sanity just as a drowning man clings to the smallest piece of driftwood. If Cat had found my master he would now know about the plans for the King's capture at the hunt. As for the rebels, she could only have reported that Otto's army was hiding somewhere, in the guise of a fair. But without a location, Cromwell's muster of loyal men couldn't march. There were probably plenty of spring fairs around the country.

My job was to get back to Hampton Court with the

information. To do so, I would have to avoid my guard who was on the other side of the door. So I'd have to find another means of getting out. I went to the back window and opened the casement. Between the house and the moat stood a small courtyard surrounded by outbuildings and a hedge strewn with washing. Leaning out of the window I examined the brickwork as best I could. It had a raised pattern, and I wondered if it would make good footholds for a swift climb down.

A sudden burst of hoof beats had me hurrying to the side window. Here I could see stables. A band of men came riding in. Amongst them was a horse tethered to the saddle of another. Someone was strapped across its back. The riders jumped from their mounts. Several of them surrounded the prisoner and pulled him from the saddle. He stood swaying, taller than them all. He wore no hat and his doublet was torn but I knew him and felt sick to my stomach. It was King Henry. They had caught their prey. I tried to take comfort from the fact that he was still alive – for the moment. They bundled him in through a door below. The horses were led into the stables.

I could hear a servant singing. I thought how strange it was to have no cares in the world, when a terrible drama was unfolding in this very house.

The song was being repeated over and over. It was an irritating and rather tuneless ditty. I tried to block it out but it grew louder and louder.

Jackdaw on the window ledge
Hey no, nonny nonny no.
Looks everywhere but in the hedge
With a hey no, nonny nonny no.

The words pounded through my head. Then I realised I recognised the voice and understood what was being said.

I ran to the back window and looked down at the hedge. And I saw a very familiar white cap with red curls spilling out.

26

I began to think I'd gone mad. Cat couldn't possibly have found me. There was no way she could have known where I'd been taken! Yet there she was, large as life.

I checked as far as I could see. No guards. But I had to be careful.

'*Jackdaw sees the ginger cat*,' I sang, trying to imitate the irritating tune. '*Hey no, nonny nonny no.*'

Cat spotted me and gave a huge grin. It was as though my guardian angel had arrived. For the first time in hours, I had a glimmer of hope. I leant out and pointed to the brickwork, although I feared I might have trouble persuading her to make the dangerous climb. Cat hated heights. To my astonishment she nodded, hitched up her skirts and began immediately. Fear of being discovered had overcome other terrors!

I held my breath and prayed that no one would come round the corner and see her.

Soon I was pulling her in through the window.

'How did you find . . . ?' I began.

'I had no idea what had happened to you after Oswyn called the guards so I decided to keep an eye on Parry instead. You said he'd be going to the meeting place so I rushed off and fetched Diablo to follow him when he left. Then we hid in one of the tents near Parry's – whoever lives in there will have a surprise when he gets back from the hunt and finds horse manure all over his floor. I was shocked when I saw you go in the tent with him. Anyway, I followed when you left and here I am!' she said as if it was a simple task. 'Cromwell wasn't back and Robert Aycliffe was still with the hunt so it was the only thing I could do.' She grinned at my astonished face. 'You had no idea I was after you, did you?'

I shook my head in wonder. 'I'll never criticise your tracking skills again! Where's Diablo?'

'I've hidden him in a barn down the road. There's plenty of hay in there.'

'I'm really pleased to see you,' I said.

'So you should be,' she retorted. 'I expect you'll be wanting my help as usual.'

'I do,' I said gratefully. 'You must go back to Hampton Court, find out where Cromwell is and deliver two important messages to him. The first is that we're at Walter Warrendon's house and the enemy army is amassed close by. They're posing as innocent traders at a spring fair, ready to march on Westminster Abbey tomorrow.'

'And the other message?'

'The King is being held captive here.'

'Here!' Cat almost screeched the word. 'Are you sure?'

'Quiet!' I warned, nodding towards the door. 'My faithful guard is outside. I know His Majesty is here. I saw them bring him in.'

'You don't think . . . they might have killed him already, do you?' Cat's whisper was filled with unimaginable horrors.

'From what I heard last night, they need him alive for the time being,' I said. 'I sense they won't do anything to him yet.'

Cat grasped me by both arms. 'As I left, some of the hunters were already back and letting it be known that the King had gone off on another of his secret adventures. They must have been Parry's men, saying it to give them more time before anyone goes looking for him! We must get him out of here. Surely that's the most important thing to do.'

'Of course it is – but that's my job. Yours is to go back, Cat.'

'I don't want to leave you here, Jack,' she said in a small voice. 'You're in such danger.'

'You needn't worry,' I said bitterly. 'I'll be perfectly safe. I have an important part to play in Parry's plot.'

'Don't be silly!' Cat scoffed. 'You're just saying that to get rid of me.'

I shook my head. 'I wish I was. Parry is planning to replace His Majesty with a puppet king who will do his bidding. Me.'

She gasped, horror all over her face.

'I'm no traitor,' I declared.

'I know that,' she said hotly, although she backed away from me and I wondered if she really believed it. 'Surely he doesn't think anyone will go along with such a story? You're not royal.' Then she stopped. 'I'm being a dolt! It happened to Lambert Simnel!'

'Who?' I said. 'And what's that got to do with . . . ?'

'In the time of our King's father, Lambert Simnel claimed that old King Henry wasn't the rightful king and that he was. He pretended he was one of those princes who were killed by King Richard. And he even got together an army.'

'What happened to Simnel? Though I'm not sure I really want to know!'

'It wasn't terrible,' said Cat. 'He got pardoned by old King Henry. Mrs Pennycod knew him. She says he used to work with her in the royal kitchens.'

'Slightly better than being put to death,' I said, feeling relieved.

'True,' said Cat chirpily. 'He was luckier than Perkin Warbeck.'

'Who's he?'

'He was the next one who tried to take the throne.

I suppose the old King got fed up with people popping up saying they were royal so in the end he had him hanged.'

'I bet Parry got his idea of an uprising from those two!' I exclaimed. 'I don't suppose they were any more royal than I am. Listen, Cat, the only way you can stop this is to get to Hampton Court.' I checked out of the window. The sun was high in the sky. 'It's about noon. With luck Cromwell will be there – and if you can't find him, Aycliffe should be back from the hunt. Go!'

Footsteps echoed on the rough floorboards of the passage. They stopped outside my room. Cat flew to the back window. 'I can't go now. There's a man standing sentry below!'

'Get behind here!' I pointed to an embroidered fire screen in a corner. Cat threw herself behind it as the latch clicked and Garth appeared in the doorway. He held a trencher with manchet bread, cheese and a tankard on it. I hadn't realised until that moment that I'd had no food or drink since last night.

'Thank you,' I said, taking it from him. But Parry's servant didn't leave. Instead, he snooped around the room, eyes narrowed, as if suspicious that something wasn't right.

I put my luncheon on the table. 'I'm going to guard this with my life!' I said conversationally. 'I've heard rats in the wainscot – and by the sound of them, they're giants. They'd have this from me before you could say poison.'

'You're welcome to them,' muttered Garth as he hurried out of the door.

Cat crept out. 'That was quick thinking!' she breathed. She broke off a big piece of bread. 'Sorry, Your Majesty,' she said, with a wicked twinkle in her eye. 'I know I shouldn't eat before you.'

'Don't joke about this,' I groaned, though now I was sure she had no doubts about my loyalty.

We ate quickly. Then Cat delved into her seamstress apron and held a pair of scissors out to me. They had long, thin blades.

'You might need a weapon,' she told me. 'This is the best I can do.'

I took them gratefully.

She checked the back window.

'The sentry's still there,' she said. 'I can hardly climb down while he's watching.'

'We'll have to create a diversion.' I took a solid piece of wood from a stack next to the fireplace. 'I'm going to throw this from the other window. With luck, he'll hear it land and go round the corner to investigate. Get ready – and leave the minute he's out of sight.'

Cat nodded, but hesitated at the window.

'What's the matter?' I asked, though I knew.

'It's even worse going down,' said Cat. 'But I'll do it for the King – the real one, that is.'

I eased open the side casement and aimed the wood to land on an old metal pail standing by the stables. It missed and fell to the ground with a dull thud.

336

I tried again – and again.

'You'll have to do better than that,' said Cat. 'He hasn't budged.'

I was running out of wood! I took a very careful aim with the last piece. If it didn't work, I could hardly start throwing furniture out.

The wood spun through the air. It hit the pail with a loud clang.

'That's it!' said Cat. 'He's heard it. I'm off.'

Down below where I was watching, the sentry appeared, looking puzzled at the pail surrounded by bits of wood. He kicked them with his foot, then glanced all about to see where they'd come from. Finally he gazed up at the sky as if he thought there'd been a plague of falling logs. I drew my head in quickly and ran to the other window. Cat was already scampering across the courtyard towards the hedge.

By the time the sentry returned, she was gone. Soon I heard faint hoof beats. Cat had got away.

27

Now to find the King – no easy matter when I was stuck at the top of this huge house.

There was only one way to get out of the room. I poked my head round the door and called for Garth. He appeared from a nearby doorway, rubbing his eyes as if I'd woken him.

'I need to use the jakes,' I said.

'Isn't there a pot in there somewhere?' said Garth.

'I can't see one,' I lied, hoping he wouldn't come in and find the large pewter one under the bed. 'Truth is I've got a bad stomach. Just show me where to go then you can get back to your nap.'

I was hoping he'd return the favour I'd done him.

Garth grunted and beckoned. 'Down the stairs. They're somewhere at the other end of the passage.' Before I could thank him, any hope of freedom from my jailer was dashed. 'I'll be right behind,' he said in my ear as I passed.

I pretended I'd forgotten Garth's directions, wandered past the stairs, turned a corner and found myself in a long, panelled passageway that led down one wing of the house. There were several doors, mostly ajar, and inside all was silent.

Garth grabbed me by the arm and swung me round. 'Wrong way,' he growled.

I headed for the stairs again. Below, another long passageway stretched away to the other end of the house. A group of men were sitting about outside a room further down. The door was padlocked. The men had their heads down, playing dice. But swords were propped against the wall, only an arm's length from them.

'What are you doing out here?' called Garth. 'Shouldn't you be in with . . . him? Making sure he doesn't come to harm?'

The men laughed – but I thought they seemed nervous.

'No chance,' said one. 'He's like a baited bear.'

'If he wasn't bound I warrant he'd have broken out by now!' said the man next to him.

So this was the King's room – and there was no one in there with him.

'I don't like it, Will,' muttered another. 'Our master should never have gone along with this business. The whole household will go down with him if it fails.'

'Curb your tongue, Ralf,' warned his neighbour,

glancing at Garth and then at me. 'Loose talk could cost us all dear.'

Garth pushed me on to the last door along the passage. He waited outside.

At the end of the row of rickety, slatted seats of the jakes was a small opening high in the wall. I climbed as quietly as I could onto the slats, making the occasional groaning noise to satisfy Garth. Some were broken and I was aware that they were the only thing between me and a drop into the moat below! The opening was scarcely big enough to poke my head through. Now I could see the row of windows on the back of the house. One of those was where the King was being held. From my trip along the passageway I judged it to be about halfway down.

Twisting my head upwards I could just make out my own open window on the next floor, at the other end of the house. There might just be a way of reaching that room from mine but the way between the two was hazardous. All over the house was the same ornate pattern of brickwork that Cat had used, but there were patches where it was crumbling.

I staggered from the jakes, clutching my stomach. I noted that Garth kept his distance!

This time the men fell silent as we passed.

Once in my room, I considered my royal rescue attempt. On the outside wall, a little way beneath my window, were mouldings. They looked like eagles – at least the newer ones did. The others, with their worn beaks and broken wings, were more like deformed ducks. I decided to avoid those. Some possible footholds presented themselves. There was no one in sight. I knew I had no choice but to risk it and hope the sentries had gone for their dinner.

Men's voices reached me. I had just stepped back when Parry and Warrendon came into view in the courtyard below.

'We march tomorrow at dawn,' Parry was saying.

'Why not now and get it over with?' said Warrendon. He sounded even more worried than when I'd arrived at his house.

'And descend on Westminster Abbey this evening when the day is all but done?' Parry was scornful. 'You are too hasty. Tomorrow we will have plenty of time to present the new monarch to London – and get him crowned. You will all be ready, I hope.' His commanding voice allowed no argument.

Warrendon's shoulders sagged. 'My whole household is at your disposal. Wright has made sure of it.'

'You have a good steward there.' Parry clapped him on the back. 'Do not forget the reward I have in store for you – as the new king's chancellor.'

I guessed that it wouldn't be long before Walter Warrendon met the same fate as Finch. I almost began to feel sorry for the man. Until I saw the ugly expression on his face. He was just as greedy for power as David Parry.

They passed out of earshot. The march was to be at dawn. My rescue could wait until after dark.

341

28

The day was the longest I'd ever known. At last the sun set. I kept checking the movements of the sentries. Once night fell they didn't stand still in the cold air but appeared now and again, walking round the courtyard and away past the stables. Each carried a burning torch. As soon as they were out of sight the darkness was intense. There was no moon and no lights shone from the windows at the back. I guessed everyone was eating in the Great Hall.

I took off my shoes, tucked Cat's scissors into my belt and waited.

A sentry came into view. He walked the length of the courtyard, briefly shone his light into the outbuildings and strode off. I made my move.

I lowered myself into the dark, testing the bricks by touch as best I could. Grasping a fearsome-looking eagle's beak I swung myself along to a drainpipe that shuddered as I clutched it. I could feel that the moulding beyond was one of the ducks – a leg fell off when I put my fingers to it. I found a hole in the brickwork and used that instead. I came to a window ledge and edged my way along, dangling from my hands.

At last I reached the place I judged to be halfway along the wall. Now to go down to the next floor. It was going to be more difficult and I'd taken a good time to get this far.

I had only inched down a brick or two when footsteps rose from below. I could do nothing but cling to the wall and hope the darkness hid me. The footsteps came close – and stopped. I sensed that the sentry was shining his light round more carefully than before. Had he heard the plaster leg falling? Would he gaze upwards? Perhaps he'd think he was dreaming if he saw a boy clinging to the wall. It was a forlorn hope.

Then at last he moved away. I willed him to hurry, but he was determined to take his time. It was only when I heard him turn the corner that I dared move.

I crept down to the window I hoped was the right one. I crawled onto the ledge and tried to see through the leaded glass panes. It was completely dark. I reasoned that the King might not have been given a candle, but that his guards would have a light out in the passageway – and the light would show under the door. I moved as quickly as I could so that I could look into the next room. Nothing there either. Was the room not where I'd thought it? I moved on again and there it was. A thin strip of flickering light. And by it I could faintly see the King slumped in a chair.

I took out Cat's scissors, jammed them under the casement and levered it open. The King started in astonishment as I lowered myself into the room. Fingers on my lips I crept to the door. Outside, the men were talking and I heard the clatter of tankards on the floorboards.

When I was satisfied that no one had heard me, I approached the King. His feet were bound to the chair legs and his hands were tied in front of him. I saw his eyes widen at the sight of Cat's scissors in my hand. It was too dark for him to identify me. He thought I'd come to harm him.

'It's Jack Briars,' I whispered. 'I'm here to set you free. With your permission, Sire, and Mistress Thimblebee's scissors, I will make a start.'

Few people were allowed to touch the King's person, but I didn't wait for his consent.

'I won't ask how you got here, Jack,' the King whispered, breathless with relief. 'But I am ever grateful to you – and to Mistress Thimblebee. I have been plunged into a nightmare. But with your help we will scupper this base plot of Parry's. Are my troops at the ready?'

I worked away at the ropes. The scissors were better at cutting cloth and I was making very slow headway. 'I am sure the troops are gathering as we speak, Your Majesty,' I said.

I hoped I was right but I could only guess that

Thomas Cromwell had mustered enough loyal men to overcome Parry's army.

'If Parry has his way I am to be brought low,' growled the King. 'He has told me I must willingly to consent to some boy being crowned in my place! Some upstart boy who claims to be descended from King Edward. Never!' He suddenly struggled to be free and I nearly cut his wrist.

Before I had a chance to admit that I was that upstart boy, I heard the click of the padlock outside.

'I'm sorry, my Liege,' I whispered, 'but I can't be found here. Your chance of escape depends on me being free.'

He appeared bewildered. I longed to stay with him but now someone was fumbling for the latch. I thought of leaving the scissors with him but bound as he was they would have been useless. I stowed them in my waistband and pulled myself out of the window just as the door opened. I clung to the wall below.

'Thought I heard talking.' I recognised the rough voice of one of Warrendon's servants.

In my haste I hadn't closed the window!

'If I speak to myself is it any wonder, you snivelling dolt?' growled the King angrily. 'I have little else to do in this accursed place.'

I was grateful for His Majesty's powers of invention!

'Release me this instant!' he ordered.

I imagined the man secretly quaking inside.

He made no answer but instead let out an oath. 'Why's that open? I'd swear on my life I shut it.

Someone has been trying to get in, I'll warrant.'

I heard footsteps come across the room. I flattened myself against the lumpy brickwork, hoping I'd be hidden by the dark shadows under the ledge.

'You can see that no one has got in here,' bellowed the King. 'And I command that you leave that window as it is. I need some air.'

His chair scraped along the floor as if he was writhing to get free. I hoped His Majesty's temper wouldn't get the better of him. If he burst from his bonds now I guessed he would not be left alone for another minute.

Again the man made no reply. The window swung wide open above my head. I saw a flicker of light. A candle was being shone out into the darkness. I tried not to breathe. My fingers were growing stiff and painful with the effort of hanging on.

Then the window was slammed shut. I prayed that the servant would leave so that I could get back to His Majesty. But from what I could tell he was still at the window. I heard muffled banging and an angry roar from the King.

When it stopped I strained my ears until I heard the door open, and close again.

I hauled myself up slowly, checking there was no light in the room. I took Cat's scissors and pushed them under the casement, just as I'd done before.

But now I understood what the banging had been. The window was nailed shut.

I could not rescue the King.

346

29

Back in my room I crawled into bed exhausted. I didn't even take my jacket off. My thoughts were wild and slipped into wilder dreams. I was trying to prise open impossible windows and always King Henry was helpless on the other side.

I was jerked awake by a loud thump.

It was still dark outside. In my befuddled state I thought it was the King's troops, come to make the rescue that I'd failed to do. I tried to gather my wits and found the reason for the noise. The door had been flung open and light spilled over me from a candle.

'It is time.' David Parry was standing there, dressed for a state occasion, all in velvet. His clothes were at odds with the steel breastplate he had strapped to his chest.

I struggled to my feet, rubbing my eyes.

'What do you think you're wearing?' he exclaimed,

347

pulling at my plain jacket. 'This is hardly the garb of a king.'

I was sure that the jacket would be covered in dirt and brick dust from my excursion. I was glad he didn't seem to have noticed it.

'You cannot be presented to your people in this!' He opened the clothes chest. At the bottom was a rich padded doublet of fine cloth, stitched all over in gold and studded with diamonds. He pulled out some breeches and a red fur-lined coat to go with it.

I was terrified he would spot the hidden scissors as I changed. I made a huge business of undoing the plain breeches and as he turned away to pick up a cap, I managed to slip the scissors between my shirt and doublet.

Parry held the cap out at arm's length with both hands. I almost shuddered to find that it bore three roaring lions – the royal arms of the King of England. He slowly lowered it onto my head.

'Get used to this, Jack,' he said. 'Soon it will be the crown.'

'I can't wait,' I said, swallowing down the bile that rose in my throat.

When I was ready he looked me up and down, and a slow, cruel smile spread over his lips. 'Perfect,' he said. 'Now to business. We shall take breakfast and then our army will join us. They are loyal to our cause and under my command.' He made the cause sound noble, but his army was made up of mercenaries – loyal only to the highest payer. 'Together we will march on London where you will be crowned king.'

'Won't His Majesty come to stop you?' I asked, playing the innocent. I had to remember I'd not been told about his capture.

Parry roared with laughter. 'King Henry will do nothing!' he said. 'Because he is here – a guest in this house.'

I made myself look as if this was astonishing news. 'A guest? Here?'

Parry waved an impatient hand that flashed with rubies. 'In truth a prisoner, but I understand that he is being as well treated as any guest. At least, he is being kept alive – for the moment. The people must see that he hands the crown over to you willingly. Thus there will be no trouble.'

I dreaded to think what would happen to His Majesty the moment his usefulness was over. Parry was rotten to the very core of his soul.

'I'm pleased to hear that you don't expect any trouble,' I said, more truthfully than he could ever know. 'I was just surprised when I saw you were wearing armour.'

'It never hurts to be prepared,' Parry replied.

'I hope I'll be fighting,' I said, pretending I was excited by the glories of war. 'Do I need my own breastplate?'

'Certainly not,' said Parry. 'You are too important to be put in any danger.'

He escorted me down the two flights of stairs to the Great Hall where we stood with Warrendon and

Wright, the steward, taking a quick breakfast of bread and meat.

'Come,' commanded Parry as soon as we'd finished.

I followed him out into the courtyard where servants were holding horses' bridles. In the dawn light, I could see a band of men, richly dressed like Parry and all carrying weapons in their belts. I recognised some of them from Court. And silently damned them to hell.

I heard a cry, 'God save the King!' Then mocking laughter. My cheeks burned with the shame of it.

A splendid grey horse was led to my side. His saddle, cloth and bridle were as sumptuous as those the King always had when he went off to hunt. And with good reason. This was His Majesty's hunter, Hyperion, captured when he was taken prisoner. What better way to present the new king to the people of London than on the royal stallion?

Wright helped me into the saddle. Hyperion began to skitter impatiently on the flagstones. But before I could ask Wright for someone to lead me in the dreaded parade, he'd left me to join Warrendon. The horse snorted and tossed his head. I grasped the saddle, fearing I'd be thrown.

The men fell silent and I heard wheels grinding along, around the house from the stables. A stocky pony came into view, pulling a rough cart. Three men sat in the back. Two carried swords. I recognised them. Will and Ralf – Warrendon's servants who'd guarded their royal prisoner so reluctantly last night.

The other was the King.

King Henry glared round at us all. He was in a high temper and I rejoiced to see it. If he was frightened, he was too angry to show it. His hands were still tied in front of him. I cursed myself for not being able to rescue him last night. I couldn't see how I would get the chance now.

'You will all die for this day's work!' bellowed the King.

Hearing his master's voice, Hyperion pricked up his ears and trotted quickly towards him. I clung on, helpless to stop the advance. The stallion came to a halt at the cart. I was face to face with the captive King. I saw fury in his eyes.

'Your betrayal is despicable, Jack Briars,' thundered King Henry. 'And you will pay for it.'

I'd not had the chance to tell him that I was to play the role of the new king. Did he believe me loyal to this dreadful band? Did my attempt to free him count for nothing? Or was he playing a part just as I was?

'I am the rightful monarch,' I retorted loudly, although the words almost choked me. 'True descendant of King Edward.'

Garth now seized the bridle and I was led to the front of the column where he left me. For once I wished he'd stay close by. The eyes of every man were on me as I struggled to control my mount.

The King let out a tirade, naming Warrendon and Parry as the most heinous traitors that ever breathed and letting them know what punishment awaited them in hell. Warrendon squirmed under the verbal attack. He too wore a breastplate but it looked as if it chafed him. I fervently hoped it did.

Parry sat on his horse and smirked.

Heads turned at a distant pounding rhythm. A cloud of dust was rising where the road disappeared into the trees. The pounding grew louder and a host of marching men appeared. Soon the road was filled with their ranks. All I could do was gape at them in pure terror. The leaders reached the bridge over the moat and called for a halt.

The men wore bright jerkins with striped sleeves and flamboyant feathers in their caps. I'd never seen such garb before. These were obviously the mercenaries. Otto was at their head. They were armed with a variety of vicious pikes and to a man had swords strapped to their sides. These men were not farm labourers who practised the longbow in case of a muster. These were trained soldiers. I prayed that the King's troops were on their way.

Otto stepped forward and raised his sword in salute. Parry rode over the bridge to meet them.

'Today we set forth to bring the true monarch to the throne of England,' he cried. 'Today will be remembered as the start of the greatest dynasty that ever ruled this fair land. We cannot fail. Victory will be ours.'

His supporters behind him gave a rousing cheer. The mercenaries raised their pikes.

'Treacherous worms . . .' The King's answer to Parry was cut short as someone tied a gag around his mouth.

A man ran forward and sounded a trumpet. The King always had harbingers to announce his arrival. This blaring note was awful to my ears.

And so King Jack began his march on London.

30

Parry and Warrendon came alongside me and we headed off on our terrible crusade. Behind us the marching feet drummed an ominous tattoo on the dry road. Hyperion kept tossing his head. He was a hunter, not used to processions, and he seemed desperate to gallop away over the fields. A tiny part of me wanted him to do just that – and carry me to safety.

'Garth, see to that horse!' commanded Parry.

The servant ran up and grasped Hyperion's bridle again. The new king on a skittering horse he couldn't control! It wasn't exactly the majestic appearance that Parry was hoping for and I took a tiny crumb of comfort from that.

As the sun rose higher we came to a small village. It was merely a duck pond and a cluster of cottages around a church. The trumpet blasted out again and the people came hurrying to the summons.

'What's this?' asked a priest, pulling a napkin from his neck. We'd obviously disturbed his breakfast.

Parry rode up to him.

'I present the true King of England,' he proclaimed. 'The grandson of Prince Edward who was our rightful monarch.'

The villagers scratched their heads and the priest looked confused.

'Is this a mummers' play?' he said. 'For everyone knows that Prince Edward died in the Tower at the hands of Richard Crookback.'

I saw Parry's back stiffen in annoyance. 'Shame on you,' he roared. 'Cry "God save the King" to your monarch.'

'King Henry is our sovereign lord, not this skinny boy,' declared the priest.

The villagers nodded.

'And there he is,' called a voice. 'Trussed like a prisoner in that cart.'

The priest looked horrified. 'Holy Mary,' he gasped. 'Shame on *you*, you traitor!'

Parry gave a signal to Otto. He stepped forward and, without a word, struck the priest hard in the face. The poor man fell to the ground, blood gushing from his mouth. The front line of mercenaries moved closer to the villagers, their weapons raised.

'God save the King,' came the feeble cry.

Our procession moved on.

'The people do not believe us,' I heard Warrendon whisper.

Parry was silent for a moment. 'Send some of your men on horseback to the next village,' he said. 'To persuade them.'

Warrendon did as he was commanded and a group of riders led by his steward went galloping off. Hyperion gave an angry whinny and made to follow. Garth was jolted into the air as he fought to control the stallion.

We came to the next village at mid-morning. Wright was arguing with a labourer who fell silent at our approach. Others had crept out, Warrendon's men surrounding them. The villagers were awed by the sight of the mercenaries. They gave a dutiful cheer for me and watched sullenly as we passed by. It happened again and again at each village and town we marched through. Warrendon's men were obviously threatening dire consequences for any who didn't proclaim loyalty to the new King.

I had no idea how His Majesty was faring. The mercenaries now surrounded the cart and when I tried to look back, I couldn't see him.

It must have been nearly midday when we arrived at the village of Hatton. We received the same almost silent treatment but as we passed someone threw a stone. It missed me and hit Warrendon on the shoulder. Parry tugged at his reins, ready to hunt down the perpetrator.

'No, David,' urged Warrendon. 'We mustn't delay.'

Parry nodded. 'I'll send Otto and his men back later,' he said grimly.

Now we were approaching a wood. The way narrowed. Warrendon dropped back and I rode silently with Parry. Behind us the mercenaries' trampling feet echoed through the overhanging trees. From somewhere ahead came a warning shout. Wright appeared, galloping towards us, panic on his face.

David Parry held up a hand to halt the procession.

'Prepare for battle!' shouted the man as he reined in his steaming horse. 'There's a force ahead!'

I could hardly keep from cheering.

'Impossible!' snapped Parry. 'No one is expecting us. Your eyes are deceiving you!'

Another scout arrived. 'Men are assembled on the open land beyond the woods,' he cried.

Parry gave a cold laugh. 'Doubtless a paltry band of labourers and swineherds. Local men who want to have their moment of glory. Let them try. They'll be no match for my army!'

At a wave of his arm we pressed forward again. My stomach knotted when we saw the bright sun between the trees that gave way to a heath. I tried not to think about the poor loyal men who would soon be crushed like ants.

They came into view the moment we cleared the forest. A motley crew as Parry had guessed. They held a selection of longbows, scythes and axes. These men had decided to make a stand for their true King. They watched us in silence although we were not too distant to see the terror on their faces.

Parry called for a halt.

'Otto, take some men and despatch this raggle-taggle lot,' he ordered. 'They will serve as a warning to others not to oppose me. Jack, stay back here with the cart where you will be protected from the fighting. I need both my kings alive . . . for the moment.'

I agreed. I hope he saw a young fool too scared to join in with the battle now it was a reality. In truth, I had no wish to attack loyal men. I began to form a desperate plan to free the King. But Garth stuck close to my side, his grip on Hyperion's bridle as strong as ever.

The mercenaries prepared to move forward. I could hardly bear to watch. The tiny, brave army were going to be slaughtered where they stood.

31

Then, behind the band of labourers, the single note of a horn sang out clearly through the air.

Horsemen came into view. A hundred, two hundred, five hundred, more. Yeomen guard and Gentlemen of the Horse, flanked by riders carrying the royal banner. Charles Brandon, the King's brother-in-law, was at their head, with Thomas Cromwell beside him.

'By Lucifer's horns!' exclaimed Parry. 'What double dealing is this? Nobody knew we were on our way.'

As we watched a new battalion appeared. A host of loyal Englishmen, all trained in the use of the longbow. Lines of archers were pulling back their bows, poised to rain their deadly arrows down on us.

'How is this possible?' wailed Warrendon. 'There are so many.'

The sight should have warmed my heart. But instead fear stabbed me like a knife. Didn't these men realise that they were aiming at their King? No, most likely they thought him in captivity somewhere – or already dead.

I did the only thing I could think of. I dug my heels into Hyperion's flanks. The grey stallion tensed beneath me – and then we were off, shedding the helpless Garth and thundering over the open ground towards the ranks of the royal army. I flattened myself to the saddle and hung on.

There were angry shouts behind me. Parry either thought I'd lost control of the horse or he'd guessed what I was doing. I soon left him in no doubt.

'Stop!' I cried, daring to let go with one hand and waving wildly. 'King Henry is there. You'll kill him.'

I wondered if Brandon would think it was a trick, but I saw Master Cromwell lean across and say something urgent.

Brandon shouted an order. The bows were lowered. The men were not to harm their true monarch.

Then came another shout. 'Charge!'

Instead of archers sending their arrows, riders surged towards us. Behind them, billmen advanced, wielding their long hooked poles. Terrified, Hyperion reared up. I clutched at his mane but I couldn't hold on. I fell, winded, onto my back as horses and men swept towards me from both sides.

Nothing could have prepared me for the terrible sound of warfare. The hooves thundering, the ground shaking, weapons clanging, men shouting and horses shrieking as they crashed to the ground. All about was confusion. I snatched up a fallen sword and turned to find myself facing an archer, his bow on his back and an axe in his hand. Instinctively I ducked as he swung the axe at me. Before he could attack again, I head-butted him hard in the stomach.

Now I found myself in the path of a rearing horse, the hooves close enough to split my skull. I dived sideways and stumbled to my feet.

I had to get to His Majesty, if I could make it alive.

Wherever I turned I met nothing but vicious blades and falling bodies. And blood. I thought the screams of the dying would stay with me for ever.

Then I spotted Hyperion, eyes wild, bleeding from a gash in his flank. I'd be safer in the saddle but I had no hope of catching him. He suddenly wheeled away from me and charged in blind terror. I could see he was trying to get to the safety of the woods. The fighters scattered as he plunged through them. I ran after him, along the path he had cleared, avoiding his bucking heels but staying as close as I could. I felt the sting of blades grazing my skin as I dodged my way behind him. I fell again and again, buffeted by fighters, thankful for my well-padded doublet that took the worst of the blows.

Suddenly Wright loomed up in front of me.

'You worm,' he hissed. His sword whipped through the air. I blocked the blow with my borrowed weapon and hit him hard under the chin with the handle. A useful trick I'd learned from Robert Aycliffe. Wright crumpled. I leapt over him and headed for the trees.

The cart was in sight. I could see the helpless horror in the King's eyes. It was matched by the look on his two guards' faces. That look gave me hope.

David Parry was close by, seated on his horse, watching the fighting. A coward who wouldn't even lead his troops. He hadn't seen me. There was a gloating expression on his face. He seemed so sure of success, despite this unexpected turn of events. The death and bloodshed meant nothing to him – as long as he was triumphant. I was going to make him answer for his crimes. But I could do nothing until the King was safe.

I ran low until I reached the back of the cart. The noise of the battle was more distant here but my ears still rang from the clashing swords. I pulled myself up into the cart. All three men turned to me. The King's eyes blazed. Will and Ralf scrabbled for their weapons, but I was quicker. I kicked them away and pointed my own sword at them.

'If you value your lives, go!' I urged them.

For a moment they sat frozen, not daring to move.

'Run, before Mister Parry sees you,' I insisted.

Now they understood. They threw themselves from the cart and vanished into the woods.

I tore off the King's gag. 'I've come to rescue you, Sire.'

'Rescue me?' growled His Majesty. 'Rescue me so that I may grovel to you and that traitor, Parry!'

His words stabbed me like a thousand knives.

'No, my Liege!' I cried. 'I have never wavered in my loyalty and service to—'

'Do not move!' It was David Parry.

32

Parry swung from his horse and leapt onto the cart.

'You are a treacherous little rat, Jack Briars,' he snarled. 'I would kill you where you stand if I didn't still need my puppet monarch.' He turned to the King. 'But I can't risk keeping you alive any more, Henry Tudor. Your rescue would ruin my plans. I will win the crown through battle alone.'

The man was truly deluded. Surely the battle could not go his way. His men were outflanked and outnumbered.

But that wouldn't save His Majesty.

Parry pulled his sword from its scabbard and raised it with both hands over his head.

'You'll have to kill me first,' I yelled.

Before he could make the fatal stroke, I brought up my own blade and knocked his aside. But the force of the blow sent my sword flying through the air.

I darted forward to make a grab for one of the servants' weapons from the bottom of the cart. I wasn't quick enough. Parry stamped on my hand, his face mad with fury.

'Get out of my way.' He spat the words, as his fingers seized the front of my doublet. He began to push me backwards to the edge of the cart. I clung to the wooden side and held on with all my strength. But Parry was stronger. I was losing the fight. And when I fell, Parry would be free to slaughter the King. I could hear His Majesty's angry shouts.

I grasped Parry's wrist with both hands and flung my body back at the same time. We hit the ground together. Parry staggered to his feet. He snatched up his sword.

'You little fool,' he bellowed. 'I always win. And if you don't want to be part of my victory then I will have to dispatch you too and find another willing orphan. What do you say? It's not as though you're armed now.'

He was wrong. But I could do nothing while his blade was pointing at my chest.

As I stared at him, I saw a movement out of the corner of my eye. A black stallion was bearing down on the cart. The rider, enclosed in a dark cloak under a wide hat, gave no clue to his allegiance.

Parry whipped round at the sound. I took my chance. I sprang onto the wheel of the cart, grabbed his hair and pulled his head back. Before he could move I whipped out Cat's scissors and held the point at his neck, where his breastplate offered no protection.

'Drop your sword,' I ordered him.

Parry stood stock still. Then his fingers released his weapon.

The black stallion arrived in a cloud of dust. There was no mistaking the flared nostrils and yellow eyes of Diablo, the devil horse. And there was only one person who rode him like that. Cat Thimblebee leapt onto the cart.

'I'll save you, Your Majesty,' she yelled. She produced a knife from her apron pocket and began to cut through his bonds.

It was only now that I realised that something had changed on the battlefield. The clamour of the fight had quietened. Some of the mercenaries were fleeing for the woods. Now all that could be heard were brisk shouted orders and the terrible groans of the wounded and dying. The King shook off his final ropes.

'We have victory,' he cried.

Parry gave a roar and tried to shake me off. I pressed the blade harder. I'd never killed a man before but this time I might not have any choice. Until this man was under arrest I couldn't let him go. Although I had the advantage, I wouldn't have the strength to hold him for long.

'It's David Parry you want,' came a desperate voice. 'It was all his idea. He forced me to go along with his terrible plans.'

Guards were marching Walter Warrendon towards us. He was bound and bloodied. Someone threw the dead body of his steward down in front of him.

Thomas Cromwell rode up, flanked by more yeomen guard.

'Remove these traitors from my sight,' said the King bitterly.

Hands pulled me away from Parry. He struggled wildly in the grip of the guards.

I watched as Warrendon and Parry were dragged away.

'Take them all,' said Cromwell grimly, pointing straight at me.

33

A nd now I sat in the condemned cell waiting for death. I hadn't written a word to Cromwell. What could I write? He knew the truth and still I was here. At first anger had burned fiercely in my belly. Anger that I was to be punished in the same way as Parry despite all I had done to protect my King. But deep down I understood that I had to be made an example. In the eyes of the world I had committed treason. Traitors could not be pardoned. I could not be allowed to live.

At least the King was safe – and Cat. I couldn't imagine how she'd found us on that battlefield. I would have given anything to be free to hear her longwinded explanation. I was sure she'd continue to work for Cromwell. She'd be very good at it.

I got up and walked around the tiny cell. Light was coming in through the narrow crack of a window and I could see marks on the stone walls. I peered closer.

They were names. Scratched into the stone. Names of those who'd been here before me. I wondered if any of them had been innocent. I doubted many of them had walked to freedom.

I heard voices down below in the courtyard. They were getting closer. They were coming for me.

For a moment, I thought my terror was going to cheat them of their execution. I could barely breathe. My heart pounded loudly in my ears.

A key turned in the door. Nicholas Mountford stood there, huge and grim. There were more yeomen behind him.

'It is time,' he said.

I gulped. I wanted to throw myself to the floor and beg for mercy. I wanted to scream and bellow that I was innocent. But it wouldn't help. A strange calmness suddenly came over me. I think my utter fear had put me in a sort of trance. I nodded and walked towards him, unable to look him in the eye, sure I would see great disgust there.

Mountford bound my hands behind my back and escorted me down into the courtyard. I squinted in the bright sunlight. I could hear the Tower ravens cawing and smelt blossom from some nearby tree. Boatmen were calling to each other on the Thames. It was so ordinary yet it made me yearn even more to stay alive.

A familiar figure was waiting for us to approach. Cromwell gave me no greeting. I could have been invisible. If I had been hoping for a glimpse of regret from my master, I would have been sorely disappointed.

'The King has commanded a private execution,' he told my guards. 'The boy does not warrant any fuss. Parry and Warrendon will make enough of a show when they walk to their deaths on the scaffold at noon.'

He turned towards the Water Gate. Mountford seized my arm and dragged me down steps to where a boat was waiting. Robert Aycliffe was already on board, the oars in his hands. Mountford pushed me to the seat opposite him. He then joined Cromwell on the bench behind me. The other guards stood back and watched as we passed under the green stained stone of the gate and into the river.

The boat swung away downstream. I couldn't help glancing back at London Bridge where the traitors' heads were displayed. David Parry had claimed that he always won. He was wrong. His head would soon be there for the crows to feast on. Was mine going to be stuck on a spike with the others?

All sat silent as we passed Limehouse and then Greenwich Palace. I wanted to ask where the deed was going to be done but I didn't dare. I had the sudden urge to throw myself overboard. With my hands tied, it would still be certain death. But better than having my head severed from my neck.

Soon the river widened and we were at a good distance from both banks. There was a tarpaulin bunched up in the front of the boat. I suddenly wondered if I was to be trussed up and thrown overboard.

'I think we're safe from prying eyes and ears now,' said Cromwell.

I was right. This was where I was going die.

I tried to stand. As I did so, the tarpaulin suddenly gave a heave and a head covered in red curls appeared behind Aycliffe.

'About time, your worshipfulness,' said Cat. 'I was suffocating under there.'

I slumped back on my seat. Had Cat come to see me die? Mountford seized my arms. I struggled.

'Keep still, Jack,' he snapped. I heard a slicing sound and suddenly my hands were free. Cat was beaming at me. Aycliffe was grinning too.

Bewildered I turned to my master.

'This ordeal is over for you, Jack,' he said. 'It will be reported that the traitor, Briars, has been executed and all will be satisfied. But that leaves us with a problem.'

I stared open-mouthed at him. He made no sense.

'The King does not wish to punish you,' he went on. 'He knows you have shown undying loyalty. But he cannot pardon a traitor. So Jack Briars is going to be put to death today.'

'Stop torturing him,' Cat burst out suddenly. 'He looks like he's waiting for the axe to fall this minute.' She grabbed my hand and squeezed it. 'It's going to be all right, Jack,' she went on. 'You're not going to die. Master Cromwell says you must have a new name and the King has sent some money and . . .'

Even with my head spinning I could see Aycliffe and

Mountford were trying not to laugh at her impetuous behaviour.

'I'm not going to die?' Stupefied, I repeated her words.

Cromwell cut in. 'Mistress Thimblebee speaks the truth, Jack. I have a different role for you to play. We're heading for a quiet mooring where you will take a ship to France.'

'France?' I mumbled stupidly, unable to take it all in.

'You're going to be a spy across the water.' Cat couldn't help butting in again. 'Still serving the King.'

'I'm sorry that we had to play out this charade,' said Cromwell. 'But that's the nature of our job.'

I understood. And for the first time in days a smile crept over my face. France! A whole new life in a foreign land lay ahead of me. 'Tell me what you want me to do,' I urged.

'That's our Jack,' said Aycliffe.

'You need a new name first,' put in Cat. 'What are you going to call yourself?'

'I'd like to stick with Jack or John for a Christian name if that's all right,' I said. 'My godfather baptised me and—' I broke off. The enormity of what was going to happen suddenly hit me. 'My godfather!' I exclaimed. 'He'll think me a traitor. It'll cause him such pain. And Mark and Mrs Pennycod.'

'Brother Matthew will receive a visitor who wishes to make confession,' said Cromwell. 'I can trust him not to speak of what he hears.'

I felt a huge wave of relief. My dear godfather would be told the truth.

'Mrs Pennycod sent you this!' Cat fished in her apron pocket and produced a squashed pie. It was the best thing I'd ever eaten in my life. 'And Mark said you're not to worry. He's going to stand up to Weasel-face.' Her eyes suddenly danced. 'Oh, and he said don't eat all those foreign onions. He heard of a boy who ate too many, burped near a candle and set the house on fire!'

I laughed. 'Tell him I will heed his words.'

Cat wriggled round to face Cromwell. 'And don't forget your promise, Master Cromwell.'

'I won't, Mistress Thimblebee,' he replied.

'I mean you can't let Weasel-face . . . I mean Oswyn Drage, give Jack's job to his brother.'

'I wouldn't dare.'

'Because that would be too mean on poor Mark Helston.'

My master put his hand on his heart. 'I swear it,' he said solemnly.

A rough mooring came into view. Our rowers took us towards a small fishing vessel.

'Once you reach France you will be met by a barrel maker,' said Cromwell. 'You will be his nephew. I will be in touch whenever I need you.'

'Good luck, Jack,' said Aycliffe as we came alongside the battered old boat. He handed me a bag. 'Clothes and money. I am certain that we will meet again.'

A sailor helped me on board the fishing boat.

'Fair winds, Jack,' called Mountford. 'And keep off those French roofs!'

'Goodbye, Jack Briars,' said Cromwell. 'It wouldn't surprise me if you were back one day – and sitting in my chair.'

As usual, my master seemed to know everything that had gone on. Then Nicholas Mountford gave me a wink.

The enormity of setting out alone and leaving everything I knew behind threatened to overwhelm me. And there still remained one more farewell. I gulped and gazed at Cat. I couldn't find the words. I was never going to see her again. Strangely the wretched girl was grinning, as if she was pleased to see me go. Suddenly hands reached down for her too and she was soon scrambling on board.

'Don't stand there gawping,' she cackled. 'I'm coming with you. I want you to hear how I rescued the King.'

'You can't come with me,' I said. 'What about your job at the palace?'

'Mister Wiltshire will have to cope,' she said. 'I'm never going to be more than a seamstress if I stay at Court. Anyway, you need me. You don't speak French.'

'Neither do you.'

'Course I do,' said the irritating girl. 'Emile in the sewing room has been teaching me.'

'Why didn't you tell me?' I said.

Cat beamed. 'You never asked!'

As ever, Cat Thimblebee had the last word.